ALSO BY

PADRAIC COLUM

THE CHILDREN OF ODIN

THE CHILDREN'S HOMER

THE GOLDEN FLEECE

THE ISLAND OF THE MIGHTY

THE ARABIAN NIGHTS

TALES OF WONDER AND MAGNIFICENCE

BY PADRAIC COLUM

ALADDIN

NEW YORK   LONDON   TORONTO   SYDNEY   NEW DELHI

ALADDIN

An imprint of Simon & Schuster Children's Publishing Division

1230 Avenue of the Americas, New York, New York 10020

This Aladdin edition September 2019

Text copyright © 1923 by The Macmillan Company

Cover illustration copyright © 2019 by Brandon Dorman

For information about special discounts for bulk purchases, please contact Simon & Schuster Special Sales at 1-866-506-1949 or business@simonandschuster.com.

The Simon & Schuster Speakers Bureau can bring authors to your live event. For more information or to book an event contact the Simon & Schuster Speakers Bureau at 1-866-248-3049 or visit our website at www.simonspeakers.com.

Series designed by Jessica Handelman

Interior designed by Tom Daly

Manufactured in the United States of America 0819 FFG

2 4 6 8 10 9 7 5 3 1

Library of Congress Control Number 2019937022

ISBN 978-1-5344-4558-1 (hc)

ISBN 978-1-5344-4557-4 (pbk)

ISBN 978-1-5344-4559-8 (eBook)

This title has previously been published with illustrations and slightly different text.

CONTENTS

The Beginning of the Stories:
Shahrazad

In the Name of God, the Merciful, the Compassionate!

Praise be to God, the Beneficent King, the Creator of the Universe, who hath raised the heavens without pillars, and spread out the earth as a bed; and blessings and peace be on the lord of apostles, our lord and our master Mohammad and his Family; blessing and peace, enduring and constant, unto the day of judgment.

To proceed: the lives of former generations are a lesson to posterity; that a man may review the remarkable events which have happened to others, and be admonished; and may consider the history of people of preceding ages, and of all that hath befallen them, and be restrained. Extolled be the perfection of Him who hath thus ordained the history of former generations to be a lesson to those which follow. Such are the "Tales of a Thousand and One Nights," with their romantic stories and fables.

There was in ancient times, in a country between China and India, a young girl who had read histories, and chronicles of ancient kings, and stories of people of old times. It is related of her (but God is all-knowing, as well as all-wise and almighty, and all-bountiful) that she had read a thousand books of histories and chronicles and stories. Her memory, too, was stored with the verses of poets and the sayings of kings and sages; moreover, this girl was wise and prudent and witty. Her name was Shahrazad.

Her father was the Wezir of the King of that country—King Shahriyar. One day the Wezir appeared in his home looking downcast, and troubled, and dejected, and ill at ease. He sighed often, he ate nothing, and it seemed that he would not be able to sleep. His daughter, having watched him for some time, went to him and asked him to tell her why he was so troubled and anxious.

He sighed heavily, and he would not speak. Thereupon Shahrazad said to him, quoting from one of the verses that were in her memory:

Tell him whom anxiety loads that anxiety will not stay:
As happiness passed, so will this, too—anxiety travels away.

Her father, hearing the verses, ceased to sigh; then looking upon his daughter, he began to speak of the troubles that oppressed him.

"Know, O my daughter," he said, "that in all the world there is no office more dreadful than the one I hold as Wezir of King Shahriyar. The King, my master, makes me his partner in deeds that have raised the people's outcry against him and that have caused fathers and mothers to flee with their daughters from his dominion. But the King's own story is a grievous one: he was deceived and injured by a wife whom he loved and trusted; not only that, but he saw his brother whom he loves deceived and injured in the same way. And it happened to the King also that he was shown a woman who had been carried away by a powerful enchanter, and it was made known to him that, although the enchanter brought this woman down to the depths of the stormy sea, she found ways to deceive him and to make him a mockery.

"King Shahriyar made a vow that he would never permit a woman to deceive him, and he made the dreadful decision that he would let his wife live only as long as he himself might be beside her. He took to marrying girl after girl, marrying one in the evening, and in the morning having her head taken off. Now for three years he has been doing this, and it will soon come about that the girls of this land will all be married by the King and slaughtered. I, who am his Wezir, have to deprive fathers and mothers of their daughters, so that he may have a bride whom he will kill. Is it a wonder, then, that I am oppressed with sorrow and solicitude?"

So the Wezir said, telling of his distress. He did not know that his daughter Shahrazad already knew of King Shahriyar—his story, and the marriages and slaughters that he made. When he had finished speaking she said to him, "O my father, take me and bring me to the King, that I may be his bride."

The Wezir was made very angry by the speech of his daughter. He turned away from her and he sat apart. But Shahrazad went to him and she said: "I have thought upon the deeds of this King, and it may be that I shall be the means of saving the girls of this land from death, and of ridding fathers and mothers of the anxiety that oppresses them. If this can be done by me, my father, I shall have a name that will be for all time remembered."

Her father would not listen to her, but Shahrazad persisted, and at last, fearful that she should imperil his life as well as her own by going before Shahriyar and letting him believe that his Wezir denied his daughter to him, he brought her to the King's palace.

Now Shahrazad had a young sister whose name was Dunyazad, and this sister went with her and was lodged in the palace. On their way, Shahrazad said, "O my sister Dunyazad, I will contrive means of having you brought into the sleeping-chamber to-night. If it happens that you are given leave to come in, sit near the end of the bed and be very quiet. Then, when it gets past the middle of the night speak up and say to me, 'O Shahrazad, my sister, if you are still awake, tell us one of your delightful stories so that we may beguile the waking hours of this, our last night together.' Say this, and it may be that it will lead to the saving of my life." Dunyazad promised that she would do all this.

When the marriage ceremony was over Shahrazad was left in the place from which so many girls had gone forth to death—in the chamber where the bride of King Shahriyar slept. The King came to her and Shahrazad made a show of weeping. He asked her why she wept, and she said:

"O King, I have a young sister, and she is at this moment lodged in the palace, and I weep because I shall not be able to take my leave of her." Then said the King: "Bid your sister come into this chamber; I give permission for you to have her with you through the hours of the night."

Thereupon Dunyazad came into the sleeping chamber.

She sat there very quietly until it was past the middle of the night; then she coughed, and she said:

"O Shahrazad, my sister, if you are still wakeful, tell us one of your delightful stories so that we may beguile the waking hours of this, our last night together." "Most willingly," said Shahrazad, "if this good King will give us leave to be talkative." The King, hearing these words and being restless, was pleased with the prospect of listening to a story, and he said, "Tell on." Thereupon Shahrazad rejoiced greatly, and at once she began.

The Story
of the Fisherman

There was a certain fisherman, advanced in age, who had a wife and three children; and though he was in indigent circumstances, it was his custom to cast his net, every day, no more than four times.

One day he went forth at the hour of noon to the shore of the sea, and put down his basket, and cast his net, and waited until it was motionless in the water, when he drew together its strings, and found it to be heavy: he pulled, but could not draw it up: so he took the end of the cord, and knocked a stake into the shore, and tied the cord to it. He then stripped himself, and dived round the net, and continued to pull until he drew it out: whereupon he rejoiced, and put on his clothes; but when he came to examine the net, he found in it the carcass of a donkey. At the sight of this he mourned, and exclaimed, There is no strength nor power but in God, the High, the Great! This is a strange piece of fortune!— And he repeated the following verse:—

O thou who occupiest thyself in the darkness of night,
and in peril! Spare thy trouble; for the support of
Providence is not obtained by toil!

He then disencumbered his net of the dead donkey, and wrung it out; after which he spread it, and descended into the sea, and—exclaiming, In the name of God!—cast it again, and waited till it had sunk and was still, when he pulled it, and found it more heavy and more difficult to raise than on the former occasion. He therefore concluded that it was full of fish: so he tied it, and stripped, and plunged and dived, and pulled until he raised it, and drew it up on the shore; when he found in it only a large jar, full of sand and mud; on seeing which, he was troubled in his heart, and repeated the following words of the poet:—

O angry fate, forbear! or, if thou wilt not forbear, relent!

Neither favor from fortune do I gain, nor profit from the work of my hands.

I came forth to seek my sustenance, but have found it to be exhausted.

How many of the ignorant are in splendor! and how many of the wise, in obscurity!

So saying, he threw aside the jar, and wrung out and cleansed his net; and, begging the forgiveness of God for his impatience, returned to the sea the third time, and threw the net, and waited till it had sunk and was motionless: he then drew it out, and found in it a quantity of broken jars and pots.

Upon this, he raised his head toward heaven, and said, O God, Thou knowest that I cast not my net more than four

times; and I have now cast it three times! Then—exclaiming,
In the name of God!—he cast the net again into the sea, and
waited till it was still; when he attempted to draw it up, but
could not, for it clung to the bottom. And he exclaimed,
There is no strength nor power but in God!—and stripped
himself again, and dived round the net, and pulled it until he
raised it upon the shore; when he opened it, and found in it
a bottle of brass, filled with something, and having its mouth
closed with a stopper of lead, bearing the impression of the
seal of our lord Suleyman.[1]

At the sight of this, the fisherman rejoiced, and said, This
I will sell in the copper-market; for it is worth ten pieces of

---

1 No man ever obtained such absolute power over the Jinn as
Suleyman Ibn-Da'ud (Solomon, the Son of David). This he did by
virtue of a most wonderful talisman, which is said to have come down
to him from heaven. It was a seal-ring, upon which was engraved "the
most great name" of God; and was partly composed of brass, and partly
of iron. With the brass he stamped his written commands to the good
Jinn; with the iron [which they greatly dread], those to the evil Jinn,
or Devils. Over both orders he had unlimited power; as well as over
the birds and the winds, and, as is generally said, the wild beasts. His
Wezir, Asaf the son of Barkhiya, is also said to have been acquainted
with "the most great name," by uttering which, the greatest miracles
may be performed; even that of raising the dead. By virtue of this
name, engraved on his ring, Suleyman compelled the Jinn to assist in
building the Temple of Jerusalem, and in various other works. Many
of the evil Jinn he converted to the true faith; and many others of this
class, who remained obstinate in infidelity, he confined in prisons.

gold. He then shook it, and found it to be heavy, and said, I must open it, and see what is in it, and store it in my bag; and then I will sell the bottle in the copper-market. So he took out a knife, and picked at the lead until he extracted it from the bottle. He then laid the bottle on the ground, and shook it, that its contents might pour out; but there came forth from it nothing but smoke, which ascended toward the sky, and spread over the face of the earth; at which he wondered excessively. And after a little while, the smoke collected together, and was condensed, and then became agitated, and was converted into an 'Efrit, whose head was in the clouds, while his feet rested upon the ground: his head was like a dome: his hands were like winnowing forks; and his legs, like masts: his mouth resembled a cavern: his teeth were like stones; his nostrils, like trumpets; and his eyes, like lamps; and he had disheveled and dust-colored hair.

When the fisherman beheld this 'Efrit,[2] the muscles of his sides quivered, his teeth were locked together, his spittle dried up, and he saw not his way. The 'Efrit, as soon as he perceived him, exclaimed, There is no deity but God: Suleyman is the Prophet of God. O Prophet of God, slay me not; for I will never again oppose thee in word, or rebel against thee in deed!—O Marid, said the fisherman, dost thou say, Suleyman is the Prophet of God? Suleyman hath been dead a thousand and eight hundred years; and we are now in the end of time. What is thy history, and what is thy tale, and what was the cause of thy entering this bottle?

---

2 'Efrit and Marid are of the Jinn: Jinn is the plural; Jinni is the singular.

When the Marid heard these words of the fisherman, he said, There is no deity but God! Receive news, O fisherman!— Of what, said the fisherman, dost thou give me news? He answered, Of thy being instantly put to a most cruel death. The fisherman exclaimed, Wherefore wouldst thou kill me? and what requires thy killing me, when I have liberated thee from the bottle, and rescued thee from the bottom of the sea, and brought thee up upon the dry land?—The 'Efrit answered, Choose what kind of death thou wilt die, and in what manner thou shalt be killed.—What is my offence, said the fisherman, that this should be my recompense from thee? The 'Efrit replied, Hear my story, O fisherman.—Tell it then, said the fisherman, and be short in thy words; for my soul hath sunk down to my feet.

Know then, said he, that I am one of the heretical Jinn: I rebelled against Suleyman the son of Da'ud; I and Sakhr the Jinni; and he sent to me his Wezir, Asaf the son of Barkhiya, who came upon me forcibly, and took me to him in bonds, and placed me before him: and when Suleyman saw me, he offered up a prayer for protection against me, and exhorted me to embrace the faith, and to submit to his authority; but I refused; upon which he called for this bottle, and confined me in it, and closed it upon me with the leaden stopper, which he stamped with the Most Great Name: he then gave orders to the Jinn, who carried me away, and threw me into the midst of the sea.

There I remained a hundred years; and I said in my heart, Whosoever shall liberate me, I will enrich him forever:—but the hundred years passed over me, and no one liberated me: and I entered upon another hundred years; and I said, Whosoever shall liberate me, I will open to him the treasures of the earth;—but no one did so; and four hundred years more passed over me, and I said, Whosoever shall liberate me, I will perform for him three wants:—but still no one liberated me. I then fell into a violent rage, and said within myself, Whosoever shall liberate me now, I will kill him; and only suffer him to choose in what manner he will die. And lo, now thou hast liberated me, and I have given thee thy choice of the manner in which thou wilt die.

When the fisherman had heard the story of the 'Efrit, he exclaimed, O Allah! that I should not have liberated thee but in such a time as this! Then said he to the 'Efrit, Pardon me, and kill me not, and so may God pardon thee; and destroy me not, lest God give power over thee to one who will destroy thee. The Marid answered, I must positively kill thee; therefore choose by what manner of death thou wilt die. The fisherman then felt assured of his death; but he again implored the 'Efrit, saying, Pardon me by way of gratitude for my liberating thee.—Why, answered the 'Efrit, I am not going to kill thee but for that very reason, because thou hast liberated me.—O Sheykh of the 'Efrits, said the fisherman, do I act kindly toward thee, and dost thou recompense me with baseness?

The 'Efrit, when he heard these words, answered by saying, Covet not life, for thy death is unavoidable. Then said the fisherman within himself, This is a Jinni, and I am a man; and God hath given me sound reason; therefore, I will now plot his destruction with my art and reason, like as he hath plotted with his cunning and perfidy. So he said to the 'Efrit, Hast thou determined to kill me? He answered, Yes. Then said he, By the Most Great Name engraved upon the seal of Suleyman, I will ask thee one question; and wilt thou answer it to me truly? On hearing the mention of the Most Great Name, the 'Efrit was agitated, and trembled, and replied, Yes; ask, and be brief. The fisherman then said, How wast thou in this bottle? It will not contain thy hand or thy foot; how then can it contain thy whole body?—Dost thou not believe that I was in it? said the 'Efrit. The fisherman answered, I will never believe thee until I see thee in it.

Upon this, the 'Efrit shook, and became converted again into smoke, which rose to the sky, and then became condensed, and entered the bottle by little and little, until it was all enclosed; when the fisherman hastily snatched the sealed leaden stopper, and, having replaced it in the mouth of the bottle, called out to the 'Efrit, and said, Choose in what manner of death thou wilt die. I will assuredly throw thee here into the sea, and build me a house on this spot; and whosoever shall come here, I will prevent his fishing in this place, and will say to him, Here is an 'Efrit, who, to any person that liberates him, will propose various kinds of death, and then give him his choice of one of them. On hearing these words of the fisherman, the 'Efrit endeavored to escape; but could not, finding himself restrained by the impression of the seal of Suleyman, and thus imprisoned by the fisherman as the vilest and filthiest and least of 'Efrits.

The fisherman then took the bottle to the brink of the sea. The 'Efrit exclaimed, Nay! nay!—to which the fisherman answered, Yea, without fail! yea, without fail! The Marid then addressing him with a soft voice and humble manner, said, What dost thou intend to do with me, O fisherman? He answered, I will throw thee into the sea; and if thou hast been there a thousand and eight hundred years, I will make thee to remain there until the hour of judgment. Did I not say to thee, spare me, and so may God spare thee; and destroy me not, lest God destroy thee? But thou didst reject my petition, and wouldest nothing but treachery; therefore God hath caused thee to fall into my hand, and I have betrayed thee.

The 'Efrit then said, Liberate me, for this is an opportunity for thee to display humanity; and I vow to thee that I will never do thee harm; but, on the contrary, will do thee a service that shall enrich thee forever.

Upon this the fisherman accepted his covenant that he would not hurt him, but that he would do him good; and when he had bound him by oaths and vows, and made him swear by the Most Great Name of God, he opened to him; and the smoke ascended until it had all come forth, and then collected together, and became, as before, an 'Efrit of hideous form. The 'Efrit then kicked the bottle into the sea. When the fisherman saw him do this, he made sure of destruction, and said, This is no sign of good:—but afterward he fortified his heart, and said, O 'Efrit, thou has covenanted with me, and sworn that thou wilt not act treacherously toward me; therefore, if thou so act, God will recompense thee; for He is jealous; He respiteth, but suffereth not to escape.

The 'Efrit laughed, and, walking on before him, said, O fisherman, follow me. The fisherman did so, not believing in his escape, until they had quitted the neighborhood of the city, and ascended a mountain, and descended into a wide desert tract, in the midst of which was a lake of water. Here the 'Efrit stopped, and ordered the fisherman to cast his net and take some fish; and the fisherman, looking into the lake, saw in it fish of different colors, white and red and blue and yellow; at which he was astonished; and he cast his net, and drew it in, and found in it four fish, each fish of a different color from the others, at the sight of which he rejoiced.

The 'Efrit then said to him, Take them to the Sultan, and present them to him, and he will give thee what will enrich thee; and for the sake of God accept my excuse, for, at present, I know no other way of rewarding thee, having been in the sea a thousand and eight hundred years, and not seen the surface of the earth until now: but take not fish from the lake more than once each day: and now I commend thee to the care of God.—Having thus said, he struck the earth with his feet, and it clove asunder, and swallowed him.

The fisherman then went back to the city, wondering at all that had befallen him with the 'Efrit, and carried the fish to his house; and he took an earthen bowl, and, having filled it with water, put the fish into it; and they struggled in the water: and when he had done this, he placed the bowl upon his head, and repaired to the King's palace, as the 'Efrit had commanded him, and, going up unto the King, presented to him the fish; and the King was excessively astonished at them, for he had never seen any like them in the course of his life; and he said, Give these fish to the cook-maid.

This maid had been sent as a present to him by the King of the Greeks, three days before; and he had not yet tried her skill. The Wezir, therefore, ordered her to fry the fish, and said to her, O maid, gratify us by a specimen of thy excellent cookery, for a person hath brought these fish as a present to the Sultan. After having thus charged her, the Wezir returned, and the King ordered him to give the fisherman four hundred pieces of gold: so the Wezir gave them to him; and he took them in his lap, and returned to his home and his wife, joyful and happy, and bought what was needful for his family.

Such were the events that befell the fisherman: now we must relate what happened to the maid.—She took the fish, and cleaned them, and arranged them in the frying-pan, and left them until one side was cooked, when she turned them upon the other side, and lo, the wall of the kitchen clove asunder, and there came forth from it a damsel of tall stature, smooth-cheeked, of perfect form; wearing a kufiyeh interwoven with blue silk; with rings in her ears, and bracelets on her wrists, and rings set with precious jewels on her fingers; and in her hand was a rod of Indian cane: and she dipped the end of the rod in the frying-pan, and said, O fish, are ye remaining faithful to your covenant? At the sight of this, the cook-maid fainted. The damsel then repeated the same words a second and a third time; after which the fish raised their heads from the frying-pan, and answered, Yes, yes. They then repeated the following verse:—

If thou return, we return; and if thou come, we come; and if thou forsake, we verily do the same.

And upon this the damsel overturned the frying-pan, and departed by the way she had entered, and the wall of the kitchen closed up again. The cook-maid then arose, and beheld the four fish burnt like charcoal; and she exclaimed, In his first encounter his staff broke!—and as she sat reproaching herself, she beheld the Wezir standing at her head; and he said to her,

Bring the fish to the Sultan:—and she wept, and informed him of what had happened.

The Wezir was astonished at her words, and exclaimed, This is indeed a wonderful event;—and he sent for the fisherman, and when he was brought, he said to him, O fisherman, thou must bring to us four fish like those which thou broughtest before. The fisherman accordingly went forth to the lake, and threw his net, and when he had drawn it in he found in it four fish as before; and he took them to the Wezir, who went with them to the maid, and said to her, Rise, and fry them in my presence, that I may witness this occurrence.

The maid, therefore, prepared the fish, and put them in the frying-pan, and they had remained but a little while, when the wall clove asunder, and the damsel appeared, clad as before, and holding the rod; and she dipped the end of the rod in the frying-pan, and said, O fish, O fish, are ye remaining faithful to your old covenant? Upon which they raised their heads, and answered as before; and the damsel overturned the frying-pan with the rod, and returned by the way she had entered, and the wall closed up again.

The Wezir then said, This is an event which cannot be concealed from the King:—so he went to him, and informed him of what had happened in his presence; and the King said, I must see this with my own eyes. He sent, therefore, to the fisherman, and commanded him to bring four fish like the former; granting him a delay of three days. And the fisherman repaired to the lake, and brought the fish thence to the King, who ordered again that four hundred pieces of gold should be given to him; and then, turning to the Wezir, said to him, Cook the fish thyself here before me.

The Wezir answered, I hear and obey. He brought the frying-pan, and, after he had cleaned the fish, threw them into it; and as soon as he had turned them, the wall clove asunder, and there came forth from it a man, in size like a bull, having in his hand a branch of a green tree; and he said, with a clear but terrifying voice, O fish, O fish, are ye remaining faithful to your old covenant? Upon which they raised their heads, and answered as before, Yes, yes:

If thou return, we return; and if thou come, we come;
and if thou forsake, we verily do the same.

The man then approached the frying-pan, and overturned it with the branch, and the fish became like charcoal, and he went away as he had come.

When he had thus disappeared from before their eyes, the King said, This is an event respecting which it is impossible to keep silence, and there must, undoubtedly, be some strange circumstance connected with these fish. He then ordered that the fisherman should be brought before him, and when he had come, he said to him, Whence came these fish? The fisherman answered, From a lake between four mountains behind this mountain which is without thy city. The King said to him, How many days' journey distant? He answered, O our lord the Sultan, a journey of half-an-hour. And the Sultan was astonished, and ordered his troops to go out immediately with him and the fisherman, who began to curse the 'Efrit.

They proceeded until they had ascended the mountain, and descended into a wide desert tract which they had never before seen in their whole lives; and the Sultan and all the troops wondered at the sight of this desert, which was between four mountains, and at the fish, which were of four colors, red and white, and yellow and blue. The King paused in astonishment, and said to the troops, and to the other attendants who were with him, Hath any one of you before seen this lake in this place? They all answered, No. Then said the King, By Allah, I will not enter my city, nor will I sit upon my throne, until I know the true history of this lake, and of its fish. And upon this he ordered his people to encamp around these mountains; and they did so.

The King disguised himself, and slung on his sword, and withdrew himself from the midst of his troops. He journeyed the whole of the night, until the morning, and proceeded until the heat became oppressive to him: he then paused to rest; after which he again proceeded the remainder of the day and the second night until the morning, when there appeared before him, in the distance, something black, at the sight of which he rejoiced, and said, Perhaps I shall there find some person who will inform me of the history of the lake and its fish.

And when he approached this black object, he found it to be a palace built of black stones, and overlaid with iron; and one of the leaves of its door was open, and the other shut. The King was glad, and he stood at the door, and knocked gently, but heard no answer; he knocked a second and a third time, but again heard no answer: then he knocked a fourth time, and with violence; but no one answered. So he said, It is doubtless empty:—and he took courage, and entered from the door into the passage, and cried out, saying, O inhabitants of the palace, I am a stranger and a traveler! have ye any provision? And he repeated these words a second and a third time; but heard no answer.

And upon this he fortified his heart, and emboldened himself, and proceeded from the passage into the midst of the palace; but he found no one there, and only saw that it was furnished, and that there was, in the center of it, a fountain with four lions of red gold, which poured forth the water from their mouths like pearls and jewels: around this were birds; and over the top of the palace was extended a net which prevented their flying out. At the sight of these objects he was astonished, and he was grieved that he saw no person there whom he could ask for information respecting the lake, and the fish, and the mountains, and the palace. He then sat down between the doors, reflecting upon these things; and as he thus sat, he heard a voice of lamentation from a sorrowful heart, chanting these verses:—

O fortune, thou pitiest me not, nor releasest me! See
my heart is straitened between affliction and peril!

Will not you [O my wife] have compassion on the
mighty whom love hath abased, and the wealthy who is
reduced to indigence?

We were jealous even of the zephyr which passed
over you: but when the divine decree is issued, the eye
becometh blind!

What resource hath the archer when, in the hour
of conflict, he desireth to discharge the arrow, but
findeth his bowstring broken?

And when troubles are multiplied upon the
nobleminded, where shall he find refuge from fate and
from destiny?

When the Sultan heard this lamentation, he sprang upon
his feet, and, seeking the direction whence it proceeded,
found a curtain suspended before the door of a chamber; and
he raised it, and beheld behind it a young man sitting on a
couch raised to the height of a cubit from the floor. He was
a handsome youth, well-shaped, and of eloquent speech, with
shining forehead, and rosy cheek, marked with a mole resembling ambergris. The King was rejoiced at seeing him, and
saluted him; and the young man (who remained sitting, and
was clad with a vest of silk, embroidered with gold, but who
exhibited traces of grief) returned his salutation, and said to
him, O my master, excuse my not rising.—O youth! said the
King, inform me respecting the lake, and its fish of various
colors, and respecting this palace, and the reason of thy being
alone in it, and of thy lamentation.

When the young man heard these words, tears trickled
down his cheeks, and he wept bitterly. And the King was
astonished, and said to him, What causeth thee to weep, O
youth? He answered, How can I refrain from weeping, when
this is my state?—and so saying, he stretched forth his hand,
and lifted up the skirts of his clothing; and lo, half of him, from
his waist to the soles of his feet, was stone; and from his waist

to the hair of his head, he was like other men. He then said, Know, O King, that the story of the fish is extraordinary; if it were engraved upon the intellect, it would be a lesson to him who would be admonished.

Here Shahrazad perceived the day approaching and she became silent and her sister said, "What a delightful story!" Shahrazad answered and said, "It is nothing to what I will tell to-morrow night, if the King let me live." And the King said to himself, "By Allah, I will not kill her until I hear the rest of the story." One night after Shahrazad began:—

The Story of the
Young King of the Black Islands

My Father was king of the city which was here situate: (said the youth) his name was Mahmud, and he was lord of the Black Islands, and of the four mountains. After a reign of seventy years, he died, and I succeeded to his throne; whereupon I took as my wife the daughter of my uncle; and she loved me excessively, so that when I absented myself from her, she would neither eat nor drink till she saw me again. She remained under my protection five years. After this, she went one day to the bath; and I had commanded the cook to prepare the supper, and entered this palace, and slept in my usual place. I had ordered two maids to fan me; and one of them sat at my head, and the other at my feet; but I was restless, because my wife was not with me; and I could not sleep.

My eyes were closed, but my spirit was awake; and I heard the maid at my head say to her at my feet, O Mes'udeh, verily our lord is unfortunate in his youth, and what a pity is it that it should be passed with our depraved, wicked mistress!—Verily, our lord is careless in not making any inquiry respecting her.—Woe to thee! said the other: hath our lord any knowledge of her conduct, or doth she leave him to his choice? Nay, on the contrary, she contriveth to defraud him by means of the cup of wine which he drinketh every night before he sleepeth, putting benj[3] into it; in consequence of which he sleepeth so soundly that he knoweth not what happeneth, nor whither she goeth, nor what she doeth; for, after she hath given him the wine to drink, she dresseth herself, and goeth out from him, and is absent until daybreak, when she returneth to him, and burneth a perfume under his nose, upon which he awaketh from his sleep.

When I heard this conversation of the maids, the light became darkness before my face, and I was hardly conscious of the approach of night, when my cousin returned from the bath. The table was prepared, and we ate, and sat awhile drinking our wine as usual. I then called for the wine which I was accustomed to drink before I lay down to sleep, and she handed to me the cup; but I turned away, and, pretending to drink it as I was wont to do, poured it into my bosom, and immediately lay down: upon which she said, Sleep on; I wish that thou wouldst never wake again! By Allah, I abhor thee, and abhor thy person, and my soul is weary of thy company!—She then arose, and attired herself in the most magnificent of her apparel, and, having perfumed herself, and slung on a sword, opened the door of the palace, and went out.

I got up immediately, and followed her until she had quitted the palace, and passed through the streets of the city, and arrived at the city-gates, when she pronounced some words that I understood not; whereupon the locks fell off, and the gates opened, and she went out, I still following her,

---

3 Bhang, hemp, a drug.

without her knowledge. Thence she proceeded to a space among the mounds, and arrived at a strong edifice, in which was a kubbeh[4] constructed of mud, with a door, which she entered. I then climbed upon the roof of the kubbeh, and, looking down upon her through an aperture, saw that she was visiting a man.

She kissed the ground before him; and he raised his head toward her, and said, Woe to thee! Wherefore hast thou remained away until this hour? She answered, O my master, and beloved of my heart, knowest thou not that I am married to my cousin, and that I abhor every man who resembles him, and hate myself while I am in his company? If I did not fear to displease thee, I would reduce the city to ruins, so that the owl and the raven should cry in it, and would transport its stones beyond Mount Kaf[5]—Thou liest, thou infamous woman, replied the man; I will no longer give thee my company, thou faithless one!

My cousin still stood weeping, and abasing herself before him, and said, O my beloved, and treasure of my heart, there remaineth to me none but thee for whom I care, and if thou cast me off, alas for me! O my beloved! O light of mine eye!— Thus she continued to weep, and to humble herself before him, until he became pacified toward her; upon which she rejoiced, and said to him, O my master, hast thou here anything that thy maid may eat? He answered, Uncover the dough-pan; it contains some cooked rats' bones: eat of them, and pick them; and take this earthen pot: thou wilt find in it

---

4   A building with a dome.

5   The chain of mountains believed by Muslims to encircle the Earth.

some buzah[6] to drink. So she arose, and ate and drank, and washed her hands.

When I saw her do this, I became unconscious of my existence, and, descending from the roof of the kubbeh, entered, and took the sword from the side of my cousin, with the intention of killing them both. I struck the man upon his neck, and thought that he was killed; but the blow, which I gave with the view of severing his head, only cut the skin and flesh; and when I thought that I had killed him, he uttered a loud snore, upon which my cousin started up, and, as soon as I had gone, took the sword, and returned it to its scabbard, and came back to the city and to the palace, in which she remained until the morning.

On the following day, I observed that my cousin had cut off her hair, and put on the apparel of mourning; and she said to me, O my cousin, blame me not for what I do; for I have received news that my mother is dead, and that my father hath been slain in a holy war, and that one of my two brothers hath died of a poisonous sting, and the other by the fall of a house: it is natural, therefore, that I should weep and mourn. On hearing these words, I abstained from upbraiding her, and said, Do what seemeth fit to thee; for I will not oppose thee. Accordingly, she continued mourning and weeping and wailing a whole year; after which she said to me, I have a desire to build for myself, in thy palace, a tomb, with a kubbeh, that I may repair thither alone to mourn, and I will call it the House of Lamentations. I replied, Do what thou seest fit.

So she built for herself a house for mourning, with a kubbeh

---

6   Barley-beer.

in the middle of it, like the tomb of a saint; after which she removed thither the man, and there she lodged him. He was in a state of excessive weakness and from the day on which I had wounded him, he had never spoken; yet he remained alive, because the appointed term of his life had not expired. My cousin every day visited him in this tomb early and late, to weep and mourn over him, and took to him wine to drink, and boiled meats; and thus she continued to do, morning and evening, until the expiration of the second year, while I patiently suffered her, till, one day, I entered her apartment unawares, and found her weeping, and slapping her face, and repeating these verses:—

I have lost my existence among mankind since your absence; for my heart loveth none but you.

Take my body, then, in mercy, to the place where you are laid; and there bury me by your side:

And if, at my grave, you utter my name, the moaning of my bones shall answer to your call.

As soon as she had finished the recitation of these verses, I said to her, holding my drawn sword in my hand, This is the language of those faithless women who renounce the ties of affinity, and regard not lawful fellowship!—and I was about to strike her with the sword, and had lifted up my arm to do so, when she rose—for she knew that it was I who had wounded the man—and, standing before me, pronounced some words which I understood not, and said, May God, by means of my enchantment, make thee to be half of stone, and half of the substance of man!—whereupon I became as thou seest, unable to move, neither dead nor alive; and when I had been reduced to this state, she enchanted the city and its markets and fields.

The inhabitants of our city were of four classes: Muslims, and Christians, and Jews, and Magians; and she transformed them into fish: the white are the Muslims; the red the Magians; the blue, the Christians; and the yellow, the Jews. She transformed, also, the four islands into four mountains, and placed them around the lake; and from that time she has continued every day to torture me, inflicting upon me a hundred lashes with a leathern whip, until the blood flows from my wounds; after which she puts on my upper half a vest of hair-cloth, beneath these garments.—Having said thus, the young man wept.

Upon this, the King, looking toward the young man, said to him, O youth, thou has increased my anxiety. And where (he added) is this woman?—The young man answered, She is in the tomb where the man is lying, in the kubbeh; and every day, before she visits him, she strips me of my clothing, and inflicts upon me a hundred lashes with the whip, while I weep and cry out, unable to move so as to stop her. After thus torturing me, she repairs early to the man, with the wine and boiled meat.—By Allah, O youth, said the King, I will do thee an act of kindness for which I shall be remembered, and a favor which historians shall record in a biography after me.

He then sat and conversed with him until the approach of night, upon which he arose, and waited till the first dawn of day, when he took off his clothes, and slung on his sword and went to the place where the man lay. After remarking the candles and lamps, and perfumes and ointments, he approached the man, and with a blow of his sword slew him: he then carried him on his back, and threw him into a well which he found in the palace, and, returning to the kubbeh, clad himself with the man's clothes, and lay down with the drawn sword by his side.

Soon after, the vile enchantress went to her cousin, and, having pulled off his clothes, took the whip, and beat him, while he cried, Ah! it is enough for me to be in this state! Have pity on me then!—Didst thou shew pity to me, she exclaimed, and didst thou spare my lover?—She then put on him the hair-cloth vest and his outer garments, and went to the kubbeh with a cup of wine, and a bowl of boiled meat. Entering the tomb, she wept and wailed, exclaiming, O my master, answer me, and speak to me!

Upon this the King, speaking in a low voice, exclaimed, Ah! Ah! there is no strength nor power but in God! On hearing these words, she screamed with joy, and fell down in a swoon; and when she recovered, she exclaimed, Possibly my master is restored to health! The King, again lowering his voice, as if from weakness, replied, Thou wretch, thou deservest not that I should address thee.—Wherefore? said she. He answered, Because all the day long thou tormentest thy husband, while he calleth out, and imploreth the aid of God, so that thou hast prevented my sleeping from the commencement of darkness until morning: thy husband hath not ceased to humble himself, and to imprecate vengeance upon thee, till he hath distracted me; and had it not been for this,

I had recovered my strength: this it is which hath prevented my answering thee.—Then, with thy permission, she replied, I will liberate him from his present sufferings.—Liberate him, said the King, and give us ease.

She replied, I hear and obey;—and immediately arose, and went out from the kubbeh to the palace, and, taking a cup, filled it with water, and pronounced certain words over it, upon which it began to boil like a cauldron. She then sprinkled some of it upon her cousin, saying, By virtue of what I have uttered, be changed from thy present state to that in which thou wast at first!—and instantly he shook, and stood upon his feet, rejoicing in his liberation, and exclaimed, I testify that there is no deity but God, and that Mohammad is God's Apostle; God bless and save him! She then said to him, Depart, and return not hither, or I will kill thee:—and she cried out in his face: so he departed from before her, and she returned to the kubbeh, and said, O my master, come forth to me that I may behold thee. He replied, with a weak voice, What hast thou done? Thou hast relieved me from the branch, but hast not relieved me from the root.—O my beloved, she said, and what is the root? He answered, The people of this city, and of the four islands: every night, at the middle hour, the fish raise their heads, and imprecate vengeance upon me and upon thee; and this is the cause that preventeth the return of vigor to my body; therefore, liberate them, and come, and take my hand, and raise me; for vigor hath already in part returned to me.

On hearing these words of the King, she said to him with joy, In the name of Allah!—and she sprang up, full of happiness, and hastened to the lake, where, taking a little of its water, she pronounced over it some unintelligible words, whereupon the fish became agitated, and raised their heads, and immediately became converted into men as before. Thus was the enchantment removed from the inhabitants of the city, and the city became repeopled, and the market-streets rebuilt, and everyone returned to his occupation: the mountains also became changed into islands as they were at the first. The enchantress then returned immediately to the King, whom she still imagined to be the man, and said to him, O my beloved, stretch forth thy honored hand, that I may kiss it.—Approach me, said the King in a low voice. So she drew near to him; and he, having his keen-edged sword ready in his hand, thrust it into her bosom.

He found the young man who had been enchanted waiting his return, and congratulated him on his safety; and the young prince kissed his hand, and thanked him. The King then said to him, Wilt thou remain in thy city, or come with me to my capital?—O King of the age, said the young man, dost thou know the distance that is between thee and thy city? The King answered, Two days and a half.—O King, replied the young man, if thou hast been asleep, awake: between thee and thy city is a distance of a year's journey to him who traveleth with diligence; and thou camest in two days and a half only because the city was enchanted: but, O King, I will never quit thee for the twinkling of an eye. The King rejoiced at his words, and said, Praise be to God, who hath in his beneficence given thee to me: thou art my son; for during my whole life, I have never been blest with a son;—and they embraced each other, and rejoiced exceedingly. They then went together into the palace, where the King who had been enchanted informed the officers of his court that he was about to perform the holy pilgrimage: so they prepared for him everything that he required; and he departed with the Sultan.

He set forth, accompanied by fifty young men, and provided with presents, and they continued their journey night and day for a whole year, after which they drew near to the city of the Sultan, and the Wezir and the troops, who had lost all hope of his return, came forth to meet him. The troops, approaching him, kissed the ground before him, and congratulated him on his safe return; and he entered the city, and sat upon the throne. He then acquainted the Wezir with all that had happened to the young King; on hearing which, the Wezir congratulated the latter, also, on his safety; and when all things were restored to order, the Sultan bestowed presents upon a number of his subjects, and said to the Wezir, Bring to me the fisherman who presented to me the fish.

So he sent to this fisherman, who had been the cause of the restoration of the inhabitants of the enchanted city, and brought him; and the King invested him with a dress of honor, and inquired of him respecting his circumstances, and whether he had any children. The fisherman informed him that he had a son and two daughters; and the King, on hearing this, took as his wife one of the daughters, and the young prince married the other. The King also conferred upon the son the office of treasurer. He then sent the Wezir to the city of the young prince, the capital of the Black Islands, and invested him with its sovereignty, dispatching with him the fifty young men who had accompanied him thence, with numerous robes of honor to all the Emirs; and the Wezir kissed his hands, and set forth on his journey; while the Sultan and the young prince remained. And as to the fisherman, he became the wealthiest of the people of his age; and his daughters continued to be the wives of the Kings until they died.

But this (added Shahrazad) is not more wonderful than what the barber told about his fifth brother.

The Story
of Alnaschar

Once, when he was judging a case, a certain King had to listen to the accounts that a barber gave of himself and his brothers. Each of his brothers had had an extraordinary event happen to him. This is the story that the barber told of his fifth brother:—

My fifth brother, Alnaschar, O Prince of the Faithful, was a pauper who begged alms by night, and subsisted upon what he thus acquired by day; and our father was a very old man, and he fell sick and died, leaving us seven hundred pieces of silver, of which each of us took his portion: namely, a hundred pieces. Now Alnaschar, when he received his share, was perplexed, not knowing what to do with it; but while he was in this state, it occurred to his mind to buy with it all kinds of articles of glass, and to sell them and make profit: so he bought glass with his hundred pieces of silver, and put it in a large tray, and sat upon an elevated place, to sell it, leaning his back against a wall. And as he sat, he meditated, and said within himself, Verily my whole stock consisteth of this glass: I will sell it for two hundred pieces of silver; and with the two hundred I will buy other glass, which I will sell for four hundred; and thus I will continue buying and selling until I have acquired great wealth. Then with this I will purchase all kinds of merchandise and essences and jewels, and so obtain vast gain. After that, I will buy a handsome house, and horses, and gilded saddles; and I will eat and drink; and I will not leave in the city a single female singer but I will have her brought to my house that I may hear her songs.—All this he calculated with the tray of glass lying before him.

Then, said he, I will send all the female betrothers to seek in marriage for me the daughters of Kings and Wezirs; and I will demand as my wife the daughter of the chief Wezir; for I have heard that she is endowed with perfect beauty and surprising loveliness; and I will give as her dowry a thousand pieces of gold. If her father consent, my wish is attained; and when I have come back to my house, I will purchase the apparel of Kings and Sultans, and cause to be made for me a saddle of gold set with jewels; after which I will ride every day upon a horse, and go about through the streets and markets to amuse myself, while the people will salute me and pray for me. Then I will pay a visit to the Wezir; and when he seeth me, he will rise to me, in humility, and seat me in his own place; and he himself will sit down below me, because I am his son-in-law. I will then order one of the servants to bring a purse containing the pieces of gold which compose the dowry, and he will place it before the Wezir; and I will add to it another purse, that he may know my spirit and excessive generosity, and that the world is contemptible in my eye: and when he addresseth me with ten words, I will answer him with two. And I will return to my house; and when any person cometh to me from the house of the Wezir, I will clothe him with a rich dress: but if any come with a present, I will return it: I will certainly not accept it.

So saying, he kicked the tray of glass, which, being upon a place elevated above the ground, fell, and all that was in it broke: there escaped nothing: and he cried out and said, All this is the result of my pride! And he slapped his face, and tore his clothes; the passers-by gazing at him, while he wept, and exclaimed, Ah! O my grief!

The people were now repairing to perform the Friday-prayers; and some merely cast their eyes at him, while others noticed him not: but while he was in this state, deprived of his whole property, and weeping without intermission, a female approached him, on her way to attend the Friday-prayers: she was of admirable loveliness; the odor of musk was diffused from her; under her was a mule with a stuffed saddle covered with gold-embroidered silk; and with her was a number of servants; and when she saw the broken glass, and my brother's state and his tears, she was moved with pity for him, and asked respecting his case. She was answered, He had a tray of glass, by the sale of which to obtain his subsistence, and it is broken, and he is afflicted as thou seest:—and upon this, she called to one of the servants, saying, Give what thou hast with thee to this poor man. So he gave him a purse, and he took it, and when he had opened it, he found in it five hundred pieces of gold, whereupon he almost died from excessive joy, and offered up prayers for his benefactress.

He returned to his house a rich man, and sat reflecting, and lo, a person knocked at the door: he rose, therefore, and opened it; and beheld an old woman whom he knew not, and she said to him, O my son, know that the time of

prayer hath almost expired, and I am not prepared by ablution; wherefore I beg that thou wilt admit me into thy house,
that I may perform it. He replied, I hear and obey;—and,
retiring within, gave her permission to enter; his mind still
wandering from joy on account of the gold; and when she
had finished the ablution, she approached the spot where he
was sitting, and there performed the prayers of two rek'ahs.
She then offered up a supplication for my brother; and he
thanked her, and offered her two pieces of gold; but when
she saw this, she exclaimed, Extolled be God's perfection!
Verily I wonder at the person who fell in love with thee in
thy beggarly condition! Take back thy money from me, and
if thou want it not, return it to her who gave it thee when
thy glass broke.—O my mother, said he, how can I contrive
to obtain access to her? She answered, O my son, she hath
an affection for thee; take then with thee all thy money, and
when thou art with her be not deficient in courteousness
and agreeable words; so shalt thou obtain of her favors and
her wealth whatever thou shalt desire.

My brother, therefore, took all the gold, and arose and
went with the old woman, hardly believing what she had
told him; and she proceeded, and my brother behind her,
until they arrived at a great door, at which she knocked;
whereupon a damsel came and opened the door, and the
old woman entered, ordering my brother to do the same.
He did so, and found himself in a large house, where he
beheld a great furnished chamber, with curtains hung in
it; and, seating himself there, he put down the gold before
him, and placed his turban on his knees; and scarcely had
he done so, when there came to him a damsel, the like of

whom had never been seen, attired in most magnificent apparel. My brother stood up at her approach; and when she beheld him, she laughed in his face, and rejoiced at his visit: then going to the door, she locked it.

She then said to him, Move not from this place until I return to thee;—and was absent from him for a short period; and as my brother was waiting for her, there came in to him a guard, of gigantic stature, with a drawn sword, the brightness of which dazzled the sight; and he exclaimed to my brother, Woe to thee! Who brought thee to this place? Thou vilest of men! Thou misbegotten wretch, and nursling of impurity!—My brother was unable to make any reply; his tongue was instantly tied; and the man laid hold upon him, and stripped him, and struck him more than eighty blows with the flat of his sword, until he fell sprawling upon the floor; when he retired from him, concluding that he was dead, and uttered a great cry, so that the earth trembled, and the place resounded at his voice, saying, Where is El-Melihah?—upon which a girl came to him, holding a handsome tray containing salt; and with this she forthwith stuffed the flesh-wounds with which my brother's skin was gashed until they gaped open; but he moved not, fearing the man would discover that he was alive, and kill him. The girl then went away, and the man uttered another cry, like the first, whereupon the old woman came to my brother, and, dragging him by the feet to a deep and dark vault, threw him into it upon a heap of slain. In this place he remained for two whole days; and God (whose perfection be extolled!) made the salt to be the means of preserving his life, by stanching the flow of blood from his veins; so, when he found that he had strength sufficient to move, he arose, and, opening a shutter in the wall, emerged from the place of the slain; and God (to whom be ascribed all might and glory!) granted him his protection. He therefore proceeded in the darkness, and concealed himself in the passage until the morning, when the old woman went forth to seek another victim, and my brother, going out after her, without her knowledge, returned to his house.

He now occupied himself with the treatment of his wounds until he was restored; and continued to watch for the old woman, and constantly saw her taking men, one after another, and conducting them to the same house. But he uttered not a word on the subject; and when his health returned, and his strength was completely renewed, he took a piece of rag, and made of it a purse, which he filled with pieces of glass: he then tied it to his waist, and disguised himself so that no one would know him, in the dress of a foreigner; and, taking a sword, placed it within his clothes; and as soon as he saw the old woman, he said to her, in the dialect of a foreigner, Old woman, hast thou a pair of scales fit for weighing nine hundred pieces of gold? The old woman answered, I have a young son, a money-changer, and he hath all kinds of scales; therefore accompany me to him before he go forth from his abode, that he may weigh for thee thy gold. So my brother said, Walk on before me:—and she went, and my brother followed her until she arrived at the door, and knocked; upon which the girl came out, and laughed in his face; and the old woman said to her, I have brought you to-day some fat meat.

The girl then took my brother's hand, and conducted him into the house (the same which he had entered before), and after she had sat with him a short time, she rose, saying to him, Quit not this place until I return to thee:—and she retired; and my brother had remained not long after when the man came to him with the drawn sword, and said to him, Rise, thou unlucky! So my brother rose, and, as the man walked before him, he put his hand to the sword which was concealed beneath his clothes, and struck the man with it, and cut off his head; after which he dragged him by his feet to the vault, and called out, Where is El-Melihah? The girl, therefore, came, having in her hand the tray containing the salt; but when she saw my brother with the sword in his hand, she turned back and fled: my brother, however, overtook her. He called out, Where is the old woman?—and she came; and he said to her, Dost thou know me, O malevolent hag? She answered, No, O my lord.—I am, said he, the man who had the pieces of gold, and in whose house thou performedst the ablution, and prayedst; after which, devising a stratagem against me, thou betrayedst me into this place.—The old woman exclaimed, Fear God in thy treatment of me!—but my brother struck her with the sword.

He then went to search for the chief damsel, and when she saw him, her reason fled, and she implored his pardon; whereupon he granted her his pardon, and said to her, What occasioned thy falling into the hands of this witch? She answered, I was a servant to one of the merchants, and this old woman used to visit me; and one day she said to me, We are celebrating a festivity, the like of which no one hath seen, and I have a desire that thou shouldest witness it. I replied, I hear and obey:—and arose, and clad myself in the best of my attire, and, taking with me a purse containing a hundred pieces of gold, proceeded with her until she entered this house, and I have continued in this state three years, through the stratagem of the old witch.

My brother then said to her, Is there any property in the house?—Abundance, she answered; and if thou canst remove it, do so:—and upon this, he arose and went with her, when she opened to him chests filled with purses, at the sight of which he was confounded; and she said to him, Go now, and leave me here, and bring some person to remove the property. So he went out, and, having hired ten men, returned; but on his arrival at the door, he found it open, and saw neither the damsel nor the purses; he found, however, some little money remaining, and the stuffs. He discovered, therefore, that she had eluded him; and he took the money that remained, and, opening the closets, took all the stuffs which they contained, leaving nothing in the house.

He passed the next night full of happiness; but when the morning came, he found at the door twenty soldiers, and on his going forth to them, they laid hold upon him, saying, the Wali[7] summoneth thee. So they took him, and conducted him to the Wali, who, when he saw him, said to him, Whence obtainedst thou these stuffs?—My brother related to him all that had befallen him with the old woman from first to last, and the flight of the damsel; adding,—and of that which I have taken, take thou what thou wilt; but leave me wherewith to

---

7   Wali, a magistrate.

procure my food. The Wali thereupon demanded the whole of the money and the stuffs; but fearing that the Sultan might become acquainted with the matter, he retained a portion only, and gave the rest to my brother, saying to him, Quit this city, or I will hang thee. My brother replied, I hear and obey:—and went forth to one of the surrounding cities.

The Story
of the Magic Horse

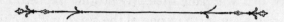

There was, in ancient times, in the country of the Persians, a mighty King, of great dignity, who had three daughters, like shining full moons and flowery gardens; and he had a male child, like the moon. He observed two annual festivals, that of the New-year's-day, and that of the Autumnal Equinox; and it was his custom, on these occasions, to open his palaces, and give his gifts, and make proclamation of safety and security, and promote the chamberlains and lieutenants: the people of his dominions also used to go in to him and salute him, and congratulate him on the festival, offering him presents, and he loved philosophy and geometry. And while the King was sitting on the throne of his dominions, on a certain day, during one of these festivals, there came in to him three sages: with one of them was a peacock of gold; and with the second, a trumpet of brass; and with the third, a horse of ivory and ebony: whereupon the King said to them, What are these things, and what is their use? The owner of the peacock answered, The use of this peacock is, that whenever an hour of the night or day passeth, it will flap its wings, and utter a cry. And the owner of the trumpet said, If this trumpet be placed at the gate of the city, it will be as a defender of it; for if an enemy enter the city, this trumpet will send forth a sound against him; so he will be known and arrested. And the owner of the horse said, O my lord, the use of this horse is, that if a man mount it, it will convey him to whatever country he desireth.

Upon this the King said, I will not bestow any favor upon you until I make trial of the uses of these things. Then he made trial of the peacock, and found it to be as its owner had said. And he made trial of the trumpet, and found it as its owner had said. He therefore said to the two sages (the owners of the peacock and the trumpet), Request of me what ye will. And they replied, We request of thee that thou marry to each of us one of thy daughters. Whereupon the King bestowed upon them two of his daughters. Then the third sage, the owner of the horse, advanced, and, having kissed the ground before the King, said to him, O King of the age, bestow upon me like as thou hast bestowed upon my companions. The King replied, When I shall have made trial of that which thou hast brought. And upon this, the King's son advanced and said, O my father, I will mount this horse, and make trial of it, and obtain proof of its use. So the King replied, O my son, try it as thou desirest.

The King's son accordingly arose, and mounted the horse, and urged it with his feet; but it moved not from its place. He therefore said, O sage, where is its rapidity of pace of which thou boastedst? And on hearing this, the sage came to him, and shewed him a turning-pin, by which to make it ascend; saying to him, Turn this pin. And the King's son turned it, and, lo, the horse moved, and soared with him toward the upper region of the sky, and ceased not its flight with him until he was out of sight of the people; whereupon the prince was perplexed at his case, and repented of his having mounted the horse. He said, The sage hath made use of a stratagem to destroy me. He began to examine all the members of the horse; and while he was doing so, he saw a thing like the head of a rooster, on the horse's right shoulder, and the same on the left shoulder: so he said, I see not any indication except these two buttons. And he turned the button that was on the right shoulder; upon which the horse bore him upward with increased velocity into the sky: so he took off his hand from that button, and, looking at the left shoulder, and seeing the button that was there, he turned it; and the movements of the horse became lessened in velocity, and changed from ascending to descending. It ceased not to descend with him toward the earth by little and little, while he continued to exercise caution for his safety; and when he saw this, and knew the uses of the horse, his heart was filled with joy and happiness, and he thanked God (whose name be exalted!) for the favor that He had shewn him in saving him from destruction. He ceased not to descend for the whole of the remainder of the day; for in his ascent, the earth had become distant from him; and he turned about the face of the horse as he desired, while it descended with him: when he would, he was carried downward by it; and when he would, he was borne by it upward.

Now when he had obtained what he desired with respect to the horse, he proceeded on it toward the earth, and began to look at its countries and cities, which he knew not; for he had never seen them before during the whole of his life. And among the objects that he beheld was a city constructed in the most excellent manner, in the midst of a land beautifully verdant, with trees and rivers: upon which he meditated in his mind, and said, Would that I knew what is the name of this city, and in what region it is. He then made a circuit around the city, viewing it attentively, right and left. The day had nearly departed, and the sun was about to set: so he said within himself, I have not found any place in which to pass the night better than this city: I will therefore pass this night in it, and in the morning I will return to my family and my royal residence, and acquaint my family and my father with that which hath happened to me, and inform him of the things that mine eyes have seen. Accordingly he began to search for a place in which he might feel secure of the safety of himself and his horse, and where no one might see him; and while he was thus engaged, lo, he beheld, in the midst of the city, a palace rising high into the air, surrounded by a large wall with high battlements; whereupon he said within himself, This place is agreeable.

He turned the button that caused the horse to descend, and ceased not to be carried downward on it until he descended steadily on the flat roof of the palace, when he alighted from the horse, and began to go around it, and to examine it, and said, By Allah, he who made thee thus was an expert sage; and if God (whose name be exalted!) extend the term of my life, and restore me to my country and my family in safety, and reunite me with my father, I will assuredly bestow every favor upon this sage, and treat him with the utmost beneficence. He then sat upon the roof of the palace until he knew that the inmates had betaken themselves to sleep. Hunger and thirst pained him; for since he had parted from his father he had not eaten food; and he said within himself, Verily such a palace as this is not devoid of the necessaries of life. He therefore left the horse in a place alone, and walked down to seek for something to eat; and finding a flight of steps, he descended by them to the lower part of the building, where he found a court paved with marble; and he wondered at this place, and at the beauty of its construction; but he heard not in the palace any sound, nor the cheering voice of an inhabitant. So he paused in perplexity, and looked to the right and left, not knowing whither to go. Then he said within himself, there is no better course for me than to return to the place in which is my horse, and to pass the night by it; and when the morning cometh, to mount and depart.

But while he was addressing himself with these words, he beheld a light approaching the place where he stood, and, looking attentively at that light, he found that it was with a party of female servants, among whom was a beautiful damsel, resembling the splendid full moon.

That damsel was the daughter of the King of this city; and her father loved her with so great an affection that he built for her this palace; and whenever her heart was contracted, she used to come hither, together with her attendants, and to remain here a day, or two days, or more; after which she returned to the palace where she generally resided. It happened that she came that night for the sake of diversion and dilatation of the mind. When the women entered the palace, they spread the furniture, and gave vent to the odors from the perfuming-vessels, and sported and rejoiced. Now while they were thus engaged, the King's son rushed upon that guard, and, taking the sword from his hand, ran upon the servants who were with the King's daughter, and dispersed them to the right and left. And when the King's daughter saw his beauty and loveliness, she said, Perhaps thou art he who demanded me in marriage yesterday, and whom my father rejected, and whom he asserted to be of hideous aspect. By Allah, my father lied in saying those words; for thou art none other than a handsome person.

Now the son of the King of India had requested her of her father, and he had rejected him, because he was disagreeable in aspect; and she imagined that the prince now before her was he who had demanded her in marriage. She then came to him, and embraced and kissed him, and seated herself with him. The servants, however, said to her, O our mistress, this is not the person who demanded thee in marriage of thy father; for that person was hideous, and this is handsome; and he who demanded thee of thy father, and whom he rejected, is not fit to be a servant to this person: but, O our mistress, verily this young man is one of high dignity.

And, after this, the servants went to the prostrated guard, and roused him; whereupon he sprang up in alarm, and searched for his sword, not finding it in his hand. So the servants said to him, He who took thy sword, and laid thee prostrate, is sitting with the King's daughter.—Now the King had charged this guard with the office of protecting his daughter, in his fear for her from misfortunes and evil accidents.—The guard therefore arose, and went to the curtain, and when he raised it, he saw the King's daughter sitting with the King's son, and they were conversing together; and as soon as he beheld them, he said to the King's son, O my master, art thou a human being or a

Jinni? To which the King's son replied, How is it that thou regardest the sons of the royal Kisras as of the unbelieving devils?—Then, taking the sword in his hand, he said to him, I am the son-in-law of the King, and he hath married me to his daughter. So when the guard heard these words from him, he said to him, O my master, if thou be of the human species, as thou hast asserted, she is suited to none but thee, and thou art more worthy of her than any other.

The guard then went shrieking to the King; and he tore his clothes, and threw dust upon his head. And when the King heard his crying, he said to him, What hath befallen thee; for thou hast agitated my heart? Acquaint me quickly, and be brief in thy words.—He therefore answered him, O King, go to the assistance of thy daughter; for a devil of the Jinn, in the garb of human beings, and having the form of the sons of the Kings, hath got possession of her: therefore seize him. And when the King heard these words from him, he thought to slay him, and said to him, How came it to pass that thou wast neglectful of my daughter, so that this event befell her? He then went to the palace wherein was his daughter, and on his arrival he found the servants standing there, and said to them, What is it that hath happened to my daughter? They answered him, O King, while we were sitting with her, suddenly there rushed upon us this young man, who resembleth the full moon, and than whom we have never seen anyone more handsome in countenance, with a drawn sword in his hand; and we inquired of him respecting his business, and he asserted that thou hadst married to him thy daughter: we know nothing more than this and we know not whether he be a human being or a Jinni. So when the King heard their words, his rage was cooled. He then raised the curtain by little and little, and looked, and beheld the King's son sitting with his daughter, conversing; and he was of most comely form, with a face like the shining full moon.

The King could not control himself, through his jealousy for his daughter. He therefore raised the curtain and entered, with a drawn sword in his hand, and rushed upon them. The King's son, on seeing him, said to her, Is this thy father? She answered, Yes. And upon this, he sprang upon his feet, and, taking his sword in his hand, shouted at the King with an amazing cry which terrified him. The King, perceiving that the prince was stronger than he, sheathed his sword, and stood until the King's son came up to him, when he met him with courtesy, and said to him, O young man, art thou a human being or a Jinni? The King's son replied, Were it not that I respect thy right and the honor of thy daughter, I had shed thy blood. How is it that thou derivest me from the devils, when I am of the sons of the royal Kisras, who, if they desired to take thy kingdom, would make thee totter from thy glory and dominion, and despoil thee of all that is in thy dwellings?—So the King, on hearing his words, dreaded and feared him; but said to him, If thou be of the sons of the Kings, as thou hast asserted, how is it that thou hast entered my palace without my permission, and dishonored me, and come unto my daughter, asserting that thou art her husband, and pretending that I had married thee to her, when I have killed the Kings and the sons of the Kings on their demanding her of me in marriage? And who will save thee from my power, when, if I cried out to my soldiers and commanded them to slay thee, they would slay thee immediately? Who then can deliver thee from my hand?

The King's son, however, when he heard these words from him, said to the King, Verily I wonder at thee, and at the smallness of thy penetration. Dost thou covet for thy daughter a husband better than myself; and hast thou seen anyone more firm of heart, and superior in requital, and more glorious in authority and troops and guards than I am?—The King answered him, No, by Allah: but I would, O young man, that thou demand her in marriage publicly, that I may marry her to thee; for if I marry her to thee privately, thou wilt disgrace me by so taking her. And the King's son replied, Thou hast said well; but, O King, if thy servants and troops were to assemble against me and slay me, as thou hast imagined, thou wouldst disgrace thyself, and the people would be divided with respect to thee, some believing, and others accusing thee by falsehood. It is my opinion that thou shouldst relinquish this idea, and adopt the course that I will point out to thee.—So the King said, Propose what thou wilt. And the King's son rejoined, What I propose to thee is this: either that thou meet me in single combat, and he who killeth the other shall be more deserving and worthy of the kingdom; or else, that thou leave me this night, and when the morning cometh, that thou send forth to me thy soldiers and troops. When the day beginneth, send them forth to me, and say to them, This person hath demanded of me my daughter in marriage on the condition that he will meet you all in combat; and he hath pretended that he will overcome and subdue you, and that ye cannot prevail against him. Then leave me with them to combat them; and if they kill me, the result will be more proper for the concealment of thy secret and the preserving of thine honor; but if I overcome and subdue them, then am I such a person as the King should desire for his son-in-law.—And when the King heard his words, he approved of his advice and accepted it, notwithstanding that he wondered at his saying, and was struck with terror at his determination to meet in combat all his army that he had described unto him.

And after this, the King called his servant, and commanded him to go forth immediately to his Wezir, and to desire him to collect all the troops, and order them to equip themselves with their arms, and to mount their horses. So the servant went to the Wezir, and acquainted him with that which the King had commanded. And upon this the Wezir summoned the chiefs of the army, and the grandees of the empire, and ordered them to mount their horses, and to go forth equipped with the weapons of war.—Meanwhile, the King continued to converse with the young man, being pleased with his conversation and sense and good breeding; and as they were talking together, the morning arrived. The King therefore arose, went to his throne, and ordered his troops to mount. Then he proceeded, with the young man before him, until they arrived at the horse-course, when the young man looked at the troops and their number. And the King called out, O companies of men, a young man hath come unto me demanding in marriage my daughter, and I have never beheld any handsomer than he, nor any stronger in heart, nor any greater in intrepidity than he: and he hath

asserted that he alone will overcome you. But when he cometh forth to combat you, receive him upon the points of your
spears, and the edges of your swords; for he hath undertaken
a great enterprise.

The King then said to the young man, O my son, do as
thou desirest with them. But he replied, O King, thou hast
not treated me equitably. How shall I go forth to combat
them when I am on foot and thy people are mounted on
horses?—So the King said to him, Take then of the horses
and choose of them that which thou wilt.—He replied,
None of thy horses pleaseth me, and I will mount none but
the horse on which I came. The King therefore said to him,
And where is thy horse? He answered him, It is on the top
of thy palace.—In what place in my palace? asked the King.
He answered, On the roof of the palace. And when the King
heard his words, he said to him, This is the first instance
that hath appeared of thine insanity. O, woe to thee! How
can the horse be upon the roof? But now will thy veracity be distinguished from thy lying.—Then the King looked
toward one of his chief officers, and said to him, Go to my
palace, and bring what thou shalt find upon the roof. And
the people wondered at the words of the young man; one
saying to another, How can this horse descend the stairs
from the roof? Verily, this is a thing the like of which we
have never heard!

Now the person whom the King had sent to the palace
ascended to its roof, and beheld the horse standing there;
and he had seen none more handsome than it; and he
approached it and examined it, and found it to be of ebony
and ivory. Some others of the chief officers of the King also

went up with this person; and when they beheld the horse, they laughed together, and said, Did the young man speak of such a horse as this? We imagine that he is no other than a madman: but his case will soon appear to us; and perhaps he may be a person of great importance.—They then raised the horse upon their hands, and carried it without stopping until they came before the King, when they placed it before him; and the people assembled around it, gazing at it, and wondering at the beauty of its make, and at the beauty of its saddle and bridle. The King also admired it, and wondered at it extremely; and he said to the King's son, O young man, is this thy horse? He answered, Yes, O King, this is my horse, and thou shalt see a wonder performed by it. The King said to him, Take thy horse and mount it. But he replied, I will not mount it unless the troops retire to a distance from it. So the King commanded the troops that were around him to retire from it as far as an arrow might be shot.

Then said the young man, O King, I am going to mount my horse, and charge upon thine army, and disperse them to the right and left, and split their hearts. The King replied, Do what thou desirest, and pity them not; for they will not pity thee. And the King's son went to the horse and mounted it. The troops were arranged in ranks before him; and one said to another, When the young man arriveth between the ranks, we will receive him with the points of the spears, and the edges of the swords. But one of them said, By Allah, it is a calamity! How shall we kill this young man?—And another said, By Allah, ye shall by no means reach him unless after a great event; and the young man hath not done these deeds but from his knowledge of his own valor and preeminence.

And when the King's son had seated himself firmly upon his horse, he turned the pin of ascent. The eyes of the spectators were strained to see what he would do; and his horse bestirred itself, and moved about with violent action, until it had performed the most extraordinary of the motions of horses, and its body became filled with air. Then it rose, and ascended into the sky. So when the King saw that he had risen, and ascended aloft, he called out to his troops, and said, Woe to you! Take him before he escape from you.—But his Wezir and lieutenants replied, O King, can anyone catch the flying bird? This is none other than a great enchanter. God hath saved thee from him: therefore praise God (whose name be exalted!) for thine escape from his hand.

The King therefore returned to his palace, after he had witnessed these acts of the King's son; and when he arrived at his palace, he went to his daughter, and acquainted her with that which had happened to him with the King's son; but he found her greatly lamenting for him, and for her separation from him; and she fell into a violent sickness, and took to her bed. So when her father saw her in this state he pressed her to his bosom, kissed her between the eyes, and said to her, O my daughter, praise God (whose name be exalted!) and thank Him for our escape from this crafty enchanter. He began to repeat to her the account of the deeds of the King's son that he had witnessed, describing to her how he had ascended into the air. But she listened to nought of her father's words; her weeping and wailing increased in violence, and afterward she said within herself, By Allah, I will not eat food, nor drink any beverage, until God reunite me with him. Therefore exceeding anxiety overcame her father the King on account of this; the state of his daughter afflicted him, and he mourned in heart for her; and every time that he addressed her with soothing words, she only increased in her passion for the young man.—Such was her case.

Now, as to the King's son, when he had ascended into the sky, being alone, he reflected upon the beauty of the damsel, and her loveliness. He had inquired of the King's people respecting the name of the city, and the name of the King, and that of his daughter; and that city was the city of San'a. He then prosecuted his journey with diligence until he came in sight of the city of his father; and after he had made a circuit around the city, he bent his course to his father's palace, and descended upon the roof. Having left his horse there, he descended to his father, and went in to him, and he found him mourning and afflicted on account of his separation: therefore, when his father saw him, he rose to him and embraced him, pressing him to his bosom, and rejoicing exceedingly at his return. And the Prince inquired of his father respecting the sage who made the horse, saying, O my father, what hath fortune done with him? His father answered him, May God not bless the sage nor the hour in which I beheld him; for he was the cause of thy separation from us, and he hath been imprisoned, O my son, since thou absentedst thyself from us.

He gave orders, however, to relieve him, and take him forth from the prison, and bring him before him; and when he came before him, he invested him with an honorary dress in token of satisfaction, and treated him with the utmost beneficence; but would not marry his daughter to him. So the sage was violently enraged at this, and repented of that which he had done, knowing that the King's son had become acquainted with the secret of the horse and the mode of its motion. Then the King said to his son, It is my opinion that thou shouldst not approach this horse henceforth, nor mount it after this day; for thou knowest not its properties, and thou art deceived respecting it. The King's son had related to his father what had happened to him with the daughter of the King, the lord of the city, and what had happened to him with her father; and his father said to him, Had the King desired to slay thee, he had slain thee; but the end of thy life was delayed.

After this, they ate and drank and were merry; and there was with the King a female musician, who played upon the lute; and she took the lute, and began to play upon it, singing of absence, before the King and his son; and she sang these verses:—

Think not that absence hath made me forget: for if I forget you, what shall I remember?

Time passeth; but never shall our love for you end: in our love for you we will die and be raised.

Then anxious thoughts were aroused in the mind of the King's son by his love of the damsel, the daughter of the King of San'a: so he rose and went to the horse and mounted it, and turned the pin of ascent; whereupon it soared with him into the air, and rose with him toward the upper region of the sky. And in the morning, his father missed him, and found him not: he therefore went up to the top of the palace, in a state of affliction, and he beheld his son mounting into the air; and upon this he grieved for his separation, and repented extremely that he had not taken the horse and concealed it. He said within himself, By Allah, if my son returns to me, I will not preserve this horse, that my heart may be at rest respecting my son. And he resumed his weeping and wailing.

But as to his son, he ceased not his course through the sky until he came to the city of San'a, when he descended in the place where he descended the first time, and he walked down stealthily until he came to the chamber of the King's daughter; but he found neither her nor her female servants, nor the man who was her guard; and the event greatly afflicted him. Then he went about searching for her through the palace, and at last he found her in a different chamber from that in which he had been with her. She had taken to the pillow, and around her were the female servants and nurses. And he went in to them and saluted them; and when the damsel heard his speech, she rose to him and embraced him. He said to her, O my mistress, thou hast rendered me desolate during this period. And she replied, Thou hast rendered *me* desolate, and had thine absence from me continued longer, I had perished without doubt.—O my mistress, he rejoined, what thoughtest thou of my conduct with thy father, and his actions to me? Were it not for my love of thee, I had slain him, and made him an example to beholders: but I love him for thy sake.—And she said to him, How couldst thou absent thyself from me? Can my life be pleasant after thy departure?—He then said to her, Wilt thou comply with my desire, and listen to my words? She answered him, Say what thou wilt; for I will consent to that which thou requirest me to do, and will not oppose thee in anything. And he said to her, Journey with me to my country and my kingdom. She replied, Most willingly.

So when the King's son heard her words, he rejoiced exceedingly, and, taking her by her hand, he made her swear by God (whose name be exalted!) that she would do so. Then he led her up to the roof of the palace, mounted his horse, and placed her on it behind him, and after he had bound her firmly, he turned the pin of ascent in the shoulder of the horse, and it ascended with them into the sky. Upon this the female servants cried out, and informed the King her father, and her mother, who thereupon came up in haste to the roof of the palace; and the King, looking up into the sky, beheld the ebony horse soaring with them in the air. The King was agitated, and his agitation increased, and he called out and said, O son of the King, I conjure thee by Allah that thou have mercy upon me, and have mercy upon my wife, and that thou make not a separation between us and our daughter! The King's son, however, answered him not; but he imagined that the damsel repented of parting from her mother and her father; so he said to her, Dost thou desire that I restore thee to thy mother and thy father?—O my love, she answered, by Allah, that is not my desire: my desire is rather to be with thee wherever thou shalt be; for I am drawn off by my love of thee from everything else, even from my father and my mother. And when the King's son heard her reply, he rejoiced exceedingly, and began to make the horse proceed gently with them, that it might not disquiet her; and he ceased not to journey on with her until he beheld a green meadow, in which was a spring of water.

There they alighted, and ate and drank; after which, the King's son mounted his horse again, took her up behind him, and bound her, in his fear for her. He then proceeded with her, and ceased not in his course through the air until he arrived at the city of his father. His joy thereat was great; and he desired to shew to the damsel the seat of his power and the dominion of his father, and to inform her that the dominion of his father was greater than that of her father. He therefore deposited her in one of the gardens in which his father diverted himself, put her in a private chamber that was furnished for his father, and placed the ebony horse at the door of that chamber, charging the damsel to guard it, and saying to her, Sit here until I send to thee my messenger; for I am going to my father, to prepare for thee a palace, and to display to thee my dominion. And the damsel rejoiced when she heard from him these words, and replied, Do what thou desirest. Then it occurred to her mind that she was not to enter the city but with respect and honor, as was suitable to persons of her rank.

So the King's son left her, and proceeded until he arrived at the city, and went in to his father; and when his father saw him, he rejoiced at his coming, and met him and welcomed him; and the King's son said to his father, Know that I have brought the King's daughter of whom I informed thee, and I have left her without the city, in one of the gardens, and come to acquaint thee with her arrival, that thou mayest prepare the procession of state, and go forth to meet her, and display to her thy dominion and thy troops and guards. The King replied, Most willingly. And immediately he commanded the people of the city to decorate the city in the most handsome manner, and rode forth in a procession equipped in the most perfect manner and with the most magnificent decorations, with all his soldiers and the grandees of his empire, and all his servants.

The King's son also took forth, from his palace, ornaments and apparel and such things as Kings treasure up, and prepared for the damsel a camel-litter of green, red, and yellow brocade, in which he displayed wonderful treasures. Then he left the camel-litter and went on before to the garden; and he entered the private chamber in which he had left the damsel, and searched for her; but found her not, nor did he find the horse. Upon this he slapped his face and rent his clothes, and began to go round about through the garden, with a mind confounded; after which, he returned to his reason, and said within himself, How did she learn the secret of this horse when I did not acquaint her with aught of it? But perhaps the Persian sage who made the horse hath found her, and taken her, as a requital for that which my father hath done unto him.—Then the King's son sought the keepers of the garden, and asked them who had passed by them, saying, Have ye seen anyone pass by you and enter this garden? And they answered, We have not seen anyone enter this garden except the Persian sage; for he entered to collect useful herbs. So when he heard their words, he was convinced that the person who had taken the damsel was that sage.

Now it happened, in accordance with destiny, that, when the King's son left the damsel in the private chamber that was in the garden, and repaired to the palace of his father to make his preparations, the Persian sage entered the garden to collect some useful herbs, and smelt the odor of musk and other perfumes with which the air was impregnated; and this sweet scent was from the odor of the King's daughter. The sage therefore proceeded in the direction of this odor until he came to the private chamber, when he saw the horse that he had made with his hand standing at the door of the chamber. So when the sage saw the horse, his heart was filled with joy and happiness; for he had mourned after it greatly since it had gone from his possession. He approached it, and examined all its limbs, and found it sound; but when he was about to mount it and depart, he said within himself, I must see what the King's son hath brought and left here with the horse. Accordingly he entered the private chamber, and found the damsel sitting there, resembling the shining sun in the clear sky. As soon as he beheld her, he knew that she was a damsel of high dignity, and that the King's son had taken her, and brought her upon the horse, and left her in that private chamber while he repaired to the city to prepare for her a stately procession, and to conduct her into the city with respect and honor.

The sage therefore went in to her, and kissed the ground before her; and she raised her eyes toward him, and, looking at him, found him to be of most hideous aspect and disagreeable form; and she said to him, Who art thou? He answered her, O my mistress, I am the messenger of the King's son, who hath sent me to thee, and commanded me to remove thee to another garden, near unto the city. And when the damsel heard from him these words, she said to him, And where is the King's son? He answered her, He is in the city, with his father, and he will come to thee immediately with a grand procession. But she said to him, O thou! could not the King's son find anyone to send to me but thee?—And the sage laughed at her words, and replied, O my mistress, let not the hideousness of my face and the disagreeableness of my aspect deceive thee; for hadst thou experienced of me what the King's son hath, thou wouldst approve of me. Verily the King's son hath especially chosen me to send to thee on account of the hideousness of my aspect and the horrible nature of my form, through his jealousy of thee, and his love of thee.

So when the damsel heard his reply, it appeared reasonable to her, and she believed it, and arose and went with him, putting her hand in his. She then said to him, O my father, what hast thou brought with thee for me to ride?—O my mistress, he answered, the horse on which thou earnest thou shalt ride. She replied, I cannot ride it by myself. And when he heard this reply from her, the sage smiled, and knew that he had got possession of her; and he said to her, I myself will ride with thee. Then he mounted, and mounted the damsel behind him, and, pressing her to him, bound her tightly, while she knew not what he desired to do with her. And after this, he turned the pin of ascent, whereupon the body of the horse became filled with air, and it moved and bestirred itself, and ascended into the sky, and continued incessantly bearing them along until it was out of sight of the city. So the damsel said to him, O thou!

what meant that which thou saidst respecting the King's son, when thou assertedst that he sent thee to me?—The sage replied, May Allah keep the King's son from everything good; for he is base and vile!—O, woe to thee! she exclaimed; how is it that thou disobeyest thy lord in that which he hath commanded thee to do? He replied, He is not my lord. And knowest thou, he added, who I am? She answered him, I know thee not but as thou hast informed me of thyself. And he said to her, Verily my telling thee this was a stratagem that I made use of against thee and against the King's son. I was lamenting constantly for this horse that is beneath thee, for it is of my making, and he had made himself master of it; but now I have obtained possession of it and of thee also, and have tortured his heart as he hath tortured mine, and he will never have it in his power henceforth. And when the damsel heard his words, she cried out, O my grief! I have neither obtained my beloved nor remained with my father and my mother! And she wept violently for that which had befallen her, while the sage incessantly proceeded with her to the country of the Greeks, until he descended with her in a verdant meadow with rivers and trees.

This meadow was near unto a city, in which was a King of great dignity; and it happened on that day that the King of the city went forth to hunt, and to divert himself, and, passing by that meadow, he saw the sage standing there, with the horse and the damsel by his side. And the sage was not aware of their approach when the servants of the King rushed upon him, and took him, together with the damsel and the horse, and placed all before the King, who, when he

beheld the hideousness of his aspect, and the disagreeableness of his appearance, and beheld the beauty of the damsel,
and her loveliness, said to her, O my mistress, what relation
is this sheykh to thee? The sage hastily answered and said,
She is my wife, and the daughter of my paternal uncle. But
the damsel declared that he was a liar, as soon as she heard
his words, and said, O King, by Allah, I know him not, and
he is not my husband; but he took me away by force and
stratagem. And when the King heard what she said, he commanded that they should carry the sage to the city, and cast
him into the prison; and so they did with him; and the King
took the damsel and the horse from him; but he knew not
the property of the horse, nor the mode of its motion.—
Thus did it befall the sage and the damsel.

As to the King's son, he put on the apparel of travel,
and, having taken what money he required, journeyed forth
in a most evil state, and quickly endeavored to trace them,
seeking them from town to town and from city to city, and
inquiring respecting the ebony horse; and everyone who
heard his mention of the ebony horse wondered at it, and
was greatly astonished at his words. Thus he continued to
do for a long period; but notwithstanding his frequent questions and his searching for them, he met with no tidings of
them. Then he journeyed to the city of the damsel's father,
and there inquired for her, but he heard no tidings of her, and
he found her father mourning for her loss. So he returned,
and repaired to the country of the Greeks, endeavoring to
trace them, and inquiring respecting them.

And it happened that he alighted at one of the khans,
and saw a party of the merchants sitting conversing; and he

seated himself near them, and heard one of them say, O my
companions, I have met with a wonderful thing.—And what
was it? they asked. He answered, I was in a certain district,
in such a city (and he mentioned the name of the city in
which was the damsel), and I heard its inhabitants talking of
a strange story, which was this:—The King of the city went
forth one day to hunt, attended by a party of his associates
and the grandees of his empire, and when they went forth
into the desert, they passed by a verdant meadow, and found
there a man standing, and by his side a woman sitting, and
with him a horse of ebony. As to the man, he was of hideous aspect, very horrible in form; and as to the woman,
she was a damsel endowed with beauty and loveliness and
elegance and perfect grace and justness of stature; and as
to the ebony horse, it was a wonderful thing: eyes have not
beheld its superior in beauty or in comeliness of make.—The
persons present said to him, And what did the King with
them? He answered, As to the man, the King took him, and
asked him respecting the damsel, and he pretended that she
was his wife, and the daughter of his paternal uncle. But
as to the damsel, she declared that he lied in his assertion.
So the King took her from him, and gave orders to cast
him into the prison. And as to the ebony horse, I know not
what became of it.—When the King's son therefore heard
these words from the merchant, he approached him, and
proceeded to question him with mildness and courtesy until
he acquainted him with the name of the city and the name of
its King; and when he knew the name of the city and that of
its King, he passed the night happy; and in the morning he
went forth on his journey.

He ceased not to prosecute his journey until he arrived at that city; but when he desired to enter it, the gate-keepers took him, and would have conducted him into the presence of the King, that he might inquire of him respecting his condition, and the cause of his coming into that city, and as to what art or trade he was skilled in; for so was the King's custom to question the strangers respecting their conditions and their arts or trades. But the arrival of the King's son at that city happened to be at eventide; and that was a time at which it was not possible to go in to the King or to consult respecting him. So the gate-keepers took him and conducted him to the prison, to put him in it. When the jailers, however, saw his beauty and loveliness, they could not bear to put him in the prison: on the contrary, they seated him with themselves, outside the prison; and when the food was brought to them, he ate with them until he was satisfied; and after they had finished eating, they sat conversing and, addressing the King's son, they said to him, From what country art thou? He answered, I am from the country of Persia, the country of the Kisras. And when they heard his answer, they laughed, and one of them said to him, O Kisrawi, I have heard the sayings of men, and their histories, and have observed their condition; but I have neither seen, nor heard of, a greater liar than this Kisrawi who is with us in the prison. And another said, Nor have I seen anyone more hideous than he in person, or more disagreeable than he in form.

So the King's son said to them, What instance of his lying hath appeared unto you? They answered, He pretendeth that he is a sage, and the King saw him as he was going to hunt, and with him a woman of surprising beauty and loveliness, and elegance and perfect grace, and justness of stature, and there was with him also a horse of black ebony, than which we have never seen any more handsome. As to the damsel, she is with the King, and he loveth her; but the woman is mad; and if that man were a sage as he pretendeth, he had cured her; for the King is striving to find her remedy, desiring to recover her of her malady. As to the ebony horse, it is in the King's treasury; and as to the man of hideous aspect, who was with it, he is with us in the prison; and when the night overshadoweth him, he weepeth and waileth in his grief for himself, and suffereth us not to sleep.

Now when the keepers of the prison acquainted the King's son with these circumstances, it occurred to his mind that he might contrive a plan by means of which to attain his desire. And when the gate-keepers desired to sleep, they put him into the prison, and closed the door upon him; and he heard the sage weeping and lamenting for himself in the Persian language, and saying in his lamentation, Woe unto me for the injustice that I have committed against myself and against the King's son, and for that which I did unto the damsel, since I neither left her nor accomplished my desire. All this arose from my ill management; for I sought for myself that which I deserved not, and which was not suited to me; and he who seeketh that which is not suited to him falleth into a calamity like that into which I have fallen.—And when the King's son heard these words of the sage, he spoke to him in the Persian language, saying, How long wilt thou continue this weeping and lamentation? Dost thou think that such a misfortune hath befallen thee as hath not befallen any beside thee?— And the sage, on hearing his words, was cheered by him, and complained to him of his case, and of the distress he experienced.

Then, when the morning came, the gate-keepers took the King's son, and conducted him to the King, and informed him that he had arrived at the city on the preceding day, at a time when it was impossible to go in unto the King. So the King questioned him, and said to him, From what country art thou, and what is thy name, and what thy art or trade, and what the reason of thy coming unto this city? And the King's son answered, As to my name, it is, in the Persian language, Harjeh; and as to my country, it is the country of Persia; and I am of the men of science, especially the science of medicine; for I cure the sick and the mad; and for this purpose I travel about through the regions and cities, to profit myself by adding science to my science; and when I see a sick person, I cure him. This is my occupation.

And when the King heard his words, he rejoiced at them exceedingly, and said to him, O excellent sage, thou hast come to us at a time when we need thee. Then he acquainted him with the case of the damsel, and said to him, If thou cure her, and recover her of her madness, thou shalt receive from me all that thou shalt desire. And the King's son, on hearing this, replied, May God confirm the power of the King! Describe to me everything that thou hast observed of her madness, and inform me how many

days ago this madness attacked her, and how thou tookest
her and the horse and the sage.—He therefore acquainted
him with the matter from beginning to end, and said to
him, The sage is in the prison. And the King's son said, O
happy King, and what hast thou done with the horse that
was with them? The King answered him, It remaineth with
me to the present time, preserved in one of the private
chambers. So the King's son said within himself, It is my
opinion that I should examine the horse before everything
else, and if it be sound, and no accident have happened
to it, all that I desire is accomplished; but if I see that its
motions are destroyed, I will yet devise some stratagem
to save my life. Then looking toward the King, he said to
him, O King, it is requisite that I see the horse which thou
hast mentioned. Perhaps I may find in it something that
will aid me to recover the damsel.—The King replied, Most
willingly. And he arose, and, taking him by the hand, led
him in to the horse; whereupon the King's son began to
go round about the horse, and to examine it and observe
its condition; and he found it sound, without any defect.
He therefore rejoiced at it exceedingly, and said, May God
confirm the power of the King! I desire to go in to the damsel, that I may see how she will act; and I beg of God that
her recovery may be effected by me, by means of the horse,
if it be the will of God, whose name be exalted!

He gave orders to take care of the horse, and the King
conducted him to the chamber in which was the damsel.
And when the King's son went in to her, he found her
beating herself, and falling down prostrate as usual; but she
was affected by no madness, and only did thus that no one

might approach her. So the King's son on seeing her in this
state, said to her, No harm shall befall thee! Then he began
to address her gently and courteously until he acquainted
her with himself; and when she knew him, she uttered a
great cry, and fell down in a fit through the violence of the
joy that she experienced; and the King imagined that this
fit was occasioned by her fear of him. And the King's son
put his mouth to her ear, and said to her, Spare my life and
thine, and be patient and firm; for this is a place wherein we
stand in need of patience and good management in devising
stratagems to make our escape from this tyrannical King.
A part of my stratagem shall be, that I go forth to him and
say to him, The disease that she suffereth ariseth from her
being possessed by a Jinni, and I promise thee her recovery.
And I will make a condition with him that he shall loose
thy bonds, and will assure him that this Jinni which hath
afflicted thee will be dispelled from thee. Therefore if he
come in to thee, address him with pleasant words, that he
may see that thou hast recovered through my means, and so
shall all that we desire be accomplished.—And she replied,
I will do so.

He then went forth from her, and, returning to the
King, full of joy and happiness, said, O fortunate King, I
have discovered, through thy good fortune, her remedy
and cure, and I have cured her for thee. Arise then and go
in to her, and speak gently and mildly to her, and promise
her that which shall rejoice her; for all that thou desirest
of her shall be accomplished for thee.—The King therefore
arose and went in to her; and when she saw him, she rose
to him, and kissed the ground before him, and welcomed

him; whereat the King rejoiced exceedingly. He ordered the servants to betake themselves to wait on her, and to prepare for her the ornaments and apparel. So they went in to her and saluted her, and she returned their salutation with the most courteous utterance and the most pleasant words. Then they attired her in royal apparel, put upon her neck a necklace of jewels, and brought her out, resembling the full moon. And when she came to the King, she saluted him, and kissed the ground before him.

The King therefore was greatly rejoiced at seeing her thus, and said to the King's son, All this is occasioned by the blessings attendant upon thee! May God increase to us thy benefactions!—And the King's son replied, O King, the perfection of her recovery and the completion of her affair must be effected by thy going forth with all thy guards and thy soldiers to the place where thou foundest her, and the ebony horse that was with her must be taken with thee, that I may there confine from her the Jinni that hath afflicted her, and imprison him and kill him, so that he may never return to her. The King said, Most willingly. Accordingly he sent forth the ebony horse to the meadow in which he had found the damsel with the horse and the Persian sage; and the King mounted with his troops, taking the damsel with him; and they knew not what he desired to do. And when they arrived at that meadow, the King's son who feigned himself a sage ordered that the damsel and the horse should be placed as far from the King and the troops as the eye could reach, and said to the King, With thy permission and leave, I desire to burn perfumes, and to recite a form of exorcism, and imprison the Jinni here, that he may never return to her. After which, I will mount the ebony horse, and mount the damsel behind me; and when I have done that, the horse will move about with violent action, and walk forward until it cometh to thee, when the affair will be finished. And when the King heard his words, he rejoiced exceedingly. Then the King's son mounted the horse, and placed the damsel behind him, while the King and all his troops looked at him. And he pressed her to him, and bound her firmly, and turned the pin of ascent; whereupon the horse rose with them into the air. The troops continued gazing at him until he disappeared from before their eyes; and the King remained half a day expecting his return to him; but he returned not: so he despaired of him, and repented greatly, and grieved for the separation of the damsel. Then he took his troops, and returned to his city.

But as to the King's son, he bent his course to the city of his father, full of joy and happiness, and ceased not in his journey until he descended upon his palace, when he took down the damsel into the palace, and felt secure of her. He then repaired to his father and his mother, and saluted them, and acquainted them with the arrival of the damsel; whereat they rejoiced exceedingly. Meanwhile, the King of the Greeks, when he returned to his city, secluded himself in his palace, mourning and afflicted. So his wezirs went in to him, and began to console him, saying to him, Verily he who took the damsel is an enchanter; and praise be to God who hath saved thee from his enchantment and craftiness. And they ceased not until he was consoled for the loss of her.

And as to the King's son, he made magnificent banquets for the people of the city, and they continued the rejoicings for a whole month; after which, he took the damsel as his wife, and they were delighted with each other exceedingly. And his father broke the ebony horse, and destroyed its motions. Then the King's son wrote a letter to the father of the damsel, and in it described to him his state, informing him that he had married the damsel, and that she was with him in the most happy condition. He sent it to him by a messenger, bearing precious presents and rarities; and when the messenger arrived at the city of the damsel's father, which was San'a of El-Yemen, he transmitted the letter, with the presents, to that King, who, on reading the letter, rejoiced exceedingly, accepted the presents, and treated the messenger with honor. He then prepared a magnificent present for his son-in-law, the King's son, and sent it to him by that messenger, who returned with it to the King's son, and informed him of the joy which the King, the father of the damsel, experienced when he brought him the news of his daughter. At this the King's son was affected with great happiness; and every year he wrote to his father-in-law, and sent him a present.

Thus they continued until the King, the father of the young man, was taken from the world; and the young man reigned after him over his dominions. He ruled his subjects with equity, and conducted himself among them in a laudable manner; the country was subject to him, and the people obeyed him: and thus they remained, passing the most delightful and most agreeable and most comfortable and most pleasant life, until they were visited by the terminator of delights and the separator of companions, the devastator of palaces and the replenisher of graves.— Extolled then be the perfection of the Living who dieth not, and in whose hands is the dominion that is apparent and the dominion that is hidden!

The Story of
Abu-Mohammad the Lazy

Harun Er-Rashid was sitting one day upon the imperial throne, when there came in to him a servant, with a crown of red gold set with pearls and jewels, comprising all kinds of jacinths and jewels such as no money would suffice to procure. This young man kissed the ground before the Khalifeh, and said to him, O Prince of the Faithful, the lady Zubeydeh saith to thee, Thou knowest that she hath made this crown, and it wanteth a large jewel to be affixed to its summit; and she hath searched among her treasures, but found not among them a large jewel such as she desireth. So the Khalifeh said to the chamberlains and lieutenants, Search for a large jewel such as Zubeydeh desireth. They therefore searched, but found nothing that suited her; and they acquainted the Khalifeh with this; in consequence of which his bosom became contracted, and he said, How is it that I am Khalifeh, and King of the Kings of the earth, and am unable to procure a jewel? Woe unto you! Inquire of the merchants.

And they inquired of the merchants; but they answered them, Our lord the Khalifeh will not find the jewel save with a man of El-Basrah, named Abu-Mohammad the Lazy. So they informed the Khalifeh of this; and he ordered his Wezir Ja'far to send a note to the Emir Mohammad

Ez-Zubeydi, the Governor of El-Basrah, desiring him to fit out Abu-Mohammad the Lazy, and to bring him before the Prince of the Faithful. The Wezir, therefore, wrote a note to that effect, and sent it by Mesrur.

Mesrur immediately repaired with it to the city of El-Basrah, and went in to the Emir Mohammad Ez-Zubeydi, who rejoiced at seeing him, and treated him with the utmost honor. He then read to him the note of the Prince of the Faithful Harun Er-Rashid, and he said, I hear and obey. He forthwith sent Mesrur with a number of his retinue to Abu-Mohammad the Lazy, and they repaired to him, and knocked at his door; whereupon one of the pages came forth to them, and Mesrur said to him, Say to thy master, The Prince of the Faithful summoneth thee. So the page went in and acquainted him with this; and he came forth, and found Mesrur, the chamberlain of the Khalifeh, attended by the retinue of the Emir Mohammad Ez-Zubeydi; upon which he kissed the ground before him, and said, I hear and obey the command of the Prince of the Faithful: but enter ye our abode. They replied, We cannot do so, unless to pay a hasty visit, as the Prince of the Faithful hath commanded us; for he is expecting thine arrival. But he said, Have patience with me a little, that I may arrange my business.

And they entered the house with him, after excessive persuasion; and they beheld in the passage curtains of blue brocade embroidered with red gold. Then Abu-Mohammad the Lazy ordered some of his pages to conduct Mesrur into the bath which was in the house; and they did so. And he saw its walls and its marble pavements to be of extraordinary construction: it was decorated with gold and silver, and its water was mixed with rose-water. The pages paid all attention to Mesrur and those who were with him, and served them in the most perfect manner; and when they came forth from the bath, they clad them with garments of brocade interwoven with gold; after which, Mesrur and his companions entered, and found Abu-Mohammad the Lazy sitting in his pavilion. Over his head were hung curtains of brocade interwoven with gold, and adorned with pearls and jewels; the pavilion was furnished with cushions embroidered with red gold; and he was sitting upon his mattress, which was upon a couch set with jewels. When Mesrur came in to him, he welcomed him and met him, and, having seated him by his side, gave orders to bring the table; and when Mesrur beheld that table, he said, By Allah, I have never seen the like of this in the palace of the Prince of the Faithful! It comprised varieties of foods, all placed in dishes of gilt China-ware.—We ate, says Mesrur, and drank, and enjoyed ourselves until the close of the day, when he gave to each of us five thousand pieces of gold. And on the following day, they clad us in clothes embroidered with gold, and treated us with the utmost honor.

Mesrur then said to Abu-Mohammad the Lazy, It is impossible for us to remain longer than this period, from our fear of the Khalifeh. But Abu-Mohammad the Lazy replied, O our lord, have patience with us until to-morrow, that we may prepare ourselves, and then we will proceed with you. So they remained that day, and passed the night until the morning; when the pages equipped a mule for Abu-Mohammad the Lazy, with a saddle of gold adorned with varieties of pearls and jewels; whereupon Mesrur said within himself, When Abu-Mohammad presenteth himself before the Khalifeh with this equipage, I wonder whether he will ask him how he obtained such wealth.

After that, they took leave of Mohammad Ez-Zubeydi, and, going forth from El-Basrah, journeyed on until they arrived at the city of Baghdad; and when they went in to the Khalifeh, and stood before him, he ordered Abu-Mohammad to seat himself. So he sat, and, addressing the Khalifeh with politeness, said, O Prince of the Faithful, I have brought with me a present in token of service: then, may I produce it, with thy permission? Er-Rashid answered, There will be no harm in that. Accordingly, Abu-Mohammad gave orders to bring a chest, which he opened, and he took forth from it some rarities, among which were trees of gold, the leaves whereof were formed of white emeralds, and its fruits of red and yellow jacinths, and white pearls; whereat the Khalifeh wondered. Then he caused a second chest to be brought, and took forth from it a tent of brocade, adorned with pearls and jacinths, and emeralds and chrysolites, and varieties of other jewels: its poles were of new Indian aloes-wood; its skirts were adorned with emeralds; and upon it were represented the forms of all living creatures, as birds and wild beasts; all these designs being adorned with jewels, jacinths and emeralds, and chrysolites and balass rubies, and all kinds of minerals. And when Er-Rashid beheld it, he rejoiced exceedingly.

Abu-Mohammad the Lazy then said, O Prince of the Faithful, imagine not that I have brought to thee this, fearing any thing or coveting aught; for the truth is, that I saw myself to be a man of the common people, and saw that this was not suitable to anyone but the Prince of the Faithful;

and if thou give me permission, I will gratify thee with the sight of some of the feats that I am able to accomplish. To this, Er-Rashid replied, Do what thou wilt, that we may see. And Abu-Mohammad said, I hear and obey. Then he moved his lips, and made a sign to the battlements of the palace; whereupon they inclined toward him; and he made another sign to them, and they resumed their proper position. After this, he made a sign with his eye, and there appeared before him private chambers with closed doors; and he addressed some words toward them, whereat the voices of birds replied to him. And Er-Rashid wondered at this extremely, and said to him, Whence obtainedst thou all this power, when thou art not known otherwise than by the appellation of Abu-Mohammad the Lazy, and they have informed me that thy father was a servant serving in a public bath, and that he left thee nothing?—O Prince of the Faithful, he answered, hear my story; for it is wonderful and extraordinary: if it were engraven on the understanding, it would be a lesson to him who would be admonished. Er-Rashid said, Relate what thou hast to tell, and acquaint me with it, O Abu-Mohammad. So he said,—

Know, O Prince of the Faithful (may God continue thy glory and power!), that the account of the people, that I am known by the surname of the Lazy, and that my father left me not any property, is true; for my father was no other than thou hast said: he worked in a public bath. In my youth I was the laziest of all beings existing upon the face of the earth. My laziness was so great that when I was sleeping in the hot season and the sun came upon me, I was too sluggish to rise and remove from the sun to the shade. Thus I

remained fifteen years, at the expiration of which period my
father was admitted to the mercy of God (whose name be
exalted!), and left me nothing. But my mother used to act as
a servant to some people, and to feed me and give me drink,
while I lay upon my side.

And it happened that my mother came in to me one
day, bringing five pieces of silver; and she said to me, O my
son, I have been told that the sheykh Abu-l-Muzaffar hath
determined to make a voyage to China. This sheykh loved
the poor, and was one of the virtuous. And my mother
said, O my son, take these five pieces of silver, and repair
with us to him, and we will request him to buy for thee
with it something from the land of China: perhaps a profit
may thence accrue to thee, of the bounty of God, whose
name be exalted! But I was too lazy to rise and go with
her. And upon this she swore by Allah, that if I did not
rise and accompany her she would not feed me nor give
me to drink nor come in to me, but would leave me to die
of hunger and thirst. So when I heard her words, Prince
of the Faithful, I knew that she would do so, on account of
her knowledge of my laziness. I therefore said to her, Seat
me. And she did so, while I wept.—Bring me my shoes,
said I. And she brought them; and I said, Put them on my
feet. And she put them on. I then said, Lift me up from
the ground. And when she had done this, said, Support
me, that I may walk. So she supported me, and I continued walking, and stumbling, until we arrived at the bank
of the river, when we saluted the sheykh, and I said to
him, O uncle, art thou El-Muzaffar? He answered, At thy
service. And I said, Take these pieces of silver, and buy

with them for me something from the land of China: perhaps God may give me a profit from it. And the sheykh
Abu-l-Muzaffar said to his companions, Do ye know this
young man? They answered, Yes: this person is known by
the name of Abu-Mohammad the Lazy; and we have never
seen him to have come forth from his house except on
this occasion. The sheykh Abu-l-Muzaffar then said, O
my son, give me the money, and may the blessing of God
(whose name be exalted!) attend it. And he received the
money from me, saying, In the name of God. After which,
I returned with my mother to the house.

The sheykh Abu-l-Muzaffar set forth on the voyage,
and with him a company of merchants, and they proceeded without interruption until they arrived at the
land of China; when the sheykh sold and bought, and set
forth to return, he and those who were with him, after
they had accomplished their desires. But when they had
continued out at sea for three days, the sheykh said to
his companions, Stay the vessel! The merchants asked,
What dost thou want? And he answered, Know that the
deposit committed to me, belonging to Abu-Mohammad
the Lazy, I have forgotten: so return with us, that we may
buy for him with it something by which he may profit. But
they replied, We conjure thee by Allah (whose name be
exalted!) that thou take us not back; for we have traversed
a very long distance, and in doing so we have experienced
great terrors, and exceeding trouble. Still he said, We
must return. They therefore said, Receive from us several
times as much as the profit of the five pieces of silver,
and take us not back. So he assented to their proposal;

and they collected for him a large sum of money.

Then they proceeded until they came in sight of an island containing a numerous population, where they cast anchor; and the merchants landed to purchase thence merchandise consisting of minerals and jewels and pearls and other things. And Abu-l-Muzaffar saw a man sitting, with a great number of apes before him; and among these was an ape whose hair was plucked off. The other apes, whenever their master was unaware, laid hold upon this plucked ape, and beat him, and threw him upon their master; who arose thereat, and beat them, and chained and tormented them, for doing this; and all these apes became enraged in consequence against the other, and beat him again. Now when the sheykh Abu-l-Muzaffar saw this ape, he grieved for him, and shewed kindness to him, and said to his owner, Wilt thou sell me this ape? The man answered, Buy. And the sheykh said, I have with me, belonging to a lad who is an orphan, five pieces of silver. Wilt thou sell him to me for that sum?—He answered, I sell him to thee. May God bless thee in him!—Then the sheykh took possession of him, and paid the money to his owner; and the servants of the sheykh took the ape, and took him to the ship.

After this, they loosed the sails, and proceeded to another island, where they cast anchor. And the divers who dived for minerals and pearls and jewels and other things came down; and the merchants gave them money as their hire for diving. So they dived; and the ape, seeing them do this, leaped from the vessel, and dived with them; whereupon Abu-l-Muzaffar exclaimed, There is no strength nor power but in God, the High, the Great! We have lost the ape, with the luck of this poor youth for whom we bought him!—They despaired of the ape; but when the party of divers came up, lo, the ape came up with them, having in his hands precious jewels; and he threw them down before Abu-l-Muzaffar, who wondered at this, and said, Verily, there is a great mystery in this ape!

Then they raised anchor, and proceeded to an island called the Island of the Zunuj. There they were captured and taken to the King, who ordered that the merchants be held prisoner. The merchants passed the night in great misery; but in the night the ape arose and came to Abu-l-Muzaffar, and loosed his chains. And when the merchants beheld Abu-l-Muzaffar loosed, they said, God grant that our liberation may be effected by thy hands, O Abu-l-Muzaffar! But he replied, Know ye that none liberated me, by the will of God (whose name be exalted!), but this ape; and I have bought my liberty of him for a thousand pieces of gold. So the merchants said, And we in like manner: each of us buyeth his liberty of him for a thousand pieces of gold, if he release us. The ape therefore arose and went to them, and began to loose one after another, until he had loosed them all from their chains; and they repaired to the ship, and embarked in it, and found it safe; nothing being lost from it.

They loosed immediately, and continued their voyage, and Abu-l-Muzaffar said, O merchants, fulfill the promise that ye have given to the ape. They replied, We hear and obey. And each of them paid him a thousand pieces of gold. Abu-l-Muzaffar also took forth from his property a thousand pieces of gold; and a great sum of money was thus collected for the ape. They then continued their voyage until they arrived at the city of El-Basrah; whereupon their companions came to meet them; and when they had landed, Abu-l-Muzaffar said, Where is Abu-Mohammad the Lazy?

The news therefore reached my mother, and while I was lying asleep, my mother came to me and said, O my son, the sheykh Abu-l-Muzaffar hath arrived, and come to the city: arise then, and repair to him and salute him, and ask him what he hath brought for thee: perhaps God (whose name be exalted!) hath blessed thee with something. So I replied, Lift me from the ground, and support me, that I may go forth and walk to the bank of the river. I walked on, stumbling upon my skirts, until I came to the sheykh Abu-l-Muzaffar; and when he beheld me, he said to me, Welcome to him whose money was the means of my liberation and the liberation of these merchants, by the will of God (whose name be exalted!). He then said to me, Take this ape; for I bought him for thee; go with him to thy house, and wait until I come to thee. I therefore took the ape before me, and went, saying within myself, By Allah, this is none other than magnificent merchandise! I entered my house, and said to my mother, Every time that I lie down to sleep, thou desirest me to arise to traffic: see then with thine eye this merchandise. Then I sat down; and while I was sitting, lo, the servants of Abu-l-Muzaffar approached me, and said to me, Art thou Abu-Mohammad the Lazy? I answered them, Yes. And behold, Abu-l-Muzaffar approached, following them. I rose to him, and kissed his hands, and he said to me, Come with me to my house. So I replied, I hear and obey. I proceeded with him until I entered the house, when he ordered his servants to bring the money; and they brought it, and he said, O my son, God hath blessed thee with this wealth as the profit of the five pieces of silver. They then carried it in the chests upon their heads, and he gave me the keys of those chests, saying to me, Walk before these men to thy house; for all this wealth is thine.

I therefore went to my mother, and she rejoiced at this, and said, O my son, God hath blessed thee with this abundant wealth; so give over this laziness, and go down into the market-street, and sell and buy. Accordingly, I relinquished my lazy habits, and opened a shop in the market-street, and the ape sat with me upon my mattress: when I ate, he ate with me; and when I drank, he drank with me; and every day he absented himself from me from morning until noon, when he came, bringing with him a purse containing a thousand pieces of gold, and he put it by my side, and sat down. Thus he ceased not to do for a long time, until abundant wealth had accrued to me: whereupon I bought, O Prince of the Faithful, possessions and rab'as,[8] and planted gardens, and many servants.

And it happened one day that I was sitting, and the ape was sitting with me upon the mattress, and, lo, he looked to the right and left; whereat I said within myself, What is the matter with this ape? And God caused the ape to speak, with an eloquent tongue, and he said, O Abu-Mohammad!

---

8   A set of dwelling-rooms over a shop: [an *appartement,* flat.]

On hearing this, I was violently terrified; but he said, Fear not. I will acquaint thee with my condition. I am a Marid of the Jinn; but I came to thee on account of thy poverty, and now thou knowest not the amount of thy wealth; and I have a want for thee to perform, the accomplishment of which will be productive of good to thee.—What is it? I asked. He answered, I desire to marry thee to a damsel like the full moon.—And how so? said I.—Tomorrow, he answered, attire thyself in thy rich clothing, mount thy mule with the saddle of gold, and repair with me to the market of the sellers of fodder: there inquire for the shop of the Sherif,[9] and seat thyself by him, and say to him, I have come to thee as a suitor, desiring thy daughter. And if he say to thee, Thou hast not wealth nor rank nor descent,—give him a thousand pieces of gold: and if he say to thee, Give me more,—do so, and excite his cupidity for money.—So I replied, I hear and obey: tomorrow I will do this, if it be the will of God, whose name be exalted!

Accordingly, when I arose in the morning, I put on the richest of my apparel, mounted the mule with the saddle of gold, and, having gone to the market of the sellers of fodder, inquired for the shop of the Sherif, and found him sitting in his shop. I therefore alighted and saluted him, and seated myself with him. I had with me some of my servants; and the Sherif said, Perhaps thou hast some business with us which we may have the pleasure of performing. So I replied, Yes: I have some business with thee.—And what is

---

9   Descendants of the Prophet enjoy the titles sherif (noble) and seyyid (master) and the privilege of the green turban.

it? he asked. I answered, I have come unto thee as a suitor,
desiring thy daughter. He replied, Thou hast not wealth
nor rank nor descent. And upon this I took forth and presented to him a purse containing a thousand pieces of red
gold, saying to him, This is my rank and descent; and he
whom may God bless and save hath said, An excellent rank
is that conferred by wealth. How good also is the saying of
the poet!—

Whoso possesseth two dirhems, his lips have
learned varieties of speech, which he uttereth:

His brethren draw near and listen to him, and thou
seest him haughty among mankind.

Were it not for his money, in which he glorieth,
thou wouldst find him in a most ignominious state.

When the rich man erreth in speech, they reply,
Thou hast spoken truly, and not uttered vanity:

But when the poor man speaketh truly, they reply,
Thou hast lied,—and make void what he hath
asserted.

Verily money, in every habitation, investeth men
with dignity and with comeliness:

It is the tongue for him who would be eloquent, and
it is the weapon for him who would fight.

And when the Sherif heard these words, and understood the verses, he hung down his head for a while toward the ground; after which, he raised his head, and said to me, If it must be, I desire of thee three thousand pieces of gold besides. So I replied, I hear and obey. I immediately sent one of the servants to my house, and he brought me the money that the Sherif had demanded; and when the Sherif saw this come to him, he arose from the shop, and said to his young men, Close it. Then he invited his companions from the market to his house, and, having performed the contract of my marriage to his daughter, said to me, After ten days I will introduce thee to her.

I returned to my house, full of joy, and in privacy informed the ape of that which had happened to me; whereupon he said, Excellently hast thou done. And when the time appointed by the Sherif approached, the ape said to me, I have a want for thee to perform: if thou accomplish it for me, thou shalt obtain of me what thou wilt.—And what is thy want? said I. He answered, At the upper end of the saloon in which thou wilt pay thy first visit to the daughter of the Sherif is a closet, upon the door of which is a ring of brass, and the keys are beneath the ring. Take them, and open the door. Thou wilt find a chest of iron, at the corners of which are four talismanic flags; in the midst is a basin filled with money, and by its side are eleven serpents, and in the basin is tied a white rooster with a cleft comb; and there is also a knife by the side of the chest. Take the knife, and kill with it the rooster, tear in pieces the flags, and empty the chest. This is what I require of thee.—And I replied, I hear and obey.

I then went to the house of the Sherif, and entering the saloon, I looked toward the closet which the ape had

described to me. And when I was left alone with the bride,
I wondered at her beauty and loveliness, and her justness of
stature and form; for she was such that the tongue cannot
describe her beauty and loveliness. When midnight came,
and the bride slept, I arose, took the keys, and opened the
closet, and, taking the knife, I killed the rooster, threw
down the flags, and overturned the chest; whereupon the
damsel awoke, and saw that the closet was opened, and the
bird killed; and she exclaimed, There is no strength nor
power but in God, the High, the Great! The Marid hath
taken me!—And her words were not ended when the Marid
encompassed the house, and snatched away the bride.
Upon this, a clamor ensued; and, lo, the Sherif approached,
slapping his face, and said, O Abu-Mohammad, what is this
deed that thou hast done unto us? Is this the recompense
that we receive from thee? I made this talisman in this
closet through my fear for my daughter from this accursed
wretch; for he was desirous of taking this damsel during a
period of six years, and could not do so. But thou shalt no
longer remain with us: so go thy way.

I therefore went forth from the house of the Sherif, and,
having returned to my own abode, searched for the ape;
but I found him not, nor saw any trace of him: so I knew
that he was the Marid who had taken my wife, and that he
had practiced a stratagem against me so that I had acted
thus with the talisman and the rooster which prevented his
taking her. I repented, and tore my clothes in pieces, and
slapped my face. No region was wide enough for me; so
I went forth immediately, seeking the desert, and stopped
not until the evening overtook me; and I knew not whither

to go. But while I was absorbed in meditation, lo, two serpents approached me; one, tawny-colored; and the other,
white; and they were contending together. I therefore took
up a stone from the ground, and struck with it the tawny
serpent, and killed it; for it was oppressing the white one.
Then the white serpent departed, and was absent for a
while; after which it returned, accompanied by ten other
white serpents; and they came to the dead serpent, and tore
it in pieces, so that there remained only its head; which
having done, they went their way.

Thereupon I laid myself prostrate on my bosom in that
place, through weariness; and while I was so lying, meditating upon my case, a being whose voice I heard, but whose
form I saw not, uttered these two verses:—

Let destiny run with slackened reins, and pass not
the night but with careless mind;

For between the closing of an eye and its opening,
God effecteth a change in the state of affairs.

On hearing this, O Prince of the Faithful, I was vehemently
affected, and inspired with the utmost trouble of mind; and I
heard a voice behind me reciting that couplet:—

O Muslim, whose guide is the Kur'an, rejoice in it; for
safety hath come to thee;

And fear not what Satan hath suggested; for we are
people whose religion is the true one.

So I said to the person who addressed me, By the Object of thy worship, inform me who thou art! Whereupon the invisible speaker assumed the form of a man, and replied, Fear not; for thy kind conduct hath become known to us, and we are a tribe of the believing Jinn; if then thou hast any want, acquaint us with it, that we may have the pleasure of performing it. I therefore said to him, Verily I have a great want; for I have been afflicted with a heavy calamity. And unto whom hath happened the like of my calamity?—And he said, Perhaps thou art Abu-Mohammad the Lazy. I replied, Yes. And he said, O Abu-Mohammad, I am a brother of the white serpent, whose enemy thou killedst. We are four brothers by the same father and mother, and we are all thankful for thy kindness. And know that he who was in the form of an ape, and who practiced this artifice with thee, is one of the Marids of the Jinn; and had he not employed this stratagem, he had never been able to take the damsel; for of a long time he hath been desirous of taking her, and this talisman prevented him; and had the talisman remained, he could not have obtained access to her. But fear not on account of this affair: we will convey thee to her, and will slay the Marid; for thy kindness is not lost upon us.

He then uttered a great cry, with a terrible voice; and, lo, a troop approached him, and he inquired of them respecting the ape; upon which one of them answered, I know his abode. He said, Where is his abode? And he answered, In the City of Brass, upon which the sun riseth not. And he said, O Abu-Mohammad, take one of our servants, and he will carry thee on his back, and will instruct thee how thou shalt take the damsel. But know that the servant is one of the Marids; and when he carrieth thee, mention not the name of God while he beareth thee; for if thou mention it, he will fly from thee, and thou wilt fall and perish.—So I replied, I hear and obey.

I took one of their servants, and he stooped, and said, Mount. And I mounted. He then soared with me into the sky until he had ascended out of sight of the world; and I saw the stars resembling the firm mountains, and heard the Angels extolling the perfection of God in Heaven. All this while the Marid was conversing with me and amusing me, and diverting me from mentioning God, whose name be exalted! But while I was in this state, lo, a person clad in green garments,[10] and having long locks of hair, and a resplendent countenance, and in his hand a spear from which sparks flew forth, approached and said to me, O Abu-Mohammad, say, There is no deity but God: Mohammad is God's Apostle—or I will smite thee with this spear. My heart was already rent in pieces by my abstaining from mentioning God (whose name be exalted!): so I said, There is no deity but God: Mohammad is God's Apostle. And immediately that person smote the Marid with the spear; whereupon he dissolved, and became ashes; and I fell from his back, and continued descending to the earth until I dropped into a roaring sea, agitated with waves.

But, lo, there was a ship, containing five sailors; and when they saw me, they came to me, and took me up into

---

10 El-Khidr, a saint who drank of the Fountain of Life and still lives. He was Wezir to Dhu-l-Karneyn, and is variously identified with Elias, Phineas, and St. George.

the vessel, and began to speak to me in a language which I knew not. I therefore made a sign to them that I knew not their language. And they proceeded on their voyage until the close of the day, when they cast a net, and caught a large fish, which they broiled; and they gave me to eat. They continued their voyage until they had conveyed me to their city; upon which they took me in to their King, and placed me before him; and I kissed the ground, and he bestowed upon me a dress of honor. Now this King was acquainted with Arabic, and he said, I appoint thee to be one of my guards. And I said to him, What is the name of this city? He answered, Its name is Henad, and it is the land of China. Then the King delivered me to the Wezir of the city, commanding him to shew me the city. The inhabitants of this city were originally infidels; in consequence of which, God (whose name be exalted!) had turned them into stones. I amused myself by taking a view of it; and have beheld nowhere a greater abundance of trees and fruits than it possessed.

I resided there for the space of a month, after which I went to a river, and seated myself upon its banks; and while I was sitting, lo, a horseman came and said, Art thou Abu-Mohammad the Lazy? I answered him, Yes. And he said, Fear not; for thy kind conduct hath become known unto us. So I asked him, Who art thou? And he answered, I am a brother of the serpent, and thou art near unto the place of the damsel to whom thou desirest to obtain access. Then he took off his clothes, and having clad me with them, said to me, Fear not; for the servant who perished beneath thee was one of our servants. And after this, the horseman took me up behind him, and conveyed me to a desert, where he said to me, Alight from behind me, and proceed between these two mountains until thou seest the City of Brass: then stop at a distance from it, and enter it not till I return to thee, and instruct thee how to act. So I replied, I hear and obey.

I alighted from behind him, and walked on until I arrived at the city, when I saw that its wall was of brass; and I went round about it, hoping to find a gate to it: but I found none. And while I was going round it, lo, the brother of the serpent approached me, and gave me a talismanic sword that would prevent anyone from seeing me. He then went his way; and he had been but a short time absent from me when cries rose, and I beheld a number of persons whose eyes were in their breasts; and when they saw me, they said, Who art thou, and what cast thee into this place? So I acquainted them with the occurrence; and they replied, The damsel whom thou hast mentioned is with the Marid in this city, and we know not what he hath done with her; and we are brothers of the serpent. Then they added, Go to that spring, see by what channel the water entereth, and enter thou with it; for it will convey thee into the city.

I therefore did so. I entered with the water into a grotto beneath the earth, and, rising thence, beheld myself in the midst of the city, and found the damsel sitting upon a couch of gold, with a canopy of brocade over her, and round the canopy was a garden containing trees of gold, the fruits of which were of precious jewels, such as rubies and chrysolites, and pearls and coral. And when the damsel saw me, she knew me; and, having saluted me first, she said to me, O my master, who brought thee to this place? So I informed her of the events that had happened; and she replied, Know that this accursed wretch, from the excess of his affection for me, hath acquainted me with that which will injure him and that which will benefit him, and hath informed me that there is in this city a talisman with which, if he desired to destroy all who are in the city, he could destroy them; and whatsoever he should order his 'Efrits to do, they would comply with his command; and that talisman is upon a pillar.—And where, said I, is the pillar? She answered, In such a place.—And what is that talisman? I asked. She answered, It is the figure of an eagle, and upon it is an inscription which I know not. Take it, and place it before thee, and take a censer with fire, and throw into it a little musk, whereupon there will rise from it a smoke which will attract the 'Efrits. If thou do so, they will all present themselves before thee; not one of them will remain absent; and they will obey thy command, and do whatsoever thou shalt order them. Arise, therefore, and do that, and may the blessing of God (whose name be exalted!) attend the act.—So I replied, I hear and obey.

I arose, and went to that pillar, and did all that she desired me to do, and the 'Efrits came and presented themselves before me, each of them saying, At thy service, O my master! Whatsoever thou commandest us to do, we will do it.—I therefore said to them, Chain the Marid who brought this damsel from her abode. And they replied, We hear and obey. They repaired immediately to that Marid, and chained him, making his bonds tight; and returned to me, saying, We have done what thou hast commanded us. And I ordered them to return. I then went back to the damsel, and, having acquainted her with what had happened, said, O my wife, wilt thou go with me? She answered, Yes. And I went forth with her by the subterranean grotto by which I had entered; and we proceeded until we came to the party who had directed me to her; when I said to them, Direct me to a route that shall lead me to my country.

Accordingly they guided me and walked with me to the shore of the sea, and placed us on board a ship; and the wind was favorable, and the ship conveyed us on until we arrived at the city of El-Basrah. And when the damsel entered the house of her father, her family saw her, and rejoiced exceedingly at her return. I then fumigated the eagle with musk, and, lo, the 'Efrits approached me from every quarter, saying, At thy service, and what dost thou desire us to do? And I commanded them to transport all that was in the City of Brass, of money and minerals and jewels, to my house which was in El-Basrah; and they did so. After that, I commanded them to bring the ape; and they brought him in an abject and despicable state; whereupon I said to him, O accursed, why didst thou act perfidiously to me? And I ordered them to put him into a bottle of brass. So they put him into a narrow bottle of brass, and stopped it over him with lead. And I resided with my wife in joy and happiness. I have now, O Prince of the Faithful, of precious treasures, and extraordinary jewels, an abundant wealth, what cannot be expressed by numbers, nor confined by limits; and if thou desire anything, of wealth or aught else, I will command the Jinn to bring it to thee immediately. All this I have received from the bounty of God, whose name be exalted!

And the Prince of the Faithful wondered at this story extremely. He gave him imperial presents in return for his gift, and treated him with the favor that was suitable to him.

The Voyages of
Es-Sindibad of the Sea

There was, in the time of the Khalifeh, the Prince of the Faithful, Harun Er-Rashid, in the city of Baghdad, a man called Es-Sindibad the Porter. He was a man in poor circumstances, who bore burdens for hire upon his head. And it happened to him that he bore one day a heavy burden, and that day was excessively hot; so he was wearied by the load, and perspired profusely, the heat violently oppressing him. In this state he passed by the door of a merchant, the ground before which was swept and sprinkled, and there the air was temperate; and by the side of the door was a wide mastaba. The porter therefore put down his burden upon that mastaba, to rest himself, and to scent the air; and when he had done so, there came forth upon him, from the door, a pleasant, gentle gale, and an exquisite odor, wherewith the porter was delighted. He seated himself upon the edge of the mastaba, and heard in that place the melodious sounds of stringed instruments, with the lute among them, and mirth-exciting voices, and varieties of distinct recitations. He heard also the voices of birds, warbling, and praising God (whose name be exalted!) with diverse tones and with all dialects; consisting of turtle-doves and hezars and blackbirds and nightingales and ring-doves and kirawans;[11] whereupon

---

11 Stone-curlews.

he wondered in his mind, and was moved with great delight. He then advanced to that door, and found within the house a great garden, wherein he beheld pages and servants and other dependents, and such things as existed not elsewhere save in the abodes of kings and sultans; and after that, there blew upon him the odor of delicious, exquisite viands, of all different kinds, and of delicious wine.

Upon this he raised his eyes toward heaven, and said, Extolled be thy perfection, O Lord! O Creator! O Supplier of the conveniences of life! Thou suppliest whom Thou wilt without reckoning! O Allah, I implore thy forgiveness of all offences, and turn to Thee repenting of all fault! O Lord, there is no animadverting upon Thee with respect to thy judgment, and thy power; for Thou art not to be questioned regarding that which Thou doest, and Thou art able to do whatsoever Thou wilt! Extolled be thy perfection! Thou enrichest whom Thou wilt, and whom Thou wilt Thou impoverishest! Thou magnifiest whom Thou wilt, and whom Thou wilt Thou abasest! There is no deity but Thou! How great is thy dignity! and how mighty is thy dominion! and how excellent is thy government! Thou hast bestowed favors upon him whom Thou choosest among thy servants, and the owner of this place is in the utmost affluence, delighting himself with pleasant odors and delicious meats and exquisite beverages of all descriptions. And Thou hast appointed unto thy creatures what Thou wilt, and what Thou hast predestined for them; so that among them one is weary, and another is at ease; and one of them is prosperous, and another is like me, in the extreme of fatigue and abjection!

And when Es-Sindibad the Porter had finished, he desired

to take up his burden and to depart. But, lo, there came forth to him from that door a young page, handsome in countenance, magnificent in apparel; and he laid hold upon the porter's hand, saying to him, Enter: answer the summons of my master; for he calleth for thee. And the porter would have refused to enter with the page; but he could not.

He therefore deposited his burden with the doorkeeper in the entrance-passage, and, entering the house with the page, he found it to be a handsome mansion, presenting an appearance of joy and majesty. And he looked toward a grand chamber, in which he beheld noblemen and great lords; and in it were all kinds of flowers, and all kinds of sweet scents, and varieties of dried and fresh fruits together with abundance of various kinds of exquisite viands, and beverage prepared from the fruit of the choicest grapevines. In it were also instruments of music and mirth. And at the upper end of that chamber was a great and venerable man, in the sides of whose beard grey hairs had begun to appear. He was handsome, with an aspect of gravity and dignity and majesty and stateliness. So, upon this, Es-Sindibad the Porter was confounded, and he said within himself, By Allah, this place is a portion of Paradise, or it is the palace of a King or sultan! Then, putting himself in a respectful posture, he saluted the assembly, prayed for them, and kissed the ground before them; after which he stood, hanging down his head in humility. But the master of the house gave him permission to seat himself. He therefore sat. And the master of the house had caused him to draw near unto him, and now began to cheer him with conversation, and to welcome him; and he put before him some of the various excellent, delicious, exquisite viands. So Es-Sindibad the Porter advanced, and, having said, In the name of God, the Compassionate, the Merciful, ate until he was satisfied and satiated, when he said, Praise be to God in every case!—and washed his hands, and thanked them for this.

The master of the house then said, Thou art welcome, and thy day is blessed. What is thy name, and what trade dost thou follow?—O my master, he answered, my name is Es-Sindibad the Porter, and I bear upon my head men's merchandise for hire. And at this, the master of the house smiled, and he said to him, Know, O porter, that thy name is like mine; for I am Es-Sindibad of the Sea. He then said to him, O porter, know that my story is wonderful, and I will inform thee of all that happened to me and befell me before I attained this prosperity and sat in this place wherein thou seest me. For I attained not this prosperity and this place save after severe fatigue and great trouble and many terrors. How often have I endured fatigue and toil in my early years! I have performed many voyages, and connected with each voyage is a wonderful tale, that would confound the mind. All that which I endured happened by fate and destiny, and from that which is written there is no escape nor flight.

The First Voyage of Es-Sindibad of the Sea

Know, O masters, O noble persons, that I had a father, a merchant, who was one of the first in rank among the people and the merchants, and who possessed abundant wealth and ample fortune. He died when I was a young child, leaving to me wealth and buildings and fields; and when I grew up, I put my hand upon the whole of the property, ate well and drank well, associated with the young men, wore handsome apparel, and passed my life with my friends and companions, feeling confident that this course would continue and profit me; and I ceased not to live in this manner for a length of time. I then returned to my reason, and recovered from my heedlessness, and found that my wealth had passed away, and my condition had changed, and all the money that I had possessed had gone. Then I arose, and collected what I had, of effects and apparel, and sold them; after which I sold my buildings and all that my hand possessed, and amassed three thousand pieces of silver; and it occurred to my mind to travel to the countries of other people; and I remembered one of the sayings of the poets, which was this:—

In proportion to one's labor, eminences are gained;
and he who seeketh eminence passeth sleepless nights.

He diveth in the sea who seeketh for pearls, and
succeedeth in acquiring lordship and good fortune.

Whoso seeketh eminence without laboring for it,
loseth his life in the search of vanity.

Upon this, I resolved, and arose, and bought for myself goods and commodities and merchandise, with such other things as were required for travel; and my mind had consented to my performing a sea voyage. So I embarked in a ship, and it descended to the city of El-Basrah, with a company of merchants; and we traversed the sea for many days and nights.

We had passed by island after island, and from sea to sea, and from land to land; and in every place by which we passed we sold and bought, and exchanged merchandise. We continued our voyage until we arrived at an island like one of the gardens of Paradise, and at that island the master of the ship brought her to anchor with us. He cast the anchor, and put forth the landing-plank, and all who were in the ship landed upon that island. They had prepared for themselves fire-pots, and they lighted the fires in them; and their occupations were various: some cooked; others washed; and others amused themselves. I was among those who were amusing themselves upon the shores of the island, and the passengers were assembled to eat and drink and play and sport.

But while we were thus engaged, lo, the master of the ship, standing upon its side, called out with his loudest voice, O ye passengers, whom may God preserve! come up quickly into the ship, hasten to embark, and leave your merchandise, and flee with your lives, and save yourselves from destruction; for this apparent island, upon which ye are, is not really an island, but it is a great fish that hath become stationary in the midst of the sea, and the sand hath accumulated upon it, so that it hath become like an island, and trees have grown upon it since times of old; and when ye lighted upon it the fire, it felt the heat, and put itself in motion, and now it will descend with you into the sea, and ye will all be drowned: then seek for yourselves escape before destruction, and leave the merchandise!— The passengers, therefore, hearing the words of the master of the ship, hastened to go up into the vessel, leaving the merchandise, and their other goods, and their copper cooking-pots, and their fire-pots; and some reached the ship, and others reached it not. The island had moved, and descended to the bottom of the sea, with all that were upon it, and the roaring sea, agitated with waves, closed over it. I was among the number of those who remained behind upon the island; so I sank in the sea with the rest who sank. But God (whose name be exalted!) delivered me and saved me from drowning, and supplied me with a great wooden bowl, of the bowls in which the passengers had been washing, and I laid hold upon it and got into it, induced by the sweetness of life, and beat the water with my feet as with oars, while the waves sported with me, tossing me to the right and left. The master of the vessel had caused her sails to be spread, and pursued his voyage with those who had embarked, not regarding such as had been submerged; and I ceased not to look at that vessel until it was concealed from my eye. I made sure of destruction, and night came upon me while I was in this state; but I remained so a day and a night, and the wind and the waves aided me until the bowl came to a stoppage with me under a high island, whereon were trees overhanging the sea. So I laid hold upon a branch of a lofty tree, and clung to it, after I had been at the point of destruction; and I kept hold upon it until I landed on the island, when I found my legs benumbed, and saw marks of the nibbling of fish upon their hams, of which I had been insensible by reason of the violence of the anguish and fatigue that I was suffering.

I threw myself upon the island like one dead, and was unconscious of my existence, and drowned in my stupefaction; and I ceased not to remain in this condition until the next day. The sun having then risen upon me, I awoke upon the island and found that my feet were swollen, and that I had become reduced to the state in which I then was. Awhile I dragged myself along in a sitting posture, and then I crawled upon my knees. And there were in the island fruits in abundance, and springs of sweet water; therefore I ate of those fruits; and I ceased not to continue in this state for many days and nights. My spirit had then revived, my soul had returned to me, and my power of motion was renewed; and I began to meditate, and to walk along the shore of the island, amusing myself among the trees with the sight of the things that God (whose name be exalted!) had created; and I had made for myself a staff from those trees, to lean upon it.

Thus I remained until I walked, one day, upon the shore of the island, and there appeared unto me an indistinct object in the distance. I imagined that it was a wild beast, or one of the beasts of the sea; and I walked toward it, ceasing not to gaze at it; and, lo, it was a mare, of superb appearance, tethered in a part of the island by the seashore. I approached her; but she cried out against me with a great cry, and I trembled with fear of her, and was about to return, when, behold, a man came forth from beneath the earth, and he called to me and pursued me, saying to me, Who art thou, and whence hast thou come, and what is the cause of thine arrival in this place? So I answered him, O my master, know that I am a stranger, and I was in a ship, and was submerged in the sea with certain others of the passengers; but God supplied me with a wooden bowl, and I got into it, and it bore me along until the waves cast me upon this island. And when he heard my words, he laid hold of my hand and said to me, Come with me. I therefore went with him, and he descended with me into a grotto beneath the earth, and conducted me into a large subterranean chamber, and, having seated me at the upper end of that chamber, brought me some food. I was hungry; so I ate until I was satiated and contented, and my soul became at ease. Then he asked me respecting my case, and what had happened to me; wherefore I acquainted him with my whole affair from beginning to end; and he wondered at my story.

And when I had finished my tale, I said, I conjure thee by Allah, O my master, that thou be not displeased with me; I have acquainted thee with the truth of my case and of what hath happened to me, and I desire of thee that thou inform me who thou art, and what is the cause of thy dwelling in this chamber that is beneath the earth, and what is the reason of thy tethering this mare by the seaside. So he replied, Know that we are a party dispersed in this island, upon its shores, and we are the grooms of the King El-Mihraj, having under our care all his horses; and every month, when moonlight commenceth, we bring the swift mares, and tether them in this island, every mare that has not foaled, and conceal ourselves in this chamber beneath the earth, that they may attract the seahorses. This is the time of the coming forth of the seahorse; and afterward, if it be the will of God (whose name be exalted!), I will take thee with me to the King El-Mihraj, and divert thee with the sight of our country. Know, moreover, that if thou hadst not met with us, thou hadst not seen anyone in this place, and wouldst have died in misery, none knowing of thee. But I will be the means of the preservation of thy life, and of thy return to thy country.

I therefore prayed for him, and thanked him for his kindness and beneficence; and while we were thus talking, the horse came forth from the sea, as he had said. And shortly after, his companions came, each leading a mare; and, seeing me with him, they inquired of me my story, and I told them what I had related to him. They then drew near to me, and spread the table, and ate, and invited me: so I ate with them; after which, they arose, and mounted the horses, taking me with them, having mounted me on a mare.

We commenced our journey, and proceeded without ceasing until we arrived at the city of the King El-Mihraj, and they went in to him and acquainted him with my story. He therefore desired my presence, and they took me in to him, and stationed me before him; whereupon I saluted him, and he returned my salutation, and welcomed me, greeting me in an honorable manner, and inquired of me respecting my case. So I informed him of all that had happened to me, and of all that I had seen, from beginning to end; and he wondered at that which had befallen me and happened to me, and said to me, O my son, by Allah, thou hast experienced an extraordinary preservation, and had it not been for the predestined length of thy life, thou hadst not escaped from these difficulties; but praise be to God for thy safety! Then he treated me with beneficence and honor, caused me to draw near to him, and began to cheer me with conversation and courtesy; and he made me his superintendent of the seaport, and registrar of every vessel that came to the coast. I stood in his presence to transact his affairs, and he favored me and benefited me in every respect; he invested me with a handsome and costly dress, and I became a person high in credit with him in intercessions, and in accomplishing the affairs of the people.

I ceased not to remain in his service for a long time; and whenever I went to the shore of the sea, I used to inquire of the merchants and travelers and sailors respecting the direction of the city of Baghdad, that perchance some one might inform me of it, and I might go with him thither and return to my country; but none knew it, nor knew anyone who went to it. At this I was perplexed, and I was weary of the length of my absence from home; and in this state I continued for a length of time, until I went in one day to the King El-Mihraj, and found with him a party of Indians. I saluted them, and they returned my salutation, and welcomed me, and asked me respecting my country; after which, I questioned them as to their country, and they told me that they consisted of various races. Among them are the Shakiriyeh, who are the most noble of their races, who oppress no one, nor offer violence to any. And among them are a class called the Brahmans, a people who never drink wine; but they are persons of pleasure and joy and sport and merriment, and possessed of camels and horses and cattle. They informed me also that the Indians are divided into seventy-two classes; and I wondered at this extremely.

And I saw, in the dominions of the King El-Mihraj, an island, among others, which is called Kasil, in which is heard the beating of tambourines and drums throughout the night. I saw too, in the sea in which is that island, a fish two hundred cubits long, and the fishermen fear it; wherefore they knock some pieces of wood, and it fleeth from them: and I saw a fish whose face was like that of the owl. I likewise saw during that voyage many wonderful and strange things, such that, if I related them to you, the description would be too long.

I continued to amuse myself with the sight of those islands and the things that they contained, until I stood one day upon the shore of the sea, with a staff in my hand, as was my custom, and, lo, a great vessel approached, wherein were many merchants; and when it arrived at the harbor of the city, and its place of anchoring, the master furled its sails, brought it to an anchor by the shore, and put forth the landing-plank; and the sailors brought out everything that was in that vessel to the shore. They were slow in taking forth the goods, while I stood writing their account, and I said to the master of the ship, Doth aught remain in thy vessel? He answered, Yes, O my master; I have some goods in the hold of the ship; but their owner was drowned in the sea at one of the islands during our voyage hither, and his goods are in our charge; so we desire to sell them, and to take a note of their price, in order to convey it to his family in the city of Baghdad, the Abode of Peace. I therefore said to the master, What was the name of that man, the owner of the goods? He answered, His name was Es-Sindibad of the Sea, and he was drowned on his voyage with us in the sea.

And when I heard his words, I looked at him with a scrutinizing eye, and recognized him; and I cried out at him with a great cry, and said, O master, know that I am the owner of the goods which thou hast mentioned, and I am Es-Sindibad of the Sea, who descended upon the island from the ship, with the other merchants who descended; and when the fish that we were upon moved, and thou calledst out to us, some got up into the vessel, and the rest sank, and I was among those who sank. But God (whose name be exalted!) preserved me and saved me from drowning by means of a large wooden bowl, of those in which the passengers were washing, and I got into it, and began to beat the water with my feet, and the wind and the waves aided me until I arrived at this island, when I landed on it, and God (whose name be exalted!) assisted me, and I met the grooms of the King El-Mihraj, who took me with them and brought me to this city. They then led me to the King El-Mihraj, and I acquainted him with my story; whereupon he bestowed benefits upon me, and appointed me clerk of the harbor of this city, and I obtained profit in his service, and favor with him. Therefore these goods that thou hast are my goods and my portion.

But the master said, There is no strength nor power but in God, the High, the Great! There is no longer faith nor conscience in anyone!—Wherefore, O master, said I, when thou hast heard me tell thee my story? He answered, Because thou heardest me say that I had goods whose owner was drowned: therefore thou desirest to take them without price; and this is unlawful to thee; for we saw him when he sank, and there were with him many of the passengers, not one of whom escaped. How then dost thou pretend that thou art the owner of the goods?—So I said to him, O master, hear my story, and understand my words, and my veracity will become manifest to thee; for falsehood is a characteristic of the hypocrites. Then I related to him all that I had done from the time that I went forth with him from the city of Baghdad until we arrived at that island upon which we were submerged in the sea, and I mentioned to him some circumstances that had occurred between me and him. Upon this, therefore, the master and the merchants were convinced of my veracity, and recognized me; and they congratulated me on my safety, all of them saying, By Allah, we believed not that thou hadst escaped drowning; but God hath granted thee a new life. They then gave me the goods, and I found my name written upon them, and nought of them was missing. So I opened them, and took forth from them something precious and costly; the sailors of the ship carried it with me, and I went up with it to the King to offer it as a present, and informed him that this ship was the one in which I was a passenger. I told him also that my goods had arrived all entire, and that this present was a part of them. And the King wondered at this affair extremely; my veracity in all that I had said became manifest to him, and he loved me greatly, and treated me with exceeding honor, giving me a large present in return for mine.

Then I sold my bales, as well as the other goods that I had, and gained upon them abundantly; and I purchased other goods and merchandise and commodities of that city. And when the merchants of the ship desired to set forth on their voyage, I stowed all that I had in the vessel, and, going in to the King, thanked him for his beneficence and kindness; after which I begged him to grant me permission to depart on my voyage to my country and my family. So he bade me farewell, and gave me an abundance of things at my departure, of the commodities of that city; and when I had taken leave of him, I embarked in the ship, and we set sail by the permission of God, whose name be exalted! Fortune served us, and destiny aided us, and we ceased not to prosecute our voyage night and day until we arrived in safety at the city of El-Basrah. There we landed, and remained a short time; and I rejoiced at my safety, and my return to my country; and after that, I repaired to the city of Baghdad, the Abode of Peace, with abundance of bales and goods and merchandise of great value. Then I went to my quarter, and entered my house, and all my family and companions came to me. I enjoyed the society of my companions and friends, exceeding my former habits, and forgot all that I had suffered from fatigue, and absence from my native country, and difficulty, and the terrors of travel. I occupied myself with delights and pleasures, and delicious meats and exquisite drinks, and continued in this state. Such were the events of the first of my voyages; and tomorrow, if it be the will of God (whose name be exalted!), I will relate to you the tale of the second of my voyages.

Es-Sindibad of the Sea then made Es-Sindibad of the Land to sup with him; after which he gave orders to present him with a hundred pieces of gold, and said to him, Thou hast cheered us by thy company this day. So the porter thanked him, and took from him what he had given him, and went his way, meditating upon the events that befell and happened to mankind, and wondering extremely. He slept that night in his abode; and when the morning came, he repaired to the house of Es-Sindibad of the Sea, and went in to him; and he welcomed him, and treated him with honor, seating him by him. And after the rest of his companions had come, the food and drink were set before them, and the time was pleasant to them, and they were merry. Then Es-Sindibad of the Sea began his narrative thus:—

The Second Voyage of Es-Sindibad of the Sea

Know, O my brother, that I was enjoying a most comfortable life, and the most pure happiness, as you were told yesterday, until it occurred to my mind, one day, to travel again to the lands of other people, and I felt a longing for the occupation of traffic, and the pleasure of seeing the countries and islands of the world, and gaining my subsistence. I resolved upon that affair, and, having taken forth from my money a large sum, I purchased with it goods and merchandise suitable for travel, and packed them up. Then I went to the bank of the river, and found a handsome, new vessel, with sails of comely canvas, and it had a numerous crew, and was superfluously equipped. So I embarked my bales in it, as did also a party of merchants besides, and we set sail that day.

The voyage was pleasant to us, and we ceased not to pass from sea to sea, and from island to island; and at every place where we cast anchor, we met the merchants and the grandees, and the sellers and buyers, and we sold and bought, and exchanged goods. Thus we continued to do until destiny conveyed us to a beautiful island, abounding with trees bearing ripe fruits, where flowers diffused their fragrance, with birds warbling, and pure rivers; but there was not in it an inhabitant, nor a blower of a fire. The master anchored our vessel at that island, and the merchants with the other passengers landed there, to amuse themselves with the sight of its trees, and to extol the perfection of God, the One, the Omnipotent, and to wonder at the power of the Almighty King. I also landed upon the island with the rest, and sat by a spring of pure water among the trees. I had with me some food, and I sat in that place eating what God (whose name be exalted!) had allotted me. The zephyr was sweet to us in that place, and the time was pleasant to me; so slumber overcame me, and I reposed there, and became immersed in sleep, enjoying that sweet zephyr, and the fragrant gales. I then arose, and found not in the place a human being nor a Jinni. The vessel had gone with the passengers, and not one of them remembered me, neither any of the merchants nor any of the sailors: so they left me in the island.

I looked about it to the right and left, and found not in it anyone save myself. I was therefore affected with violent vexation, not to be exceeded, and my gall-bladder almost burst by reason of the severity of my grief and mourning and fatigue. I had not with me aught of worldly goods, neither food nor drink, and I had become desolate, weary in my soul, and despairing of life; and I said, Not every time doth the jar escape unbroken; and if I escaped the first time, and found him who took me with him from the shore of the island to the inhabited part, far, far from me this time is the prospect of my finding him who will convey me to inhabited lands! Then I began to weep and wail for myself until vexation overpowered me; and I blamed myself for that which I had done, and for my having undertaken this voyage and fatigue after I had been reposing at ease in my abode and my country, in ample happiness, and enjoying good food and good drink and good apparel, and had not been in want of anything, either of money or goods or merchandise. I repented of my having gone forth from the city of Baghdad, and having set out on a voyage over the sea, after the fatigue that I had suffered during my first voyage, and I felt at the point of destruction, and said, Verily to God we belong, and verily unto Him we return! And I was in the predicament of the mad.

After that, I rose and stood up, and walked about the island to the right and left, unable to sit in one place. Then I climbed up a lofty tree; and began to look from it to the right and left; but saw nought save sky and water, and trees and birds, and islands and sands. Looking, however, with a scrutinizing eye, there appeared to me on the island a white object, indistinctly seen in the distance, of enormous size: so I descended from the tree, and went toward it, and proceeded in that direction without stopping until I arrived at it; and, lo, it was a huge white dome, of great height and large circumference. I drew near to it, and walked round it; but perceived no door to it; and I found that I had not strength nor activity to climb it, on account of its exceeding smoothness. I made a mark at the place where I stood, and went round the dome measuring its circumference; and, lo, it was fifty full paces; and I meditated upon some means of gaining an entrance into it.

The close of the day, and the setting of the sun, had now drawn near; and, behold, the sun was hidden, and the sky became dark, and the sun was veiled from me. I therefore imagined that a cloud had come over it; but this was in the season of summer; so I wondered; and I raised my head, and, contemplating that object attentively, I saw that it was a bird, of enormous size, bulky body, and wide wings, flying in the air; and this it was that concealed the body of the sun, and veiled it from view upon the island. At this my wonder increased, and I remembered a story which travelers and voyagers had told me long before, that there is, in certain of the islands, a bird of enormous size, called the rukh, that feedeth its young ones with elephants. I was convinced, therefore, that the dome which I had seen was one of the eggs of the rukh. I wondered at the works of God (whose name be exalted!); and while I was in this state, lo, that bird alighted upon the dome, and brooded over it with its wings, stretching out its legs behind upon the ground; and it slept over it.—Extolled be the perfection of Him who sleepeth not!

Thereupon I arose, and unwound my turban from my head, and folded it and twisted it so that it became like a rope; and I girded myself with it, binding it tightly round my waist, and tied myself by it to one of the feet of that bird, and made the knot fast, saying within myself, Perhaps this bird will convey me to a land of cities and inhabitants, and that will be better than my remaining in this island. I passed the night sleepless, fearing that, if I slept, the bird would fly away with me when I was not aware; and when the dawn came, and morn appeared, the bird rose from its egg, and uttered a great cry, and drew me up into the sky. It ascended and soared up so high that I imagined it had reached the highest region of the sky; and after that, it descended with me gradually until it alighted with me upon the earth, and rested upon a lofty spot. So when I reached the earth, I hastily untied the bond from its foot, fearing it, though it knew not of me nor was sensible of me; and after I had loosed my turban from it, and disengaged it from its foot, shaking as I did so, I walked away. Then it took something from the face of the earth in its talons, and soared to the upper region of the sky; and I looked attentively at that thing, and, lo, it was a serpent, of enormous size, of great body, which it had taken and carried off toward the sea; and I wondered at that event.

After this, I walked about that place, and found myself upon an eminence, beneath which was a large, wide, deep valley; and by its side, a great mountain, very high; no one could see its summit by reason of its excessive height, and no one had power to ascend it. I therefore blamed myself for that which I had done, and said, Would that I had remained in the island, since it is better than this desert place; for in the island are found, among various fruits, what I might have eaten, and I might have drunk of its rivers; but in this place are neither trees nor fruits nor rivers: and there is no strength nor power but in God, the High, the Great! Verily every time that I escape from a calamity, I fall into another that is greater and more severe!

Then I arose, and emboldened myself, and walked in that valley; and I beheld its ground to be composed of diamonds, with which they perforate minerals and jewels, and with which also they perforate porcelain and the onyx; and it is a stone so hard that neither iron nor rock have any effect upon it, nor can anyone cut off aught from it, or break it, unless by means of the lead-stone. All that valley was likewise occupied by serpents and venomous snakes, every one of them like a palm-tree; and by reason of its enormous size, if an elephant came to it, it would swallow it. Those serpents appeared in the night, and hid themselves in the day, fearing lest the rukh and the vulture should carry them off, and after that tear them in pieces; and the cause of that I know not. I remained in that valley, repenting of what I had done, and said within myself, By Allah, I have hastened my own destruction! The day departed from me, and I began to walk along that valley, looking for a place in which to pass the night, fearing those serpents, and forgetting my food and drink and subsistence, occupied only by care for my life. And there appeared to me a cave near by; so I walked thither, and I found its entrance narrow. I therefore entered it, and, seeing a large stone by its mouth, I pushed it, and stopped with it the mouth of the cave while I was within it; and I said within myself, I am safe now that I have entered this place; and when daylight shineth upon me, I will go forth, and see what destiny will do. Then I looked within the cave, and beheld a huge serpent sleeping at the upper end of it over its eggs. At this my flesh quaked, and I raised my head, and committed my case to fate and destiny; and I passed all the night sleepless, until the dawn rose and shone, when I removed the stone with which I had closed the entrance of the cave, and went forth from it, like one intoxicated, giddy from excessive sleeplessness and hunger and fear.

I then walked along the valley; and while I was thus occupied, lo, a great slaughtered animal fell before me, and I found no one. So I wondered thereat extremely; and I remembered a story that I had heard long before from certain of the merchants and travelers, and persons in the habit of journeying about,—that in the mountains of the diamonds are experienced great terrors, and that no one can gain access to the diamonds, but that the merchants who import them know a stratagem by means of which to obtain them; that they take a sheep, and slaughter it, and skin it, and cut up its flesh, which they throw down from the mountain to the bottom of the valley: so, descending fresh and moist, some of these stones stick to it. Then the merchants leave it until midday, and birds of the large kind of vulture and the aquiline vulture descend to that meat, and, taking it in their talons, fly up to the top of the mountain; whereupon the merchants come to them, and cry out at them, and they fly away from the meat. The merchants then advance to that meat, and take from it the stones sticking to it; after which they leave the meat for the birds and the wild beasts, and carry the stones to their countries. And no one can procure the diamonds but by means of this stratagem.

Therefore when I beheld that slaughtered animal, and remembered this story, I arose and went to the slaughtered beast. I then selected a great number of these stones, and put them into my pocket, and within my clothes.

And while I was doing thus, lo, another great slaughtered animal. So I bound myself to it with my turban, and laying myself down on my back, placed it upon my bosom, and grasped it firmly. Thus it was raised high above the ground; and, behold, a vulture descended upon it, seized it with its talons, and flew up with it into the air, with me attached to it; and it ceased not to soar up until it had ascended with it to the summit of the mountain, when it alighted with it, and was about to tear off some of it.

And thereupon a great and loud cry arose from behind that vulture, and something made a clattering with a piece of wood upon the mountain; whereat the vulture flew away in fear, and soared into the sky.

I therefore disengaged myself from the slaughtered animal, with the blood of which my clothes were polluted; and I stood by its side. And, lo, the merchant who had cried out at the vulture advanced to the slaughtered animal, and saw me standing there. He spoke not to me; for he was frightened at me, and terrified; but he came to the slaughtered beast, and turned it over; and, not finding anything upon it, he uttered a loud cry, and said, Oh, my disappointment! There is no strength nor power but in God! We seek refuge with God from Satan the accursed!—He repented, and struck hand upon hand, and said, Oh, my grief! What is this affair?

So I advanced to him, and he said to me, Who art thou, and what is the reason of thy coming to this place? I answered him, Fear not, nor be alarmed; for I am a human being, of the best of mankind; and I was a merchant, and my tale is marvelous, and my story extraordinary, and the cause of my coming to this mountain and this valley is wondrous to relate. Fear not; for thou shalt receive of me what will rejoice thee; I have with me abundance of diamonds, of which I will give thee as much as will suffice thee, and every piece that I have is better than all that would come to thee by other means: therefore be not timorous nor afraid.

And upon this the man thanked me, and prayed for me, and conversed with me; and, lo, the other merchants heard me talking with their companion; so they came to me. Each merchant had thrown down a slaughtered animal; and when they came to us, they saluted me, and congratulated me on my safety, and took me with them; and I acquainted them with my whole story, relating to them what I had suffered on my voyage, and telling them the cause of my arrival in this valley. Then I gave to the owner of the slaughtered animal to which I had attached myself an abundance of what I had brought with me; and he was delighted with me, and prayed for me, and thanked me for that; and the other merchants said to me, By Allah, a new life hath been decreed thee; for no one ever arrived at this place before thee and escaped from it; but praise be to God for thy safety!—They passed the next night in a pleasant and safe place, and I passed the night with them, full of the utmost joy at my safety and my escape from the valley of serpents and my arrival in an inhabited country.

And when day came, we arose, and journeyed over that great mountain, beholding in that valley numerous serpents; and we continued to advance until we arrived at a garden in a great and beautiful island, wherein were camphor-trees, under each of which trees a hundred men might shade themselves. When anyone desireth to obtain some camphor from one of these trees, he maketh a perforation in the upper part of it with something long, and catcheth what descendeth from it. The liquid camphor floweth from it, and becomes like gum. It is the juice of that tree; and after this operation, the tree drieth, and becometh firewood.

In that island too is a kind of wild beast called the rhinoceros, which pastureth there like oxen and buffaloes in our country; but the bulk of that wild beast is greater than the bulk of the camel, and it eateth the tender leaves of trees. It is a huge beast, with a single horn, thick, in the middle of its head, a cubit in length, wherein is the figure of a man. And in that island are some animals of the ox-kind. Moreover, the sailors and travelers, and persons in the habit of journeying about in the mountains and the lands, have told us, that this wild beast which is named the rhinoceros lifteth the great elephant upon its horn, and pastureth with it upon the island and the shores, without being sensible of it; and the elephant dieth upon its horn; and its fat, melting by the heat of the sun, and flowing upon its head, entereth its eyes, so that it becometh blind. Then it lieth down upon the shore, and the rukh cometh to it, and carrieth it off [with the elephant] in its talons to its young ones, and feedeth them with it and with that which is upon its horn [namely the elephant]. I saw also in that island abundance of the buffalo-kind, the like of which existeth not among us.

The valley before mentioned containeth a great quantity of diamonds such as I carried off and hid in my pockets. For these the people gave me in exchange goods and commodities belonging to them; and they conveyed them for me, giving me likewise pieces of silver and pieces of gold; and I ceased not to proceed with them, amusing myself with the sight of different countries, and of what God hath created, from valley to valley and from city to city, we, in our way, selling and buying, until we arrived at the city of El-Basrah. We remained there a few days, and then I came to the city of Baghdad, the Abode of Peace, and came to my quarter, and entered my house, bringing with me a great quantity of diamonds, and money and commodities and goods in abundance. I met my family and relations, bestowed alms and gifts, made presents to all my family and companions, and began to eat well and drink well and wear handsome apparel. I associated with friends and companions, forgot all that I had suffered, and ceased not to enjoy a pleasant life and joyful heart and dilated bosom, with sport and merriment. Everyone who heard of my arrival came to me, and inquired of me respecting my voyage, and the states of the different countries: so I informed him, relating to him what I had experienced and suffered; and he wondered at the severity of my sufferings, and congratulated me on my safety.

This is the end of the account of the events that befell me and happened to me during the second voyage; and to-morrow, if it be the will of God (whose name be exalted!), I will relate to you the events of the third voyage.

The Third Voyage of Es-Sindibad of the Sea

Know, O my brother (and hear from me the story of the third voyage, for it is more wonderful than the preceding stories, hitherto related—and God is all-knowing with respect to the things which He hideth, and omniscient), that, in the times past, when I returned from the second voyage, and was in a state of the utmost joy and happiness, rejoicing in my safety, having gained great wealth, as I related to you yesterday, God having compensated me for all that I had lost, I resided in the city of Baghdad for a length of time in the most perfect prosperity and delight, and joy and happiness.

Then my soul became desirous of travel and diversion, and I longed for commerce and gain and profits, the soul being prone to evil. So I meditated, and bought an abundance of goods suited for a sea voyage, and packed them up, and departed with them from the city of Baghdad to the city of El-Basrah. There, coming to the bank of the river, I beheld a great vessel, in which were many merchants and other passengers, people of worth, and comely and good persons, people of religion and kindness and probity. I therefore embarked with them in that vessel, and we departed in reliance on the blessing of God (whose name be exalted!), and his aid and favor, rejoicing in expectation of good fortune and safety. We ceased not to proceed from sea to sea, and from island to island, and from city to city; at every place by which we passed diverting ourselves, and selling and buying, in the utmost joy and happiness. Thus we did until we were, one day, pursuing our course in the midst of the roaring sea, agitated with waves, when, lo, the master, standing at the side of the vessel, looked at the different quarters of the sea, and then slapped his face, furled the sails of the ship, cast its anchors, plucked his beard, rent his clothes, and uttered a great cry. So we said to him, O master, what is the news? And he answered, Know, O passengers, whom may God preserve! that the wind hath prevailed against us, and driven us out of our course in the midst of the sea, and destiny hath cast us, through our evil fortune, toward the Mountain of Apes. No one hath ever arrived at this place and escaped, and my heart is impressed with the conviction of the destruction of us all.

And the words of the master were not ended before the apes had come to us and surrounded the vessel on every side, numerous as locusts, dispersed about the vessel and on the shore. We feared that, if we killed one of them, or struck him, or drove him away, they would kill us, on account of their excessive number; for numbers prevail against courage; and we feared them lest they should plunder our goods and our commodities. They are the most hideous of beasts, and covered with hair like black felt, their aspect striking terror. No one understandeth their language or their state, they shun the society of men, have yellow eyes, and black faces, and are of small size, the height of each one of them being four spans.

They climbed up the cables, and severed them with their teeth, and they severed all the ropes of the vessel in every part; so the vessel inclined with the wind, and stopped at their mountain, and on their coast. Then, having seized all the merchants and the other passengers, and landed upon the island, they took the vessel with the whole of its contents, and went their way with it.

They left us upon the island, the vessel became concealed from us, and we knew not whither they went with it. And while we were upon that island, eating of its fruits and its herbs, and drinking of the rivers that were there, lo, there appeared to us an inhabited house in the midst of the island. We therefore went toward it, and walked to it; and, behold, it was a pavilion, with lofty angles, with high walls, having an entrance with folding doors, which were open; and the doors were of ebony. We entered this pavilion, and found in it a wide, open space, like a wide, large court, around which were many lofty doors, and at its upper end was a high and great mastaba. There were also in it utensils for cooking, hung over the fire-pots, and around them were many bones. But we saw not there any person; and we wondered at that extremely. We sat in the open space in that pavilion a little while, after which we slept; and we ceased not to sleep from near the mid-time between sunrise and noon until sunset.

And, lo, the earth trembled beneath us, and we heard a confused noise from the upper air, and there descended upon us, from a summit of the pavilion, a person of enormous size, in human form, and he was like a great palm-tree: he had two eyes like two blazes of fire, and tusks like the tusks of swine, and a mouth of prodigious size, like the mouth of a well, and lips like the lips of the camel, hanging down upon his bosom, and he had ears like two mortars, hanging down upon his shoulders, and the nails of his hands were like the claws of the lion. So when we beheld him thus, we became unconscious of our existence, our fear was vehement, and our terror was violent, and through the violence of our fear and dread and terror we became as dead men. And after he had descended upon the ground, he sat a little while upon the mastaba. Then he arose and came to us, and, seizing me by my hands from among my companions, the merchants, lifted me up from the ground in his hand, and felt me and turned me over; and I was in his hand like a little mouthful. He continued to feel me as the butcher feeleth the sheep that he is about to slaughter; but he found me infirm from excessive affliction, and lean from excessive fatigue and from the voyage; having no flesh. He therefore let me go from his hand, and took another, from among my companions; and he turned him over as he had turned me over, and felt him as he had felt me, and let him go. He ceased not to feel us and turn us over, one after another, until he came to the master of our ship, who was a fat, stout, broad-shouldered man; a person of strength and vigor: so he pleased him, and he seized him as the butcher seizeth the animal that he is about to slaughter, and, having thrown him on the ground, put his foot upon his neck, which he thus broke. Then he roasted him, and ate him. He then threw himself down, and slept upon that mastaba; and he slept uninterruptedly until the morning, when he went his way.

As soon, therefore, as we were sure that he was far from us, we conversed together, and wept for ourselves, saying, Would that we had been drowned in the sea, or that the apes

had eaten us; for it were better than the roasting of a man
upon burning coals! By Allah, this death is a vile one! But
what God willeth cometh to pass, and there is no strength
nor power but in God, the High, the Great! We die in sorrow, and no one knoweth of us; and there is no escape for
us from this place!—We then arose and went forth upon the
island, to see for us a place in which to hide ourselves, or to
flee; and it had become a light matter to us to die, rather than
that our flesh should be roasted with fire. But we found not
for us a place in which to hide ourselves; and the evening
overtook us. So we returned to the pavilion, by reason of the
violence of our fear, and sat there a little while; and, lo, the
earth trembled beneath us, and the giant approached us, and,
coming among us, began to turn us over, one after another,
as on the former occasion, and to feel us, until one pleased
him; whereupon he seized him, and did with him as he did
with the master of the ship the day before. He roasted him,
and ate him upon that mastaba, and slept that night upon that
mastaba again; and when the day came, he arose and went his
way, leaving us as usual.

Upon this we assembled together and conversed, and said,
one to another, By Allah, if we cast ourselves into the sea
and die drowned, it will be better than our dying burnt; for
this mode of being put to death is abominable! And one of
us said, Hear my words. Verily we will contrive a stratagem
against him and kill him, and be at ease from apprehension of
his purpose. So I said to them, Hear, O my brothers. If we
must kill him, we will transport this wood, and remove some
of this firewood, and make for ourselves rafts, each to bear
three men; after which we will contrive a stratagem to kill

him, and embark on the rafts, and proceed over the sea to whatsoever place God shall desire. Or we will remain in this place until a ship shall pass by, when we will embark in it. And if we be not able to kill him, we will embark on our rafts, and put out to sea; and if we be drowned, we shall be preserved from being roasted over the fire, and from being slaughtered. If we escape, we escape.—To this they all replied, By Allah, this is a right opinion and a wise proceeding. And we agreed upon this matter, and commenced the work. We removed the pieces of wood out of the pavilion, and constructed rafts, attached them to the seashore, and stowed upon them some provisions; after which we returned to the pavilion.

And when it was evening, lo, the earth trembled with us, and the giant came in to us, like the biting dog. He turned us over and felt us, one after another, and, having taken one of us, did with him as he had done with the others before him. He ate him; then slept upon the mastaba. So thereupon we arose, and took two iron spits, of those which were set up, and put them in the fierce fire until they were red-hot, and became like burning coals; when we grasped them firmly, and we thrust them into his eyes. Thus his eyes were destroyed, and he uttered a great cry, whereat our hearts were terrified. Then he arose resolutely from that mastaba and began to search for us, while we fled from him to the right and left, and he saw us not; for his sight was blinded; but we feared him with a violent fear, and made sure, in that time, of destruction, and despaired of safety. And upon this he sought the door, feeling for it, and went forth from it, crying out, while we were in the utmost fear of him; and, lo, the earth shook beneath us, by reason of the vehemence of his cry. So when he went forth from the pavilion, we followed him, and he went his way, searching for us.

Then he returned, accompanied by a female, greater than he, and more hideous in form; and when we beheld him, and her who was with him, more horrible than he in appearance, we were in the utmost fear. As soon as the female saw us, we hastily loosed the rafts that we had constructed, and embarked on them, and pushed them forth into the sea. But each of the giants had a mass of rock, and they cast at us until the greater number of us died from the casting, there remaining of us only three persons, I and two others; and the raft conveyed us to another island.

I then walked along the island until I came to the extremity of it; when I cast a glance toward the sea, and beheld a ship at a distance, in the midst of the deep. So I took a great branch of a tree, and made a sign with it to the passengers, calling out to them; and when they saw me, they said, We must see what this is. Perhaps it is a man.—Then they approached me, and heard my cries to them. They therefore came to me, and took me with them in the ship and asked me respecting my state: so I informed them of all that had happened to me from beginning to end, and of the troubles that I had suffered; whereas they wondered extremely. They clad me with some of their clothes, attiring me decently; and after that, they put before me some provisions, and I ate until I was satisfied. They also gave me to drink some cool and sweet water, and my heart was revived, my soul became at ease, and I experienced great comfort. God (whose name be exalted!) had raised me to life after my death; so I praised Him (exalted be his name!) for his abundant favors, and thanked Him. My courage was strengthened after I had made sure of destruction, so that it seemed to me that all which I then experienced was a dream.

We proceeded on our voyage, and the wind was fair to us by the permission of God (whose name be exalted!) until we came in sight of an island called the Island of Es-Selahit, where sandalwood is abundant, and there the master anchored the ship, and the merchants and other passengers landed, and took forth their goods to sell and buy. And I beheld in that sea which we navigated, namely the Sea of India, many wonders and strange things that cannot be numbered nor calculated. Among the things that I saw there were a fish in the form of the cow, and a creature in the form of the donkey; and I saw a bird that cometh forth from a seashell, and layeth its eggs and hatcheth them upon the surface of the water, and never cometh forth from the sea upon the face of the earth.—After this we continued our voyage, by permission of God (whose name be exalted!), and the wind and voyage were pleasant to us, until we arrived at El-Basrah, where I remained a few days. Then I came to the city of Baghdad, and repaired to my quarter, entered my house, and saluted my family and companions and friends. I rejoiced at my safety and my return to my country and my family and city and district, and I gave alms and presents, and clad the widows and the orphans, and collected my companions and friends. And I ceased not to live thus, eating and drinking, and sporting and making merry, associating familiarly and mingling in society; and I forgot all that had happened to me, and the distresses and horrors that I had suffered.

Such were the most wonderful of the things that I beheld

during that voyage; and to-morrow, if it be the will of God (whose name be exalted!), thou shalt come, O Sindibad of the Land, and I will relate the story of the fourth voyage; for it is more wonderful than the stories of the preceding voyages.

The Fourth Voyage of Es-Sindibad of the Sea

Know, O my brother, that when I returned to the city of Baghdad, and met my companions and my family and my friends, and was enjoying the utmost pleasure and happiness and ease, and had forgotten all that I had experienced, and had become immersed in sport and mirth, and the society of friends and companions leading the most delightful life, my wicked soul suggested to me to travel again to the countries of other people, and I felt a longing for associating with the different races of men, and for selling and gains. So I resolved upon this, and purchased precious goods, suitable to a sea-voyage, and, having packed up many bales, more than usual, I went from the city of Baghdad to the city of El-Basrah, where I embarked my bales in a ship, and joined myself to a party of the chief men of El-Basrah, and we set forth on our voyage.

The vessel proceeded with us, confiding in the blessing of God (whose name be exalted!), over the roaring sea agitated with waves, and the voyage was pleasant to us; and we ceased not to proceed in this manner for a period of nights and days, from island to island and from sea to sea, until a contrary wind rose against us one day. The master therefore cast the anchors, and stayed the ship in the midst of the sea, fearing that she would sink in the midst of the deep. And

while we were in this state, supplicating, and humbling ourselves to God (whose name be exalted!), there rose against us
a great tempest, which rent the sails in strips, and the people
were submerged with all their bales and their commodities
and wealth. I was submerged among the rest, and I swam in
the sea for half a day, after which I abandoned myself; but
God (whose name be exalted!) aided me to lay hold upon a
piece of one of the planks of the ship, and I and a party of
the merchants got upon it. We continued sitting upon this
plank, striking the sea with our feet, and the waves and the
wind helping us; and we remained in this state a day and a
night. And on the following day, shortly before the mid-time
between sunrise and noon, a wind rose against us, the sea
became boisterous, the waves and the wind were violent, and
the water cast us upon an island: and we were like dead men,
from excess of sleeplessness and fatigue, and cold and hunger,
and fear and thirst.

We walked along the shores of that island, and found
upon it abundant herbs; so we ate some of them to stay our
departing spirits, and to sustain us; and passed the next night
upon the shore of the island. And when the morning came,
and diffused its light and shone, we arose and walked about
the island to the right and left, and there appeared to us a
building in the distance. We therefore proceeded over the
island in the direction of that building which we had seen
from a distance, and ceased not to proceed until we stood at
its door. And while we were standing there, lo, there came
forth to us from that door a group of men, who, without
speaking to us, seized us, and took us to their King, and he
commanded us to sit. So we sat; and they brought to us some

food, such as we knew not, nor in our lives had we seen the like of it; wherefore my stomach consented not to it, and I ate none of it in comparison with my companions, and my eating so little of it was owing to the grace of God (whose name be exalted!), in consequence of which I have lived to the present time. For when my companions ate of that food, their minds became stupefied, and they ate like madmen, and their states became changed. Upon this, therefore, I was confounded respecting their case, and grieved for them, and became extremely anxious by reason of the violence of my fear for myself.

Accordingly I turned away, and, seeing a road on my right hand, I proceeded along it, and ceased not to go on, sometimes running by reason of fear, and sometimes walking at my leisure until I had taken rest. Thus I continued to do until I was hidden from the eyes of the man who directed me to the way, and I saw him not nor did he see me. The sun had disappeared from me, and darkness approached; wherefore I sat to rest, and desired to sleep; but sleep came not to me that night on account of the violence of my fear and hunger and fatigue. And when it was midnight, I arose and walked on over the island, and I ceased not to proceed until day arrived, and the morning came and diffused its light and shone, and the sun rose over the tops of the high hills and over the low gravelly plains. I was tired and hungry and thirsty: so I began to eat of the herbs and vegetables that were upon the island, and continued to eat of them till I was satiated, and my departing spirit was stayed; after which I arose and walked on again over the island; and thus I ceased not to do all the day and the next night; whenever I was hungry, eating of the vegetables.

In this manner I proceeded for the space of seven days with their nights; and on the morning of the eighth day, I cast a glance, and beheld a faint object in the distance. So I went toward it, and ceased not to proceed until I came up to it, after sunset; and I looked at it with a scrutinizing eye, while I was yet distant from it, and with a fearful heart in consequence of what I had suffered first and after, and, lo, it was a party of men gathering pepper. And when I approached them, and they saw me, they hastened to me, and came to me and surrounded me on every side, saying to me, Who art thou, and whence hast thou come? I answered them, Know ye, O people, that I am a poor foreigner. And I informed them of my whole case, including how they had taken my companions, and fed them with food of which I did not eat. And they congratulated me on my safety, and wondered at that which had befallen me. Then they made me sit among them until they had finished their work, and they brought me some nice food. I therefore ate of it, being hungry, and rested with them awhile; after which they took me and embarked with me in a vessel, and went to their island and their abodes. They then took me to their King, and I saluted him, and he welcomed me and treated me with honor, and inquired of me my story. So I related to him what I had experienced, and what had befallen me and happened to me from the day of my going forth from the city of Baghdad until I had come unto him. And the King wondered extremely at my story, and at the events that had happened to me; he, and all who were present in his assembly. After that, he ordered me to sit with him. Therefore I sat; and he gave orders to bring the food, which accordingly they brought, and I ate of it as much as sufficed me, and washed my hands, and offered up thanks for the favor of God (whose name be exalted!), praising Him and glorifying Him. I then rose from the presence of the King, and diverted myself with a sight of his city; and, lo, it was a flourishing city, abounding with inhabitants and wealth, and with food and markets and goods, and sellers and buyers.

So I rejoiced at my arrival at that city, and my heart was at ease; I became familiar with its inhabitants, and was magnified and honored by them and by their King above the people of his dominions and the great men of his city. And I saw that all its great men and its small rode excellent and fine horses without saddles; whereat I wondered; and I said to the King, Wherefore, O my lord, dost thou not ride on a saddle; for therein is ease to the rider, and additional power? He said, What kind of thing is a saddle? This is a thing that in our lives we have never seen, nor have we ever ridden upon it.

And I said to him, Wilt thou permit me to make for thee a saddle to ride upon and to experience the pleasure of it? He answered me, Do so. I therefore said to him, Furnish me with some wood. And he gave orders to bring me all that I required. Then I asked for a clever carpenter, and sat with him, and taught him the construction of the saddle, and how he should make it. Afterward I took some wool, and teased it, and made felt of it; and I caused some leather to be brought, and covered the saddle with it, and polished it. I then attached its straps, and its girth: after which I brought the blacksmith, and described to him the form of the stirrups, and he forged an excellent pair of stirrups; and I filed them, and tinned them. Then I attached fringes of silk. Having done this, I arose and brought one of the best of the King's horses, girded upon him that saddle, attached to it the stirrups, bridled him, and brought him forward to the King; and it pleased him, and was agreeable to him. He thanked me, and seated himself upon it, and was greatly delighted with that saddle; and he gave me a large present as a reward for that which I had done for him. And when his Wezir saw that I had made that saddle, he desired of me one like it. So I made for him a saddle like it. The grandees and dignitaries likewise desired of me saddles, and I made for them. I taught the carpenter the construction of the saddle; and the blacksmith, the mode of making stirrups; and we employed ourselves in making these things, and sold them to the great men and masters. Thus I collected abundant wealth, and became in high estimation with them, and they loved me exceedingly.

I continued to enjoy a high rank with the King and his attendants and the great men of the country and the lords of the state, until I sat one day with the King, in the utmost happiness and honor; and while I was sitting, the King said to me, Know, O thou, that thou hast become magnified and honored among us, and hast become one of us, and we cannot part with thee, nor can we suffer thee to depart from our city; and I desire of thee that thou obey me in an affair, and reject not that which I shall say. So I said to him, And what dost thou desire of me, O King? For I will not reject that which thou shalt say, since thou hast shewn favor and kindness and beneficence to me, and (praise be to God!) I have become one of thy servants.

And he answered, I desire to marry thee among us to a

beautiful, lovely, elegant wife, possessed of wealth and loveliness, and thou shalt become a dweller with us, and I will lodge thee by me in my palace: therefore oppose me not, nor reject what I say. And when I heard the words of the King, I was abashed at him, and was silent, returning him no answer, by reason of the exceeding bashfulness with which I regarded him. So he said, Wherefore dost thou not reply to me, O my son? And I answered him, O my master, it is thine to command, O King of the age! And upon this he sent immediately and caused the Kadi and the witnesses to come, and married me forthwith to a woman of noble rank, of high lineage, possessing abundant wealth and fortune, of great origin, of surprising loveliness and beauty, owner of dwellings and possessions and buildings. Then he gave me a great, handsome house, standing alone, and he gave me servants and other dependents, and assigned me supplies and salaries. Thus I became in a state of the utmost ease and joy and happiness, forgetting all the fatigue and affliction and adversity that had happened to me; and I said within myself, When I set forth on my voyage to my country, I will take her with me. But every event that is predestined to happen to man must inevitably take place, and no one knoweth what will befall him. I loved her and she loved me with a great affection, concord existed between me and her, and we lived in a most delightful manner, and most comfortable abode, and ceased not to enjoy this state for a length of time.

Then God (whose name be exalted!) caused to die the wife of my neighbor, and he was a companion of mine. So I went in to him to console him for the loss of his wife, and beheld him in a most evil state, anxious, weary in soul and heart;

and upon this I consoled him and comforted him, saying to him, Mourn not for thy wife. God will happily compensate thee by giving thee one better than she, and thy life will be long if it be the will of God, whose name be exalted!—But he wept violently, and said to me, O my brother, return to thy reason, and do not announce how can God compensate me by giving me a better than she, when but one day remaineth of my life? So I replied, O my brother, return to thy reason, and do not announce thine own death; for thou art well, in prosperity and health. But he said to me, O my companion, by thy life, to-morrow thou wilt lose me, and never in thy life wilt thou see me again.—And how so? said I. He answered me, This day they will bury my wife, and they will bury me with her in the sepulchre; for it is our custom in our country, when the wife dieth, to bury with her husband alive; and when the husband dieth, they bury with him his wife alive; that neither of them may enjoy life after the other. I therefore said to him, By Allah, this custom is exceedingly vile, and none can endure it!

And while we were thus conversing, lo, most of the people of the city came, and proceeded to console my companion for the loss of his wife and for himself. They began to prepare her body for burial according to their custom, brought a bier, and carried the woman in it, with all her apparel and ornaments and wealth, taking the husband with them; and they went forth with them to the outside of the city, and came to a place in the side of a mountain by the sea. They advanced to a spot there, and lifted up from it a great stone, and there appeared, beneath the place of this, a margin of stone, like the margin of a well. Into this they threw down that woman; and, lo, it was a great pit beneath the mountain. Then they brought the man, tied him beneath his bosom by a rope of fibers of the palm-tree, and let him down into the pit. They also let down to him a great jug of sweet water, and seven cakes of bread; and when they had let him down, he loosed himself from the rope, and they drew it up, and covered the mouth of the pit with that great stone as it was before, and went their ways, leaving my companion with his wife in the pit.

So I said within myself, By Allah, this death is more grievous than the first death. I then went to their King, and said to him, O my lord, how is it that ye bury the living with the dead in your country? And he answered me, Know that this is our custom in our country: when the husband dieth, we bury with him his wife; and when the wife dieth, we bury her with her husband alive; that we may not separate them in life nor in death; and this custom we have received from our forefathers. And I said, O King of the age, and in like manner the foreigner like me, when his wife dieth among you do ye with him as ye have done with this man? He answered me, Yes: we bury him with her, and do with him as thou hast seen. And when I heard these words from him, my gall-bladder almost burst by reason of the violence of my grief and mourning for myself; my mind was stupefied, and I became fearful lest my wife should die before me and they should bury me alive with her. Afterward, however, I comforted myself, and said, Perhaps I shall die before her: and no one knoweth which will precede and which will follow. And I proceeded to beguile myself with occupations.

And but a short time had elapsed after that when my wife fell sick, and she remained so a few days, and died. So the

greater number of the people assembled to console me, and
to console her family for her death; and the King also came
to console me for the loss of her, as was their custom. They
then brought for her a woman to wash her, and they washed
her, and decked her with the richest of her apparel, and ornaments of gold, and necklaces and jewels. And when they had
attired my wife, and put her in the bier, and carried her and
gone with her to that mountain, and lifted up the stone from
the mouth of the pit, and cast her into it, all my companions,
and the family of my wife, advanced to bid me farewell and to
console me for the loss of my wife. I was crying out among
them, I am a foreigner, and am unable to endure your custom!
But they would not hear what I said, nor pay any regard to
my words. They laid hold upon me and bound me by force,
tying with me seven cakes of bread and a jug of sweet water,
according to their custom, and let me down into that pit.
And, lo, it was a great cavern beneath that mountain. They
said to me, Loose thyself from the ropes. But I would not
loose myself. So they threw the ropes down upon me, and
covered the mouth of the pit with the great stone that was
upon it, and went their ways.

I knew not night from day; and I sustained myself with
little food, not eating until hunger almost killed me, nor drinking until my thirst became violent, fearing the exhaustion of
the food and water that I had with me. I said, There is no
strength nor power but in God, the High, the Great! What
tempted me to marry in this city? And every time that I say, I
have escaped from a calamity, I fall into a calamity that is more
mighty than the preceding one! By Allah, my dying this death
is unfortunate! Would that I had been drowned in the sea, or

had died upon the mountains! It had been better for me than this evil death!

And I continued in this manner, blaming myself. I laid myself down upon the bones of the dead, begging aid of God (whose name be exalted!), and wished for death, but I found it not, by reason of the severity of my sufferings. Thus I remained until hunger burned my stomach, and thirst inflamed me; when I sat, and felt for the bread, and ate a little of it, and I swallowed after it a little water. Then I rose and stood up, and walked about the sides of the cavern; and I found that it was spacious sideways, and with vacant cavities; but upon its bottom were numerous dead bodies, and rotten bones, that had lain there from old times. And upon this I made for myself a place in the side of the cavern, remote from the fresh corpses, and there I slept.

I remained in that cavern a length of time, until I was sleeping one day, and I awoke from my sleep, and heard something make a noise in a side of the cavern. So I said, What can this be? I then arose and walked toward it, taking with me a long bone of a dead man; and when it was sensible of my presence, it ran away, and fled from me; and, lo, it was a wild beast. But I followed it to the upper part of the cavern, and thereupon a light appeared to me from a small spot, like a star. Sometimes it appeared to me, and sometimes it was concealed from me. Therefore when I saw it, I advanced toward it; and the nearer I approached to it, the larger did the light from it appear to me. So upon this I was convinced that it was a hole in that cavern, communicating with the open country; and I said within myself, There must be some cause for this: either it is a second mouth, like that from which they let me down, or it is a fissure in this place. I meditated in my mind awhile, and advanced toward the light; and, lo, it was a perforation in the back of that mountain, which the wild beasts had made, and through which they entered this place. When I saw it, therefore, my mind was quieted, my soul was tranquilized, and my heart was at ease; I made sure of life after death, and became as in a dream.

Then I managed to force my way through that perforation, and found myself on the shore of the sea, upon a great mountain, which formed a barrier between the sea on the one side, and the island and city on the other, and to which no one could gain access. So I praised God (whose name be exalted!), and thanked Him, and rejoiced exceedingly, and my heart was strengthened.

Afterward, as I was sitting, one day, upon the shore of the sea, meditating upon my case, lo, a vessel passed along in the midst of the roaring sea agitated with waves. So I took in my hand a white garment, of the clothes of the dead, and tied it to a staff, and ran with it along the seashore, making a sign to the people with that garment, until they happened to look, and saw me upon the summit of the mountain. They therefore approached me, and heard my voice, and sent to me a boat in which was a party of men from the ship; and when they drew near to me they said to me, Who art thou, and what is the reason of thy sitting in this place, and how didst thou arrive at this mountain; for in our lives we have never seen anyone who hath come unto it? So I answered them, I am a merchant. The vessel that I was in was wrecked, and I got upon a plank, together with my things, and God facilitated my landing at this place, with my things, by means of my exertion and my skill, after severe toil. They therefore took me with them in the boat, and they proceeded with me until they took me up into the ship, to the master.

And the master said to me, O man, how didst thou arrive at this place, which is a great mountain, with a great city behind it? All my life I have been accustomed to navigate this sea, and to pass by this mountain; but have never seen anything there except the wild beasts and the birds.—I answered him, I am a merchant. I was in a great ship, and it was wrecked, and all my merchandise, consisting of these stuffs and clothes which thou seest, was submerged; but I placed it upon a great plank, one of the planks of the ship, and destiny and fortune aided me, so that I landed upon this mountain, where I waited for some one to pass by and take me with him.—And I acquainted them not with the events that had befallen me in the city, or in the cavern; fearing that there might be with them in the ship some one from that city.

We ceased not to proceed on our voyage from island to island and from sea to sea. I hoped to escape, and was rejoiced at my safety; but every time that I reflected upon my abode in the cavern with my wife, my reason left me. We pursued our course until we arrived at the Island of the Bell, whence we proceeded to the Island of Kela in six days. Then we came to the kingdom of Kela, which is adjacent to India, and in it are a mine of lead, and places where the Indian cane groweth, and excellent camphor; and its King is a King of great dignity, whose dominion extendeth over the Island of the Bell. In it is a city called the City of the Bell, which is two days' journey in extent.

At length, by the providence of God, we arrived in safety at the city of El-Basrah, where I landed, and remained a few days; after which I came to the city of Baghdad, and to my quarter, and entered my house, met my family and my companions, and made inquiries respecting them; and they rejoiced at my safety, and congratulated me. I stored all the commodities that I had brought with me in my magazines, gave alms and presents, and clad the orphans and the widows; and I became in a state of the utmost joy and happiness, and returned to my former habit of associating with familiars and companions and brothers, and indulging in sport and merriment.

Such were the most wonderful of the events that happened to me in the course of the fourth voyage. But, O my brother, sup thou with me, and observe thy custom by coming to me to-morrow, when I will inform thee what happened to me and what befell me during the fifth voyage; for it was more wonderful and extraordinary than the preceding voyages.

The Fifth Voyage of Es-Sindibad of the Sea

Know, O my brothers, that when I returned from the fourth voyage, and became immersed in sport and merriment and joy, and had forgotten all that I had experienced, and what had befallen me, and what I had suffered, by reason of my excessive joy at the gain and profit and benefits that I had obtained, my mind again suggested to me to travel, and to divert myself with the sight of the countries and the islands of other people. So I arose and meditated upon that subject, and brought precious goods, suited for a sea voyage. I packed up the bales, and departed from the city of Baghdad to the city of El-Basrah; and, walking along the bank of the river, I saw a great, handsome, lofty vessel, and it pleased me; wherefore I purchased it. Its apparatus was new, and I hired for it a master and sailors, over whom I set my servants as superintendents, and I embarked in it my bales. And there came to me a company of merchants, who also embarked their bales in it, and paid me hire. We set sail in the utmost joy and happiness, and rejoicing in the prospect of safety and gain, and ceased not to pursue our voyage from island to island and from sea to sea, diverting ourselves with viewing the islands and landing at them and selling and buying.

Thus we continued to do until we arrived one day at a large island, destitute of inhabitants. There was no person upon it: it was deserted and desolate; but on it was an enormous white dome, of great bulk; and we landed to amuse ourselves with a sight of it, and, lo, it was a great egg of a rukh. Now when the merchants had landed, and were diverting themselves with viewing it, not knowing that it was the egg of a rukh, they struck it with stones; whereupon it broke, and there poured down from it a great quantity of liquid, and the young rukh appeared within it. So they pulled it and drew it forth from the shell, and killed it, and took from it abundance of meat. I was then in the ship, and knew not of it, and they acquainted me not with that which they did. But in the meantime one of the passengers said to me, O my master, arise and divert thyself with the sight of this egg which we imagined to be a dome. I therefore arose to take a view of it, and found the merchants striking the egg. I called out to them, Do not this deed; for the rukh will come and demolish our ship, and destroy us. But they would not hear my words.

And while they were doing as above related, behold, the sun became concealed from us, and the day grew dark, and there came over us a cloud by which the sky was obscured. So we raised our heads to see what had intervened between us and the sun, and saw that the wings of the rukh were what veiled from us the sun's light, so that the sky was darkened. And when the rukh came, and beheld its egg broken, it cried out at us; whereupon its mate, the female bird, came to it, and they flew in circles over the ship, crying out at us with a voice more vehement than thunder. So I called out to the master and the sailors, and said to them, Push off the vessel, and seek safety before we perish. The master therefore hastened, and, the merchants having embarked, he loosed the ship, and we departed from that island.

And when the rukhs saw that we had put forth to sea, they absented themselves from us for a while. We proceeded, and made speed, desiring to escape from them, and to quit their country; but, lo, they had followed us, and they now approached us, each of them having in its claws a huge mass of rock from a mountain; and the male bird threw the rock that he had brought upon us. The master, however, steered away the ship, and the mass of rock missed her by a little space. It descended into the sea by the ship, and the ship went up with us, and down, by reason of the mighty plunging of the rock, and we beheld the bottom of the sea in consequence of its vehement force. Then the female threw upon us the rock that she had brought, which was smaller than the former one, and, as destiny had ordained, it fell upon the stern of the ship, and crushed it, making the rudder fly into twenty pieces, and all that was in the ship became submerged in the sea.

I strove to save myself, impelled by the sweetness of life, and God (whose name be exalted!) placed within my reach one of the planks of the ship; so I caught hold of it, and, having got upon it, began to row upon it with my feet, and the wind and the waves helped me forward. The vessel had sunk near an island in the midst of the sea, and destiny cast me, by permission of God (whose name be exalted!), to that island. I therefore landed upon it; but I was at my last breath, and in the state of the dead, from the violence of the fatigue and distress and hunger and thirst that I had suffered. I then threw myself down upon the shore of the sea, and remained lying there awhile, until my soul felt at ease, and my heart was tranquilized, when I walked along the island, and saw that it resembled one of the gardens of Paradise. Its trees bore ripe fruits, its rivers were flowing, and its birds were warbling the praises of Him to whom belongeth might and permanence. Upon that island was an abundance of trees and fruits, with varieties of flowers. So I ate of the fruits until I was satiated, and I drank of those rivers until I was satisfied with drink; and I praised God (whose name be exalted!) for this, and glorified Him. I then remained sitting upon the island till evening came, and night approached; whereupon I rose; but I was like a slain man, by reason of the fatigue and fear that I had experienced; and I heard not in that island a voice, nor did I see in it any person.

I slept there without interruption until the morning, and then rose and stood up, and walked among the trees; and I saw a streamlet, by which sat an old man, a comely person, who was clad from the waist downward with a covering made of the leaves of trees. So I said within myself, Perhaps this old man hath landed upon this island and is one of the ship-wrecked persons with whom the vessel fell to pieces. I then approached him and saluted him, and he returned the salutation by a sign, without speaking; and I said to him, O sheykh, what is the reason of thy sitting in this place? Whereupon he shook his head, and sighed, and made a sign to me with his hand, as though he would say, Carry me upon thy neck, and transport me from this place to the other side of the streamlet. I therefore said within myself, I will act kindly with this person, and transport him to this place to which he desireth to go: perhaps I shall obtain for it a reward in heaven.

Accordingly I advanced to him, and took him upon my shoulders, and conveyed him to the place that he had indicated to me; when I said to him, Descend at thine ease. But he descended not from my shoulders. He had twisted his legs round my neck, and I looked at them, and I saw that they were like the hide of the buffalo in blackness and roughness. So I was frightened at him, and desired to throw him down from my shoulders; but he pressed upon my neck with his feet, and squeezed my throat, so that the world became black before my face, and I was unconscious of my existence, falling upon the ground in a fit, like one dead. He then raised his legs, and beat me upon my back and my shoulders; and I suffered violent pain; wherefore I rose with him. He still kept his seat upon my shoulders, and I had become fatigued with bearing him; and he made a sign to me that I should go in among the trees, to the best of the fruits. When I disobeyed him, he inflicted upon me, with his feet, blows more violent than those of whips; and he ceased not to direct me with his hand to every place to which he desired to go, and to that place I went with him. If I loitered, or went leisurely, he beat me; and I was as a captive to him. We went into the midst of the island, among the trees, and he descended not from my shoulders by night nor by day: when he desired to sleep, he would wind his legs round my neck, and sleep a little, and then he would arise and beat me, whereupon I would arise with him quickly, unable to disobey him, by reason of the severity of that which I suffered from him; and I blamed myself for having taken him up, and having had pity on him.

I continued with him in this condition, enduring the most violent fatigue, and said within myself, I did a good act unto this person, and it hath become an evil to myself! By Allah, I will never more do good unto anyone as long as I live!—I begged of God (whose name be exalted!), at every period and in every hour, that I might die, in consequence of the excessive fatigue and distress that I suffered.

Thus I remained for a length of time, until I carried him one day to a place in the island where I found an abundance of pumpkins, many of which were dry. Upon this I took a large one that was dry, and, having opened its upper extremity, and cleansed it, I went with it to a grapevine, and filled it with the juice of the grapes. I then stopped up the aperture, and put it in the sun, and left it for some days, until it had become pure wine; and every day I used to drink of it, to help myself to endure the fatigue that I underwent with that obstinate devil; for whenever I was intoxicated by it, my energy was strengthened.

So, seeing me one day drinking, he made a sign to me with his hand, as though he would say, What is this? And I answered him, This is something agreeable, that invigorateth the heart, and dilateth the mind. Then I ran with him, and danced among the trees; I was exhilarated by intoxication, and clapped my hands, and sang, and was joyful. Therefore when he beheld me in this state, he made a sign to me to hand him the pumpkin, that he might drink from it; and I feared him, and gave it to him; whereupon he drank what remained in it, and threw it upon the ground, and, being moved with merriment, began to shake upon my shoulders. He then became intoxicated, and drowned in intoxication; all his limbs, and the muscles of his sides, became relaxed, and he began to lean from side to side upon my shoulders. So when I knew that he was drunk, and that he was unconscious of existence, I put my hand to his feet, and loosed them from my neck. Then I stooped with him, and sat down, and threw him upon the ground. I scarcely believed that I had liberated myself and escaped from the state in which I had been; but I feared him, lest he should arise from his intoxication, and torment me. I therefore took a great mass of stone from among the trees, and, coming to him, struck him upon his head as he lay asleep. May no mercy of God be on him!

After that, I walked about the island, with a happy mind, and came to the place where I was before, on the shore of the sea. And I remained upon that island, eating of its fruits, and drinking of the water of its rivers, for a length of time, and watching to see some vessel passing by me, until I was sitting one day, reflecting upon the events that had befallen me and happened to me, and I said within myself, I wonder if God will preserve me in safety, and if I shall return to my country, and meet my family and my companions. And, lo, a vessel approached from the midst of the roaring sea agitated with waves, and it ceased not in its course until it anchored at that island; whereupon the passengers landed there. So I walked toward them; and when they beheld me, they all quickly approached me and assembled around me, inquiring respecting my state, and the cause of my coming to that island. I therefore acquainted them with my case, and with the events that had befallen me; whereat they wondered extremely.

And they said to me, This man who rode upon thy shoulders is called the Old Man of the Sea, and no one ever was beneath his limbs and escaped from him except thee; and praise be to God for thy safety! Then they brought me some food, and I ate until I was satisfied; and they gave me some clothing, which I put on, covering myself decently. After this, they took me with them in the ship; and when we had proceeded days and nights, destiny drove us to a city of lofty buildings, all the houses of which overlooked the sea. That city is called the City of the Apes; and when the night cometh, the people who reside in it go forth from the doors that open upon the sea, and, embarking in boats and ships, pass the night upon the sea, in their fear of the apes, lest they should come down upon them in the night from the mountains.

I landed to divert myself in this city, and the ship set sail without my knowledge. So I repented of my having landed there, remembering my companions, and what had befallen them from the apes, first and afterward; and I sat weeping and mourning. And thereupon a man of the inhabitants of the city advanced to me and said to me, O my master, it seemeth that thou art a stranger in this country. I therefore replied, Yes: I am a stranger, and a poor man.

Upon this the man brought me a cotton bag, and said to me, Take this bag, and fill it with pebbles from this city, and go forth with a party of the inhabitants. I will associate thee with them, and give them a charge respecting thee, and do thou as they shall do. Perhaps thou wilt accomplish that by means of which thou wilt be assisted to make thy voyage, and to return to thy country.

Then that man took me and led me forth from the city, and I picked up small pebbles, with which I filled that bag. And, lo, a party of men came out from the city, and he associated me with them, giving them a charge respecting me, and saying to them, This is a stranger; so take him with you, and teach him the mode of gathering. Perhaps he may gain the means of subsistence, and ye will obtain from God a reward and recompense.

And they replied, We hear and obey. They welcomed me, and took me with them, and proceeded, each of them having a bag like mine, filled with pebbles; and we ceased not to pursue our way until we arrived at a wide valley, wherein were many lofty trees, which no one could climb. In that valley were also many apes, which, when they saw us, fled from us, and ascended those trees. Then the men began to pelt the apes with the stones that they had with them in the bags; upon which the apes began to pluck off the fruits of those trees, and to throw them at the men; and I looked at the fruits which the apes threw down, and, lo, they were cocoa-nuts. Therefore when I beheld the party do thus, I chose a great tree, upon which were many apes, and, advancing to it, proceeded to pelt those apes with stones; and they broke off nuts from the tree and threw them at me. So I collected them as the rest of the party did, and the stones were not exhausted from my bag until I had collected a great quantity. And when the party had ended this work, they gathered together all that was with them, and each of them carried off as many of the nuts as he could.

We then returned to the city during the remainder of the day, and I went to the man, my companion, who had associated me with the party, and gave him all that I had collected, thanking him for his kindness. But he said to me, Take these and sell them, and make use of the price. And afterward he gave me the key of a place in his house, and said to me, Put here these nuts that thou hast remaining with thee, and go forth every day with the party as thou hast done this day; and of what thou bringest, separate the bad, and sell them, and make use of their price; and the rest keep in thy possession in this place. Perhaps thou wilt accumulate of them what will aid thee to make thy voyage.—So I replied, Thy reward is due from God, whose name be exalted!

I did as he told me, and continued every day to fill the bag with stones, and to go forth with the people, and do as they did. They used to commend me, one to another, and to guide me to the tree upon which was abundance of fruit; and I ceased not to lead this life for a length of time, so that I collected a great quantity of good cocoa-nuts, and I sold a great quantity, the price of which became a large sum in my possession. I bought everything that I saw and that pleased me, my time was pleasant, and my good fortune increased throughout the whole city.

I remained in this state for some time; after which, as I was standing by the seaside, lo, a vessel arrived at that

city, and cast anchor by the shore. In it were merchants,
with their goods, and they proceeded to sell and buy, and
to exchange their goods for cocoa-nuts and other things.
So I went to my companion, informed him of the ship that
had arrived, and told him that I desired to make the voyage
to my country. And he replied, It is thine to determine. I
therefore bade him farewell, and thanked him for his kindness to me. Then I went to the ship, and, accosting the
master, engaged with him for my passage, and embarked in
that ship the cocoa-nuts and other things that I had with
me, after which they set sail that same day. We continued
our course from island to island and from sea to sea, and at
every island at which we cast anchor I sold some of those
cocoa-nuts, and exchanged; and God compensated me with
more than I had before possessed and lost.

And we came after that to the pearl-fisheries; whereupon
I gave to the divers some cocoa-nuts, and said to them, Dive
for my luck and lot. Accordingly they dived in the bay there,
and brought up a great number of large and valuable pearls;
and they said to me, O my master, by Allah, thy fortune is
good! So I took up into the ship what they had brought up
for me, and we proceeded, relying on the blessing of God
(whose name be exalted!), and continued our voyage until we
arrived at El-Basrah, where I landed, and remained a short
time. I then went thence to the city of Baghdad, entered my
quarter, came to my house, and saluted my family and companions, who congratulated me on my safety. I stored all the
goods and commodities that I had brought with me, clothed
the orphans and the widows, bestowed alms and gifts, and
made presents to my family and my companions and my

friends. God had compensated me with four times as much as I had lost, and I forgot what had happened to me, and the fatigue that I had suffered, by reason of the abundance of my gain and profits, and resumed my first habits of familiar intercourse and fellowship.

Such were the most wonderful things that happened to me in the course of the fifth voyage: but sup ye, and tomorrow come again, and I will relate to you the events of the sixth voyage; for it was more wonderful than this.

The Sixth Voyage of Es-Sindibad of the Sea

Know, O my brother and my friends and my companions, that when I returned from that fifth voyage, and forgot what I had suffered, by reason of sport and merriment and enjoyment and gaiety, and was in a state of the utmost joy and happiness, I continued thus until I was sitting one day in exceeding delight and happiness and gaiety; and while I sat, lo, a party of merchants came to me, bearing the marks of travel. And upon this I remembered the days of my return from travel, and my joy at meeting my family and companions and friends, and at entering my country; and my soul longed again for travel and commerce. So I determined to set forth. I bought for myself precious, sumptuous goods, suitable for the sea, packed up my bales, and went from the city of Baghdad to the city of El-Basrah, where I beheld a large vessel, in which were merchants and great men, and with them were precious goods. I therefore embarked my bales with them in this ship, and we departed in safety from the city of El-Basrah.

We continued our voyage from place to place and from

city to city, selling and buying, and diverting ourselves with viewing different countries. Fortune and the voyage were pleasant to us, and we gained our subsistence, until we were proceeding one day, and, lo, the master of the ship vociferated and called out, threw down his turban, slapped his face, plucked his beard, and fell down in the hold of the ship by reason of the violence of his grief and rage. So all the merchants and other passengers came together to him and said to him, O master, what is the matter? And he answered them, Know, O company, that we have wandered from our course, having passed forth from the sea in which we were, and entered a sea of which we know not the routes; and if God appoint not for us some means of effecting our escape from this sea, we all perish: therefore pray to God (whose name be exalted!) that He may save us from this case. Then the master arose and ascended the mast, and desired to loose the sails; but the wind became violent upon the ship, and drove her back, and her rudder broke near a lofty mountain; whereupon the master descended from the mast, and said, There is no strength nor power but in God, the High, the Great! No one is able to prevent what is predestined! By Allah, we have fallen into a great peril, and there remaineth to us no way of safety or escape from it!

So all the passengers wept for themselves: they bade one another farewell, because of the expiration of their lives, and their hope was cut off. The vessel drove upon that mountain, and went to pieces; its planks were scattered, and all that was in it was submerged; the merchants fell into the sea, and some of them were drowned, and some caught hold upon that mountain, and landed upon it.

I was of the number of those who landed upon the mountain; and, lo, within it was a large island. By it were many vessels broken in pieces, and upon it were numerous goods, on the shore of the sea, things thrown up by the sea from the ships that had been wrecked, and the passengers of which had been drowned. Upon it was an abundance, that confounded the reason and the mind, of commodities and wealth that the sea cast upon its shores. I ascended to the upper part of the island, and walked about it, and I beheld in the midst of it a stream of sweet water, flowing forth from beneath the nearest part of the mountain, and entering at the furthest part of it, on the opposite side of the valley. Then all the other passengers went over that mountain to the interior of the island, and dispersed themselves about it, and their reason was confounded at that which they beheld. They became like madmen in consequence of what they saw upon the island of commodities and wealth lying on the shore of the sea.

I beheld also in the midst of the above-mentioned stream an abundance of various kinds of jewels and minerals, with jacinths and large pearls, suitable to Kings. They were like gravel in the channels of the water which flowed through the fields; and all the bed of that stream glittered by reason of the great number of minerals and other things that it contained. We likewise saw on that island an abundance of the best kind of Sanfi aloes-wood, and Kamari aloes-wood. And in that island is a gushing spring of crude ambergris, which floweth like wax over the side of that spring through the violence of the heat of the sun, and spreadeth upon the seashore, and the monsters of the deep come up from the sea and swallow it, and descend with it into the sea; but it becometh hot in their stomachs, therefore they eject it from their mouths into the sea, and it congealeth on the surface of the water. Upon this, its color and its qualities become changed, and the waves cast it up on the shore of the sea: so the travelers and merchants who know it take it and sell it. But as to the crude ambergris that is not swallowed, it floweth over the side of that fountain, and congealeth upon the ground; and when the sun shineth upon it, it melteth, and from it the odor of the whole of that valley becometh like the odor of musk. Then, when the sun withdraweth from it, it congealeth again. The place wherein is this crude ambergris no one can enter: no one can gain access to it: for the mountain surroundeth that island.

We continued to wander about the island, diverting ourselves with the view of the good things which God (whose name be exalted!) had created upon it, and perplexed at our case, and at the things that we beheld, and affected with violent fear. We had collected upon the shore of the sea a small quantity of provisions, and we used it sparingly, eating of it every day, or two days, only one meal, dreading the exhaustion of our stock, and our dying in sorrow, from the violence of hunger and fear. Each one of us that died we washed, and shrouded in some of the clothes and linen which the sea cast upon the shore of the island; and thus we did until a great number of us had died, and there remained of us but a small party, who were weakened by a colic occasioned by the sea. After this, we remained a short period, and all my associates and companions died, one after another, and each of them who died we buried. Then I was alone on that island, and there remained with me but little of the provisions, after there had been much.

So I wept for myself, and said, Would that I had died before my companions, and that they had washed me and buried me! There is no strength nor power but in God, the High, the Great!—And I remained a short time longer; after which I arose and dug for myself a deep grave on the shore of the island, and said within myself, When I fall sick, and know that death hath come to me, I will lie down in this grave, and die in it, and the wind will blow the sand upon me, and cover me; so I shall become buried in it. I blamed myself for my little sense, and my going forth from my country and my city, and my voyaging to foreign countries, after what I had suffered in the first instance, and the second and the third and the fourth and the fifth; and when I had not performed one of my voyages without suffering in it horrors and distresses more troublesome and more difficult than the horrors preceding. I believed not that I could escape and save myself, and repented of undertaking sea-voyages, and of my returning to this life when I was not in want of wealth, but had abundance, so that I could not consume what I had, nor spend half of it during the rest of my life; having enough for me, and more than enough.

Then I meditated in my mind, and said, This river must have a beginning and an end, and it must have a place of egress into an inhabited country. The right plan in my opinion will be for me to construct for myself a small raft, of sufficient size for me to sit upon it, and I will go down and cast it upon this river, and depart on it. If I find safety, I am safe, and escape, by permission of God (whose name be exalted!); and if I find no way of saving myself, it will be better for me to die in this river than in this place.—And I sighed for myself. Then I arose and went and collected pieces of wood that were upon that island, of Sanfi and Kamari aloes-wood, and bound them upon the shore of the sea with some of the ropes of the ships that had been wrecked; and I brought some straight planks, of the planks of the ships, and placed them upon those pieces of wood. I made the raft to suit the width of the river, less wide than the latter, and bound it well and firmly; and, having taken with me some of those minerals and jewels and goods, and of the large pearls that were like gravel, as well as other things that were upon the island, and some of the crude, pure, excellent ambergris, I put them upon that raft, with all that I had collected upon the island, and took with me what remained of the provisions.

I departed upon the raft along the river, meditating upon what might be the result of my case, and proceeded to the place where the river entered beneath the mountain. I propelled the raft into that place, and became in intense darkness within it, and the raft continued to carry me in with the current to a narrow place beneath the mountain, where the sides of the raft rubbed against the sides of the channel of the river, and my head rubbed against the roof of the channel. I was unable to return thence, and I blamed myself for that which I had done, and said, If this place become narrower to the raft, it will scarcely pass through it, and it cannot return: so I shall perish in this place in sorrow, inevitably! I threw myself upon my face on the raft, on account of the narrowness of the channel of the river, and ceased not to proceed, without knowing night from day, by reason of the darkness in which I was involved beneath that mountain, together with my terror and fear for myself lest I should perish. In this state I continued my course along the river, which sometimes widened and at other times contracted; but the intensity of the darkness wearied me excessively, and slumber overcame me in consequence of the violence of my distress. So I lay upon my face on the raft, which ceased not to bear me along while I slept, and knew not whether the time was long or short.

At length I awoke, and found myself in the light; and, opening my eyes, I beheld an extensive tract, and the raft tied to the shore of an island, and around me a company of men. When they saw that I had risen, they rose and came to me, and spoke to me in their language; but I knew not what they said, and imagined that it was a dream, and that this occurred in sleep, by reason of the violence of my distress and vexation. And when they spoke to me and I understood not their speech, and returned them not an answer, a man among them advanced to me, and said to me, in the Arabic language, Peace be on thee, O our brother! What art thou, and whence hast thou come, and what is the cause of thy coming to this place? We are people of the sown lands and the fields, and we came to irrigate our fields and our sown lands, and found thee asleep on the raft: so we laid hold upon it, and tied it here by us, waiting for thee to rise at thy leisure. Tell us then what is the cause of thy coming to this place.

I replied, I conjure thee by Allah, O my master, that thou bring me some food; for I am hungry; and after that, ask of me concerning what thou wilt. And thereupon he hastened, and brought me food, and I ate until I was satiated and was at ease, and my fear subsided, my satiety was abundant, and my soul returned to me. I therefore praised God (whose name be exalted!) for all that had occurred, rejoiced at my having passed forth from that river, and having come to these people; and I told them of all that had happened to me from beginning to end, and of what I had experienced upon that river, and of its narrowness.

They then talked together, and said, We must take him with us and present him to our King, that he may acquaint him with what hath happened to him. Accordingly they took me with them, and conveyed with me the raft, together with all that was upon it, of riches and goods, and jewels and minerals, and ornaments of gold, and they took me in to their King, who was the King of Sarandib, and acquainted him with what had happened; whereupon he saluted me and welcomed me, and asked me respecting my state, and respecting the events that had happened to me. I therefore acquainted him with all my story, and what I had experienced, from first to last; and the King wondered at this narrative extremely, and congratulated me on my safety. Then I arose and took forth from the raft a quantity of the minerals and jewels, and aloes-wood and crude ambergris, and gave it to the King; and he accepted it from me, and treated me with exceeding honor, lodging me in a place in his abode. I associated with the best and the greatest of the people, who paid me great respect, and I quitted not the abode of the King.

The island of Sarandib is under the equinoctial line; its night being always twelve hours, and its day also twelve hours. Its length is eighty leagues; and its breadth, thirty; and it extendeth largely between a lofty mountain and a deep valley. This mountain is seen from a distance of three days, and it containeth varieties of jacinths, and different kinds of minerals, and trees of all sorts of spices, and its surface is covered with emery, wherewith jewels are cut into shape: in its rivers also are diamonds, and pearls are in its valleys. I ascended to the summit of the mountain, and diverted myself with a view of its wonders, which are not to be described; and afterward I went back to the King, and begged him to give me permission to return to my country. He gave me permission after great pressing, and bestowed upon me an abundant present from his treasuries, and he gave me a present and a sealed letter, saying to me, Convey these to the Khalifeh Harun Er-Rashid, and give him many salutations from us. So I replied, I hear and obey. Then he wrote for me a letter on skin of the khawi, which is finer than parchment, of a yellowish color; and the writing was in ultramarine. And the form of what he wrote to the Khalifeh was this:—Peace be on thee, from the King of India, before whom are a thousand elephants, and on the battlements of whose palace are a thousand jewels. To proceed: we have sent to thee a trifling present: accept it then from us. Thou art to us a brother and sincere friend, and the affection for you that is in our hearts is great: therefore favor us by a reply. The present is not suited to thy dignity; but we beg of thee, O brother, to accept it graciously. And peace be on thee!—And the present was a cup of ruby, a span high, the inside of which was embellished with precious pearls; and a bed covered with the skin of the serpent that swalloweth the elephant, which skin hath spots, each like a piece of gold, and whosoever sitteth upon it never becometh diseased; and a hundred thousand mithkals of Indian aloes-wood; and a servant girl like the shining full moon. Then he bade me farewell, and gave a charge respecting me to the merchants and the master of the ship.

So I departed thence, and we continued our voyage from island to island and from country to country until we arrived at Baghdad, whereupon I entered my house, and met my family and my brethren; after which I took the present, with a token of service from myself for the Khalifeh. On entering his presence, I kissed his hand, and placed before him the whole, giving him the letter; and he read it, and took the present, with which he was greatly rejoiced, and he treated me with the utmost honor. He then said to me, O Sindibad, is that true which this King hath stated in his letter? And I kissed the ground, and answered, O my lord, I witnessed in his kingdom much more than he hath mentioned in his letter. On the day of his public appearance, a throne is set for him upon a huge elephant, eleven cubits high, and he sitteth upon it, having with him his chief officers and pages and guests, standing in two ranks, on his right and on his left. At his head standeth a man having in his hand a golden javelin, and behind him a man in whose hand is a great mace of gold, at the top of which is an emerald a span in length, and of the thickness of a thumb. And when he mounteth, there mount at the same time with him a thousand horsemen clad in gold and silk; and as the King proceedeth, a man before him proclaimeth, saying, This is the King of great dignity, of high authority! And he proceedeth to repeat his praises in terms that I remember not, at the end of his panegyric saying, This is the King the owner of the crown the like of which neither Suleyman nor the Mihraj possessed! Then he is silent; and one behind him proclaimeth, saying, He will die! Again I say, He will die! Again I say, He will die!—And the other saith, Extolled be the perfection of the Living who dieth not!—Moreover, by reason of his justice and good government and intelligence, there is no Kadi in his city; and all the people of his country distinguish the truth from falsity.—And the Khalifeh wondered at my words, and said, How great is this King! By Allah, he hath been endowed with wisdom and dominion!

Then the Khalifeh conferred favors upon me, and commanded me to depart to my abode. So I came to my house, and gave the legal and other alms, and continued to live in the same pleasant circumstances as at present. I forgot the arduous troubles that I had experienced, discarded from my heart the anxieties of travel, rejected from my mind distress, and betook myself to eating and drinking, and pleasures and joy.

And when Es-Sindibad of the Sea had finished his story, he ordered his servant to give to Es-Sindibad of the Land a hundred pieces of gold, and said to him, How now, O my brother? Hast thou heard of the like of these afflictions and calamities and distresses, or have such troubles as have befallen me befallen anyone else, or hath anyone else suffered such hardships as I have suffered? Know then that these pleasures are a compensation for the toil and humiliations that I have experienced.

And upon this, Es-Sindibad of the Land advanced, and kissed his hands, and said to him, O my lord, by Allah, thou hast undergone great horrors, and hast deserved these abundant favors: continue then, O my lord, in joy and security; for God hath removed from thee the evils of fortune; and I beg of God that He may continue to thee thy pleasures, and bless thy days.—And upon this, Es-Sindibad of the Sea bestowed favors upon him, and made him his boon-companion; and he quitted him not by night nor by day as long as they both lived.

Praise be to God, the Mighty, the Omnipotent, the Strong, the Eminent in power, the Creator of the heaven and the earth, and of the land and the seas!

The Story of Bedr Basim and Jawharah, the Daughter of the King of the Sea

There was in olden time and in an ancient age and period, in the land of the Persians, a King named Shah-Zeman, and the place of his residence was Khurasan. Once a beautiful servant girl was brought to the King; he married her, but for long she would not speak to her husband nor to anyone in the palace. Months passed, and then, when a child was to be born to her, she spoke to her husband, Shah-Zeman, and said:—

Know, O fortunate King, that my name is Jullanar of the Sea. My father was one of the Kings of the Sea, and he died, and left us the kingdom; but while we were enjoying it, one of the Kings came upon us, and took the kingdom from our hands. I have also a brother named Salih, and my mother is of the women of the sea; I quarreled with my brother, and swore that I would throw myself into the hands of a man of the inhabitants of the land. Accordingly I came forth from the sea, and sat upon the shore of an island in the moonlight. But had not thy heart loved me, I had not remained with thee one hour; for I should have cast myself into the sea from this window, and gone to my mother and my people.

Afterward Jullanar's brother, Salih, and her mother and sisters came to visit her in King Shah-Zeman's palace, and when her son, Bedr Basim, was born, these people of the sea watched over him. The old King, the husband of Jullanar, fell sick and died, and then Bedr Basim, at the age of sixteen, became King in his stead. The story then goes on to say:—

After this, it happened that Salih came in one night to Jullanar, and saluted her; whereupon she rose to him and embraced him, and seated him by her side, and said to him, O my brother, how art thou, and how are my mother and the daughters of my uncle? He answered her, O my sister, they are well, in prosperity and great happiness, and nothing is wanting to them but the sight of thy face. Then she offered him some food, and he ate; and, conversation ensuing between them, they mentioned the King Bedr Basim, and his beauty and loveliness, and his stature and justness of form, and his horsemanship and intelligence and polite accomplishments. Now the King Bedr Basim was reclining; and when he heard his mother and his uncle mentioning him and conversing respecting him, he pretended that he was asleep, and listened to their talk. And Salih said to his sister Jullanar, The age of thy son is seventeen years, and he hath not married, and we fear that something may happen to him, and he may not have a son. I therefore desire to marry him to one of the Queens of the Sea, that shall be like him in beauty and loveliness.—So Jullanar replied, Mention them to me; for I know them. Accordingly he proceeded to enumerate them to her, one after another, while she said, I approve not of this for my son, nor will I marry him save to her who is like him in beauty and loveliness, and intelligence and religion, and polite accomplishments and kindness of nature, and dominion and rank and descent. And he said to her, I know not one more of the daughters of the Kings of the Sea, and I have enumerated to thee more than a hundred damsels, yet not one of them pleaseth thee: but see, O my sister, whether thy son be asleep or not. She therefore felt him, and she found that he bore the appearance of sleep: so she said to him, He is asleep: what then hast thou to say, and what is thy desire with regard to his sleeping?

He answered her, O my sister, know that I have remembered a damsel, of the damsels of the Sea, suitable to thy son; but I fear to mention her, lest thy son should be awake, and his heart should be entangled by love of her, and perhaps we may not be able to gain access to her: so he and we and the lords of his empire would be wearied, and trouble would befall us in consequence thereof.

And when his sister heard his words, she replied, Tell me what is the condition of this damsel, and what is her name; for I know the damsels of the Sea, the daughters of Kings and of others; and if I see her to be suitable to him, I will demand her in marriage of her father, though I expend upon her all that my hand possesseth. Acquaint me therefore with her, and fear not aught; for my son is asleep.—He said, I fear that he may be awake; and the poet hath said,—

I loved her when her qualities were described; for sometimes the ear loveth before the eye.

But Jullanar replied, Say, and be brief, and fear not, O my brother. And he said, By Allah, O my sister, none is suitable to thy son except the Queen Jawharah, the daughter of the

King Es-Semendel, and she is like him in beauty and loveliness and elegance and perfection, and there existeth not in the sea nor on the land anyone more graceful or more sweet in natural endowments than she. When she looketh aside, she putteth to shame the wild cows and the gazelles; and when she walketh with a vacillating gait, the willow-branch is envious; and when she displayeth her countenance, she confoundeth the sun and the moon, and captivateth every beholder: she is sweet-lipped, gentle in disposition.—And when she heard the words of her brother, she replied, Thou hast spoken truth, O my brother. By Allah, I have seen her many times, and she was my companion when we were little children; but now we have no acquaintance with each other, because of the distance between us; and for eighteen years I have not seen her. By Allah, none is suitable to my son except her.

Now when Bedr Basim heard their words, and understood what they said from first to last in description of the damsel that Salih mentioned, Jawharah the daughter of the King Es-Semendel, he became enamored of her by the ear; but he pretended to them that he was asleep. A flame of fire was kindled in his heart on her account, and he was drowned in a sea of which neither shore nor bottom was seen. Then Salih looked toward his sister Jullanar, and said to her, By Allah, O my sister, there is not among the Kings of the Sea anyone more stupid than her father, nor is there any of greater power than he. Therefore acquaint not thy son with the case of this damsel until we demand her in marriage for him of her father; and if he favor us by assenting to our proposal, we praise God (whose name be exalted!); and if he reject us, and marry her not to thy son, we will remain at ease, and demand in marriage another.—And when Jullanar heard what her brother Salih said, she replied, Excellent is the opinion that thou hast formed. Then they were silent; and they passed that night. In the heart of the King Bedr Basim was a flame of fire, kindled by his passion for the Queen Jawharah; but he concealed his case, and said not to his mother nor to his uncle aught respecting her, though he was tortured by love of her as though he were on burning coals. And when they arose in the morning, the King and his uncle entered the bath, and washed: then they came forth, and drank some wine, and the attendants placed before them the food: so the King Bedr Basim and his mother and his uncle ate until they were satisfied, and washed their hands. And after that, Salih rose upon his feet, and said to the King Bedr Basim and his mother Jullanar, With your permission, I would go to my mother; for I have been with you a period of days, and the hearts of my family are troubled respecting me, and they are expecting me. But the King Bedr Basim said to his uncle Salih, Remain with us this day. And he complied with his request.

Bedr Basim then said, Arise with us, O my uncle, and go forth with us to the garden. So they went to the garden, and proceeded to divert and recreate themselves; and the King Bedr Basim seated himself beneath a shady tree, desiring to rest and sleep; but he remembered what his uncle Salih had said, describing the damsel and her beauty and loveliness, and he shed many tears, and recited these verses:—

Were it said to me, while the flame is burning within me, and the fire blazing in my heart and bowels,

Wouldst thou rather that thou shouldst behold them,
or a draught of pure water?—I would answer, Them.

Then he lamented and groaned and wept, and recited these
two other verses:—

Who will save me from the love of a charming gazelle,
with a face like the sun: nay, more lovely?

My heart was at ease, free from love of her; but now
burneth with passion for the daughter of Es-Semendel.

So when his uncle Salih heard what he said, he struck hand
upon hand, and said, There is no deity but God: Mohammad
is the Apostle of God: and there is no strength nor power
but in God, the High, the Great! Then he said to him, Didst
thou hear, O my son, what I and thy mother said respecting
the Queen Jawharah, and our mention of her qualities? Bedr
Basim answered, Yes, O my uncle, and I became enamored
of her from hearsay, when I heard what ye said. My heart is
devoted to her, and I have not patience to remain absent from
her.—Salih therefore said to him, O King, let us return to thy
mother and acquaint her with the case, and I will ask her to
permit me to take thee with me and to demand in marriage
for thee the Queen Jawharah. Then we will bid her farewell,
and I will return with thee; for I fear that, if I took thee and
went without her permission, she would be incensed against
me; and she would be right, as I should be the cause of your
separation, like as I was the cause of her separation from us.
The city, too, would be without a King, its people having none

to govern them, and to see to their cases: so the state of the empire would become adverse unto thee, and the kingdom would depart from thy hand.—But when Bedr Basim heard the words of his uncle Salih, he replied, Know, O my uncle, that if I return to my mother and consult her on this subject, she will not allow me to do it; therefore I will not return to her, nor consult her ever. And he wept before his uncle, and said to him, I will go with thee, and I will not inform her, and then I will return. So when Salih heard the words of his sister's son, he was perplexed at his case, and said, I beg aid of God (whose name be exalted!) in every circumstance.

Then Salih, seeing his sister's son in this state, and knowing that he desired not to return to his mother, but would go with him, took from his finger a seal-ring on which were engraved some of the names of God (whose name be exalted!), and handed it to the King Bedr Basim, saying to him, Put this upon thy finger, and thou wilt be secure from drowning and from other accidents, and from the noxiousness of the beasts of the sea and its great fishes. So the King Bedr Basim took the seal-ring from his uncle Salih, and put it upon his finger; after which, they plunged into the sea, and ceased not in their course until they arrived at the palace of Salih, when they entered it, and Bedr Basim's grandmother, the mother of his mother, saw him, as she sat, attended by her relations. When they went in to them, they kissed their hands; and as soon as Bedr Basim's grandmother saw him, she rose to him and embraced him, kissed him between the eyes, and said to him, Thine arrival is blessed, O my son! How didst thou leave thy mother Jullanar?—He answered her, Well; in prosperity and health; and she saluteth thee and the daughters of her uncle. Then Salih acquainted his mother with that which had occurred between him and his sister Jullanar, and that the King Bedr Basim had become enamored of the Queen Jawharah, the daughter of the King Es-Semendel, from hearsay. He related to her the story from beginning to end, and said, He hath not come but for the purpose of demanding her in marriage of her father, and marrying her.

But when the grandmother of the King Bedr Basim heard the words of Salih, she was violently incensed against him, and was agitated and grieved, and she said to him, O my son, thou hast erred in mentioning the Queen Jawharah, the daughter of the King Es-Semendel, before the son of thy sister; for thou knowest that the King Es-Semendel is stupid, overbearing, of little sense, of great power, niggardly of his daughter Jawharah toward those who demand her in marriage; for all the Kings of the Sea have demanded her of him, and he refused, and approved not one of them, but rejected them all, and said to them, Ye are not equal to her in beauty nor in loveliness, nor in other qualities than those. And we fear to demand her in marriage of her father; for he would reject us as he hath rejected others; and we are people of kindness; so we should return broken-hearted.—And when Salih heard what his mother said, he replied, O my mother, what is to be done? For the King Bedr Basim became enamored of this damsel when I mentioned her to my sister Jullanar, and he said, We must demand her in marriage of her father though I should give away all my kingdom. And he hath asserted that if he marry her not he will die of love and desire for her.—Then Salih said to his mother, Know that the son of my sister is more beautiful and more lovely than she, and that his father was King of all the Persians, and he is now their King, and Jawharah is not suitable to any but him. I have resolved that I will take to her father some jewels, consisting of jacinths and other gems, and convey a present befitting him, and demand her of him in marriage. If he allege as a pretext to us that he is a King, so also is he a King, the son of a King. And if he allege as a pretext to us her loveliness, he is more lovely than she. Again, if he allege as a pretext to us the extent of dominions, he hath more extensive dominions than she and than her father, and hath more numerous troops and guards; for his kingdom is greater than the kingdom of her father. I must endeavor to accomplish this affair of the son of my sister, though my life be lost thereby, since I was the cause of this event; and as I cast him into the seas of her love, I will strive to effect his marriage to her; and may God (whose name be exalted!) aid me to do that!—So his mother said to him, Do as thou wilt, and beware of speaking rudely to him when thou addressest him; for thou knowest his stupidity and his power, and I fear lest he make a violent attack upon thee, since he knoweth not the dignity of anyone. And he replied, I hear and obey.

He then arose, and took with him two leathern bags full of jewels and jacinths, and oblong emeralds, and precious minerals of all kinds of stones, and, having made his young men carry them, he proceeded with them, he and the son of his sister, to the palace of the King Es-Semendel. He asked permission to go in to him, and permission was given him; and when he entered, he kissed the ground before him, and saluted with the best salutation. And when the King Es-Semendel saw him, he rose to him, treated him with the utmost honor, and ordered him to sit. So he sat, and after he had been seated awhile, the King said to him, Thine arrival is blessed. Thou hast made us desolate by thine absence, O Salih. What is thy want, that thou hast come unto us? Acquaint me with thy want, that I may perform it for thee.— And upon this he rose, and kissed the ground a second time, and said, O King of the age, my want respecteth God, and the magnanimous King, and the bold lion, the report of whose good qualities the caravans have borne abroad, and whose fame hath been published in the provinces and cities, for liberality and beneficence, and pardon and clemency and obliging conduct. Then he opened the two leathern bags, and took forth from them the jewels and other things, and scattered them before the King Es-Semendel, saying to him, O King of the age, perhaps thou wilt accept my present, and shew favor to me, and comfort my heart by accepting it from me. Upon this, the King Es-Semendel said to him, For what reason hast thou presented to me this present? Tell me thine affair, and acquaint me with thy want; and if I be able to perform it, I will perform it for thee this instant, and not oblige thee to weary thyself; but if I be unable to perform it, God imposeth not upon a person aught save what he is able to accomplish.—Then Salih rose, and kissed the ground three times, and said, O King of the age, verily the thing that I require thou art able to perform, and it is in thy power, and thou art master of it. I impose not upon the King a difficulty, nor am I mad, that I should ask of the King a thing that he is unable to do; for one of the sages hath said, If thou desire that thy request should be complied with, ask that which is possible. Now as to the thing that I have come to demand, the King (may God preserve him!) is able to do it.—So the

King said to him, Ask the thing that thou requirest, and explain thine affair, and demand what thou desirest. And he said to him, O King of the age, know that I have come to thee as a marriage-suitor, desiring the unique pearl, and the hidden jewel, the Queen Jawharah, the daughter of our lord; then disappoint not, O King, him who applieth to thee.

But when the King heard his words, he laughed so that he fell backward, in derision of him, and replied, O Salih, I used to think thee a man of sense, and an excellent young man, who attempted not aught but what was right, and uttered not aught but what was just. What hath happened to thy reason, and urged thee to this monstrous thing, and great peril, that thou demandest in marriage the daughters of Kings, the lords of cities and provinces? Art thou of a rank to attain to this high eminence, and hath thy reason decreased to this extreme degree that thou confrontest me with these words?—So Salih said, May God amend the state of the King! I demanded her not in marriage for myself; yet if I demanded her for myself, I am her equal; nay more; for thou knowest that my father was one of the Kings of the Sea, if thou art now our King. But I demanded her not in marriage save for the King Bedr Basim, lord of the provinces of Persia, whose father was the King Shah-Zeman, and thou knowest his power. If thou assert that thou art a great King, the King Bedr Basim is a greater King: and if thou boastest that thy daughter is lovely, the King Bedr Basim is more lovely than she, and more beautiful in form, and more excellent in rank and descent; and he is the horseman of his age. So if thou assent to that which I have asked of thee, thou wilt, O King of the age, have put the thing in its proper place; and if thou behave arrogantly toward us, thou treatest us not equitably, nor pursuest with us the right way. Thou knowest, O King, that this Queen Jawharah, the daughter of our lord the King, must be married; for the sage saith, The inevitable lot of the damsel is either marriage or the grave;—and if thou design to marry her, the son of my sister is more worthy of her than all the rest of men.—But when the King Es-Semendel heard the words of the King Salih, he was violently enraged; his reason almost departed, and his soul almost quitted his body, and he said to him, O dog of men, doth such a one as thyself address me with these words, and dost thou mention my daughter in the assemblies, and say that the son of thy sister Jullanar is her equal? Who then art thou, and who is thy sister, and who is her son, and who was his father, that thou sayest to me these words, and addressest me with this discourse? Are ye, in comparison with her, aught but dogs?—Then he called out to his young men, and said, O young men, take the head of this young wretch!

So they took the swords and drew them, and sought to slay him; but he turned his back in flight, seeking the gate of the palace; and when he arrived at the gate of the palace, he saw the sons of his uncle, and his relations and tribe and young men, who were more than a thousand horsemen, buried in iron and in coats of mail put one over another, and having in their hands spears and bright swords. On their seeing Salih in this state, they said to him, What is the news? He therefore told them his story. And his mother had sent them to his assistance. So when they heard his words, they knew that the King was stupid and of great power, and they alighted from their horses, and drew their swords, and went in to the King Es-Semendel. They saw him sitting upon the throne of his kingdom, heedless of these people, and violently enraged against Salih; and they saw his servants and his young men and his guards unprepared; and when he beheld them, with the drawn swords in their hands, he called out to his people, saying, O! woe to you! Take ye the heads of these dogs!—But there had not elapsed more than a little while before the party of the King Es-Semendel were routed, and betook themselves to flight; and Salih and his relations had seized the King Es-Semendel, and bound his hands behind him.

Now Jawharah, awaking from sleep, was informed that her father was taken a captive, and that his guards had been slain. So she went forth from the palace, and fled to one of the islands, where she repaired to a lofty tree, and she concealed herself upon it. And when these two parties contended together, some of the young men of the King Es-Semendel fled, and Bedr Basim, seeing them, asked them respecting their case; whereupon they acquainted him with that which had happened. Therefore, on his hearing that the King Es-Semendel had been seized, he turned his back in flight, fearing for himself, and said in his heart, Verily this disturbance originated on my account, and none is the object of search but myself. He turned back in flight, seeking safety, and knew not whither to go. But the destinies fixed from all eternity drove him to that island upon which was Jawharah, the daughter of the King Es-Semendel; and he came to the tree, and threw himself down like one slain, desiring to take rest by his prostrate position, and not knowing that every one who is an object of search resteth not; and none knoweth what is hidden from him in the secrets of destiny. And when he lay down, he turned up his eyes toward the tree, and his eye met that of Jawharah: so he looked at her, and saw her to be like the moon when it shineth; and he said, Extolled be the perfection of the Creator of this surprising form! and He is the Creator of everything, and is Almighty! Extolled be the perfection of God, the Great, the Creator, the Maker, the Former! By Allah, if my imagination tell me truth, this must be Jawharah the daughter of the King Es-Semendel. I suppose that when she heard of the conflict happening between the two parties, she fled, and came to this island, and hid herself upon this tree; but if this be not the Queen Jawharah, this is more beautiful than she.—Then he proceeded to meditate upon her case, and said within himself, I will rise and ask her respecting her state; and if this be she, I will ask for her in marriage of herself, and this is the thing I seek. So he stood erect upon his feet, and said to Jawharah, O utmost object of desire, who art thou, and who brought thee unto this place? And Jawharah, looking at Bedr Basim, saw him to be like the full moon when it appeareth from behind the black clouds, of elegant stature, comely in his smile. She therefore said to him, O thou endowed with comely qualities, I am the Queen Jawharah, the daughter of the King Es-Semendel, and I have fled to this place because Salih and his troops have fought with my father and slain his troops, and made him a captive, together with some of his troops: so I fled, in fear for myself. Then the Queen Jawharah said to the King Bedr Basim, And I came not to this place save in flight, fearing slaughter; and I know not what fortune hath done with my father. And when Bedr Basim heard her words, he wondered extremely at this strange coincidence, and said, No doubt I have attained my desire by the capture of her father. He then looked at her, and said to her, Descend, O my mistress; for I am a victim of thy love, and thine eyes have captivated me. On account of me and thee were this disturbance and these conflicts. Know that I am the King Bedr Basim, the King of Persia, and that Salih is my maternal uncle, and he is the person who came to thy father and demanded thee of him in marriage. I have left my kingdom on thine account, and our meeting now is a wonderful coincidence. Arise then, and descend to me, that I may go with thee to the palace of thy father, and ask my uncle Salih to release him, and marry thee lawfully.

But when Jawharah heard the words of Bedr Basim, she said within herself, On account of this base young wretch hath this event happened, and my father hath been made a captive, and his chamberlains and his attendants have been slain, and I have become separated from my palace, and come forth an exile from my country to this island. If now I employ not some stratagem with him, thereby to defend myself from him, he will gain possession of me, and attain his desire; for he is in love; and the lover, whatever he doth, is not to be blamed for it.—Then she beguiled him with words, and with soft discourse, and he knew not what artifices she had devised against him; and she said to him, O my master, and light of mine eye, art thou the King Bedr Basim, the son of the Queen Jullanar? So he answered her, Yes, O my mistress. And she said, May God cut off my father, and deprive him of his kingdom, and not comfort his heart, nor restore him from estrangement, if he desire a person more comely than thou, and aught more comely than these charming endowments! By Allah, he is of little sense and judgment!—She then said to him, O King of the age, blame not my father for that which he hath done.

If the measure of thy love for me be a span, that of my love for thee is a cubit. I have fallen into the snare of thy love, and become of the number of thy victims. The love that thou hadst is transferred to me, and there remaineth not of it with thee aught save as much as the tenth part of what I feel.— Then she descended from the tree, and drew near to him, and came to him and embraced him. So when the King Bedr Basim saw what she did to him, his love for her increased. And he said to her, O Queen, by Allah, my uncle Salih did not describe to me the quarter of the tenth part of thy loveliness, nor the quarter of a kirat of four and twenty kirats.[12] Then Jawharah pressed him close, and uttered some words not to be understood; after which, she said to him, Be changed from this human form into the form of a bird, the most beautiful of birds, with white feathers, and red bill and feet. And her words were not ended before the King Bedr Basim became transformed into the shape of a bird, the most beautiful that could be of birds; and he shook, and stood upon his feet, looking at Jawharah. Now she had with her a damsel, one of her female servants, named Marsineh, and she looked at her and said, By Allah, were it not that I fear on account of my father's being a captive with his uncle, I had slain him, and may God not recompense him well; for how unfortunate was his coming unto us; all this disturbance having been effected by his means! But, O girl, take him, and convey him to the Thirsty Island, and leave him there that he may die of thirst.— So the servant took him, and conveyed him to the island, and was about to return from him; but she said within herself, By

---

12 Not a quarter of a carat out of the whole twenty-four.

Allah, the person endowed with this beauty and loveliness deserveth not to die of thirst. Then she took him forth from the Thirsty Island, and brought him to an island abounding with trees and fruits and rivers, and, having put him upon it, returned to her mistress, and said to her, I have put him upon the Thirsty Island.—Such was the case of Bedr Basim.

But as to Salih, the uncle of the King Bedr Basim, when he had got possession of the King Es-Semendel, and slain his guards and servants, and the King had become his captive, he sought Jawharah, the King's daughter; but found her not. So he returned to his palace, to the presence of his mother, and said, O my mother, where is the son of my sister, the King Bedr Basim? She answered, O my son, by Allah, I have no knowledge of him, nor know I whither he hath gone; for when he was told that thou hadst fought with the King Es-Semendel, and that conflicts and slaughter had ensued between you, he was terrified, and fled. So when Salih heard the words of his mother, he grieved for the son of his sister, and said, O my mother, by Allah, we have acted negligently with respect to the King Bedr Basim, and I fear that he will perish, or that one of the soldiers of the King Es-Semendel may fall upon him, or that the King's daughter, Jawharah, may fall upon him, and shame will betide us from his mother, and good will not betide us from her; for I took him without her permission. Then he sent guards and spies after him, through the sea and in other directions, but they met with no tidings of him; wherefore they returned, and informed the King Salih thereof; and his anxiety and grief increased, and his bosom became contracted on account of the King Bedr Basim.—Thus was it with them.

Next, with regard to Bedr Basim's mother, Jullanar of

the Sea, when her son had descended into the sea with his uncle Salih, she waited expecting him; but he returned not to her, and tidings of him were long kept from her. So she remained many days expecting him; after which she arose, and descended into the sea, and came to her mother; and when her mother saw her, she rose to her, and kissed her and embraced her, as did also the daughters of her uncle. She then asked her mother respecting the King Bedr Basim, and her mother answered her, O my daughter, he came with his uncle, and his uncle took jacinths and jewels and went with them, he and Bedr Basim, to the King Es-Semendel, and demanded in marriage his daughter: but the King assented not to his proposal, and he was violent to thy brother in his words. I therefore sent to thy brother about a thousand horsemen, and a conflict ensued between them and the King Es-Semendel; but God aided thy brother against them, and he slew his guards and his troops, and made the King Es-Semendel a captive. So tidings of this event reached thy son, and apparently he feared for himself; wherefore he fled from us without our will, and he returned not to us after that, nor have we heard any tidings of him.—Then Jullanar inquired of her respecting her brother Salih, and she informed her, saying, He is sitting upon the throne of the kingdom in the place of the King Es-Semendel, and he hath sent in every direction to search for thy son and the Queen Jawharah. So when Jullanar heard the words of her mother, she mourned for her son violently, and her anger was fierce against her brother Salih, because he had taken her son and descended with him into the sea without her permission. She then said, O my mother, verily I fear for our kingdom; for I came to you and informed not anyone of the people of the empire, and I dread, if I remain long away from them, that the kingdom will be alienated from us, and that the dominion will depart from our hands. The right opinion is, that I should return, and govern the empire until God shall order for us the affair of my son; and forget not ye my son, nor neglect his case: for if mischief befall him, I perish inevitably; since I regard not the world save in connection with him, nor delight save in his life.—So her mother replied, With feelings of love and honor will I comply, O my daughter. Inquire not what we suffer by reason of his separation and absence.— Then her mother sent to search for him, and Bedr Basim's mother returned with mourning heart and weeping eye to the empire. The world had become strait to her, her heart was contracted, and her case was grievous.

Now again as to the King Bedr Basim, when the Queen Jawharah had enchanted him, and sent him with her servant to the Thirsty Island, saying to her, Leave him upon it to die of thirst—the servant put him not save upon a verdant, fruitful island, with trees and rivers. So he betook himself to eating of the fruits, and drinking of the rivers; and he ceased not to remain in this state for a period of days and nights, in the form of a bird, not knowing whither to go, nor how to fly. And while he was one day upon that island, lo, there came thither a fowler, to catch something wherewith to sustain himself; and he saw the King Bedr Basim in the form of a bird, with white feathers and with red bill and feet, captivating the beholder, and astonishing the mind. So the fowler looked at him, and he pleased him, and he said within himself, Verily this bird is beautiful: I have not seen a bird like it in its beauty, nor in its form. Then he cast the net over him, and caught him, and he went with him into the city, saying within himself, I will sell it, and receive its price. And one of the people of the city met him, and said to him, For how much is this bird to be sold, O fowler? The fowler said to him, If thou buy it, what wilt thou do with it? The man answered, I will kill it and eat it. But the fowler said to him, Whose heart would be pleased to kill this bird and eat it? Verily I desire to present it to the King, and he will give me more than the sum that thou wouldst give me as its price, and will not kill it, but will divert himself with beholding it, and observing its beauty and loveliness; for during my whole life, while I have been a fowler, I have not seen the like of it among the prey of the sea nor among the prey of the land. If thou be desirous of it, the utmost that thou wouldst give me as its price would be a piece of silver; and I, by Allah the Great, will not sell it.—Then the fowler went with him to the palace of the King; and when the King saw him, his beauty and loveliness pleased him, and the redness of his bill and his feet; so he sent a servant to purchase the bird. The servant asked him, Wilt thou sell this bird? The fowler answered, No; it is for the King, as a present from me unto him. The servant therefore took him, and went with him to the King, and acquainted him with that which he had said; whereupon the King took the bird, and gave to the fowler ten pieces of gold; and he received them, and kissed the ground, and departed. The servant then brought the bird to the King's pavilion, put him in a handsome cage, hung it up, and put with him what he might eat and drink. And when the King came down, he said, Where is the bird? Bring it that I may see it. By Allah, it is beautiful!—So the man brought him, and put him before the King; and he saw that, of the food that was with him, he had not eaten aught; wherefore the King said, By Allah, I know not what it will eat, that I may feed it. Then he gave orders to bring the repast. The tables therefore were brought before him, and the King ate of the repast; and when the bird looked at the flesh-meat and other viands, and the sweetmeats and fruits, he ate of all that was upon the table before the King, and the King was amazed at him, and wondered at his eating, as did also the other persons who were present. And upon this the King said to the servants who were around him, In my life I have never seen a bird eat like this bird.

The King then commanded that his wife should come to divert herself with the sight of him. So a servant went to bring her; and when he saw her, he said to her, O my mistress, the King desireth thy presence, in order that thou mayest divert thyself with the sight of this bird that he hath bought; for when we brought the repast, it flew from the cage, and pitched upon the table, and ate of all that was upon it. Arise then, O my mistress; divert thyself with the sight of it; for it is beautiful in appearance, and it is a wonder among the wonders of the age.—Therefore when she heard the words, she came quickly; but as soon as she looked at the bird, and discovered him, she veiled her face, and turned back. So the King rose and followed her, and said to her, Wherefore didst thou cover thy face, when there are not in thy presence any but the women who serve thee, and thy husband? And she answered, O King, verily this is not a bird; but it is a man like thee. But when he heard the words of his wife, he said to her, Thou utterest falsehood. How much dost thou jest! How can it be aught but a bird?—She replied, By Allah, I jested not with thee, nor did I tell thee anything but truth. Verily this bird is the King Bedr Basim, the son of the King Shah-Zeman, lord of the countries of the Persians, and his mother is Jullanar of the Sea.—And how, said he, hath he become transformed into this shape? She answered him, The Queen Jawharah, the daughter of the King Es-Semendel, hath enchanted him. Then she related to him what had happened to him from first to last, telling him that he had demanded Jawharah in marriage of her father, and that her father consented not thereto, and that his maternal uncle Salih had fought with the King Es-Semendel, and that Salih had overcome him, and made him a captive. And when the King heard the words of his wife, he wondered extremely. Now this Queen, his wife, was the most skillful in enchantment among the people of her age. The King therefore said to her, By my life, I conjure thee to free him from his enchantment, and not leave him tormented. May God (whose name be exalted!) cut off the hand of Jawharah! How vile is she, and how little is her religion, and how great are her deceit and her artifice!—His wife replied, Say to him, O Bedr Basim, enter this closet. So the King ordered him to enter the closet; and when he heard the King's words, he entered it. Then the wife of the King arose, and, having veiled her face, took in her hand a cup of water, and entered, the closet; and she uttered over the water some words not to be understood, and sprinkling him with it said to him, By virtue of these great names, and excellent verses of the Kur'an, and by the power of God (whose name be exalted!), the Creator of the heavens and the earth, and the Reviver of the dead, and the Distributor of the means of subsistence and the terms of life, quit this form in which thou now art, and return to the form in which God created thee! And her words were not ended when he shook violently, and returned to his original form, whereupon the King beheld him a comely young man, than whom there was not upon the face of the earth one more beautiful.

When the King Bedr Basim beheld this thing, he said, There is no deity but God: Mohammad is the Apostle of God! Extolled be the perfection of the Creator of all creatures, and the Ordainer of their means of subsistence and their terms of life!—Then he kissed the hands of the King, and prayed for long life for him; and the King kissed the head of Bedr Basim, and said to him, O Bedr Basim, relate to me thy story from beginning to end. So he related to him his story, not concealing from him aught; and the King wondered thereat, and said to him, O Bedr Basim, God hath delivered thee from enchantment; what then doth thy good pleasure demand, and what dost thou desire to do? He answered him, O King of the age, I desire of thy beneficence that thou wouldst prepare for me a ship, and a company of thy servants, and all that I require; for I have been absent a long time, and I fear that the empire may depart from me. Moreover, I imagine not that my mother is alive, on account of my separation. What seems most probable to me is, that she hath died in consequence of her mourning for me; since she knoweth not what hath happened to me, nor whether I be living or dead. I therefore beg thee, O King, to complete thy beneficence to me by granting that which I have requested of thee.—And when the King considered his beauty and loveliness and his eloquence, he replied and said to him, I hear and obey. He then prepared for him a ship, transported to it what he required, and dispatched with him a company of his servants. So he embarked in the ship, after he had bidden farewell to the King, and they proceeded over the sea.

The wind aided them, and they ceased not to proceed for ten days successively; but on the eleventh day, the sea became violently agitated, the ship began to rise and pitch, and the sailors were unable to manage her. They continued in this state, the waves sporting with them, until they drew near to one of the rocks of the sea, and the ship fell upon that rock, and broke in pieces, and all who were in her were drowned, except the King Bedr Basim; for he mounted upon one of the planks, after he had been at the point of destruction. The plank ceased not to bear him along the sea, and he knew not whither he was going, nor had he any means of checking the motion of the plank: it carried him with the water and the wind, and continued to do so for a period of three days. But on the fourth day, the plank was cast with him upon the shore of the sea, and he found there a city, white as a very white pigeon, built upon an island by the shore of the sea, with lofty angles, beautiful in construction, with high walls, and the sea beat against its walls. So when the King Bedr Basim beheld the island upon which was this city, he rejoiced greatly; and he had been at the point of destruction by reason of hunger and thirst. He therefore landed from the plank, and desired to go up to the city; but there came to him mules and donkeys and horses, numerous as the grains of sand, and they began to strike him, and to prevent his going up from the sea to the city. So he swam round behind that city, and landed upon the shore, and he found not there anyone; wherefore he wondered, and said, To whom doth this city belong, not having a King nor anyone in it, and whence are these mules and donkeys and horses that prevented me from landing? And he proceeded to meditate upon his case as he walked along, not knowing whither to go.

Then, after that, he saw a sheykh, a grocer; and when the King Bedr Basim saw him, he saluted him; and the sheykh returned the salutation, and, looking at him, saw him to be a comely person: so he said to him, O young man, whence hast thou come, and what brought thee to this city? He therefore related to him his story from beginning to end; and he wondered at it, and said to him, O my son, didst thou not see anyone in thy way? He answered him, O my father, I only wonder at this city seeing that it is devoid of people. And the shekyh said to him, O my son, come up into the shop, lest thou perish. So Bedr Basim went up, and seated himself in the shop. And the sheykh arose, and brought him some food, saying to him, O my son, come into the inner part of the shop. Extolled be the perfection of Him who hath preserved thee from this she-devil!—The King Bedr Basim therefore feared violently. He then ate of the food of the sheykh until he was satisfied, and washed his hands, and, looking at the sheykh, said to him, O my master, what is the reason of these words? For thou hast made me to be frightened at this city and its people.—And the sheykh answered him, O my son, know that this city is the City of the Enchanters, and in it is a Queen who is an enchantress, like a she-devil; she is a sorceress, a great enchantress, abounding in artifice, exceedingly treacherous, and the horses and mules and donkeys that thou sawest, all these are like me and thee of the sons of Adam;

but they are strangers; for whoever entereth this city, and is a young man like thyself, this infidel enchantress taketh him, and she remaineth with him forty days, and after the forty days she enchanteth him, and he becometh a mule or a horse or a donkey, of these animals that thou hast seen upon the shore of the sea. Therefore when thou desiredst to land, they feared for thee lest she should enchant thee like them, and they said to thee by signs, Land not, lest the enchantress see thee—in pity for thee; for perhaps she might do unto thee as she did unto them.—And the grocer said, She got possession of this city from her family by enchantment: and her name is the Queen Lab; the meaning of which in Arabic is Esh-Shems (that is, The Sun).

Now when the King Bedr Basim heard these words from the sheykh, he feared violently, and began to tremble like the reed that is shaken by the wind; and he said to him, I believed not that I had escaped from the calamity in which I was involved by enchantment, and now destiny casteth me into situation more abominable than that! And he proceeded to reflect upon his case, and upon the events that had happened to him; and when the sheykh looked at him, he saw that his fear was violent; so he said to him, O my son, arise and sit at the threshold of the shop, and look at those creatures and at their dress and their forms, and the states in which they are through enchantment; but fear not; for the Queen, and everyone in the city, loveth me and regardeth me, and agita-teth not my heart, nor wearieth my mind. Therefore when the King Bedr Basim heard these words of the sheykh, he went forth and sat at the door of the shop, diverting himself; and there passed by him people, and he beheld creatures not to be numbered. And when the people saw him, they advanced to the sheykh, and said to him, O sheykh, is this thy captive, and a prey that thou hast taken during these days? But he answered them, This is the son of my brother. I heard that his father had died; so I sent for him, and caused him to come, that I might enjoy his company.—They replied, Verily this young man is a comely youth; but we fear for him on account of the Queen Lab, lest she turn upon thee with treachery and take him from thee; for she loveth the comely young men. The sheykh however said to them, Verily the Queen will not thwart me: she regardeth me favorably, and loveth me; and when she knoweth that he is the son of my brother, she will not offer him any injury, nor afflict me with respect to him, nor trouble my heart on his account.—And King Bedr Basim remained with the sheykh for a period of months, and the sheykh loved him greatly.

After this, Bedr Basim was sitting at the shop of the sheykh one day as was his custom, and, lo, a thousand soldiers, with drawn swords in their hands, clad in various kinds of apparel, having upon their waists girdles adorned with jewels, riding upon Arab horses; and they came to the shop of the sheykh, and saluted him, and passed on. Then, after them, came a thousand damsels, like moons, clad in various dresses of silk and satin embroidered with gold and adorned with varieties of jewels, and all of them were armed with spears; and in the midst of them was a damsel riding upon an Arab mare, upon which was a saddle of gold set with varieties of jewels and jacinths. They ceased not to proceed until they arrived at the shop of the sheykh, when they saluted him, and passed on. And, lo, the Queen Lab approached, in a magnificent procession, and she came to the shop of the sheykh; whereupon she saw the King Bedr Basim sitting at the shop, resembling the moon at the full. So when the Queen Lab beheld him, she was confounded at his beauty and loveliness, and amazed, and she became distracted with love of him. She came to the shop, and alighted, and, having seated herself by the King Bedr Basim, she said to the sheykh, Whence obtainedst thou this person? He answered, This is the son of my brother: he came to me a short time ago. And she said, Let him be with me that I may converse with him. The sheykh said to her, Wilt thou take him from me and not enchant him? She answered, Yes. He said, Swear to me. And she swore to him that she would not hurt him nor enchant him. Then she gave orders to bring forward to him a handsome horse, saddled, and bridled with a bridle of gold, and all that was upon him was of gold set with jewels; and she presented to the sheykh a thousand pieces of gold, saying to him, Seek aid for thyself therewith. The Queen Lab then took the King Bedr Basim, and departed with him; and he was like the moon in its fourteenth night. He proceeded with her; and the people, as often as they looked at him, and observed his beauty, were pained for him, and said, By Allah, this young man doth not deserve that this accursed woman should enchant him! And the King Bedr Basim heard the words of the people; but he was silent, and had committed his case to God, whose name be exalted!

He ceased not to proceed with the Queen Lab and her retinue until they arrived at the gate of the palace; when the emirs and servants and the great men of the empire alighted. She had commanded the chamberlains to order all the great men of the empire to depart: so they kissed the ground and departed. And the Queen, with her servants, entered the palace; and when the King Bedr Basim looked at the palace, he beheld a palace of which he had never seen the like. Its walls were constructed of gold, and in the midst of it was a great pool, abounding with water, in a great garden; and the King Bedr Basim looked at the garden, and saw in it birds warbling with all varieties of tongues and voices, mirth-exciting and plaintive, and those birds were of all forms and colors. The King Bedr Basim beheld great majesty, and he said, Extolled be the perfection of God for his bounty and his clemency! He sustaineth the person who worshippeth other than Himself!— The Queen seated herself at a lattice-window overlooking the garden. She was on a couch of ivory, upon which was magnificent furniture; and the King Bedr Basim sat by her side. She ordered the female servants to bring a table; whereupon there was brought a table of red gold set with large pearls and with jewels, and upon it were dishes of all kinds of viands. So they ate until they were satisfied, and washed their hands. The servants next brought vessels of gold and silver and crystal, and they brought also all kinds of flowers, and plates of dried fruits; after which the Queen gave orders to bring singing-women; and there came ten damsels like moons, with all kinds of musical instruments in their hands. Then the Queen filled a cup, and drank it; and she filled another, and handed it to the King Bedr Basim, who took it and drank it; and they ceased not to do thus, drinking until they were satisfied; when the Queen ordered the women to sing. So they sang all kinds of melodies, and it seemed to the King Bedr Basim as though the palace danced with delight at the sounds. His reason was captivated, and his bosom was dilated, and he forgot his estrangement

from his country, and said, Verily this Queen is a comely damsel! I will never henceforth quit her; for her kingdom is larger
than mine, and she is preferable to the Queen Jawharah.—He
ceased not to drink with her until it was evening, and the
lamps and candles were lighted, and the attendants gave vent
to the fumes of the sweet-scented substances in the censers.

The next morning she caused him to be clad in the most
beautiful apparel, and gave orders to bring the drinking-
vessels. Accordingly the servants brought them, and they
drank; after which the Queen arose, and took the hand of the
King Bedr Basim, and they sat upon the throne, and she gave
orders to bring the food: so they ate, and washed their hands.
The servants then brought to them the drinking-vessels, and
the fresh fruits and the flowers and the dried fruits; and they
ceased not to eat and drink, while the women sang various
melodies, till evening.

They continued eating and drinking, and delighting themselves, for a period of forty days; after which she said to him,
O Bedr Basim, is this place the more pleasant, or the shop of
thine uncle the grocer? He answered her, By Allah, O Queen,
this is pleasant; for my uncle is a poor man who selleth beans.
And she laughed at his words. But in the morning, the King
Bedr Basim awoke from his sleep and found not the Queen
Lab: so he said, Whither can she have gone? He became sad
on account of her absence, and perplexed respecting his case;
and she had been absent from him a long time, and had not
returned; wherefore he said within himself, Whither hath she
gone? He then proceeded to search for her; but he found
her not; and he said within himself, Perhaps she hath gone to
the garden. He therefore went to the garden, and he saw in

it a running river, by the side of which was a white bird, and
on the bank of that river was a tree, whereon were birds of
various colors. So he looked at the birds; but they saw him
not; and, lo, a black bird alighted by that white bird, and began
to feed her with his bill like a pigeon; and after a while, the
latter bird became changed into a human form, at which he
looked attentively, and, lo, she was the Queen Lab. He therefore knew that the black bird was an enchanted man, and that
she loved him, and for that reason transformed herself by
enchantment into a bird; in consequence of which, jealousy
seized him, and he was incensed against the Queen Lab, on
account of the black bird. Then he returned to his place, and
after a while she returned to him, and began to jest with him;
but he was violently incensed against her, and uttered not to
her a single word. So she knew what he felt, and was convinced that he saw her when she became a bird. She however
did not manifest to him anything; but concealed her feelings.

After this, he said to her, O Queen, I desire thee to permit me to go to the shop of my uncle; for I have conceived
a desire to visit him, and for forty days I have not seen him.
And she replied, Go to him; but be not long absent from me,
since I cannot part with thee, nor endure to be away from
thee for one hour. So he said to her, I hear and obey. He
then mounted, and went to the shop of the sheykh, the grocer, who welcomed him and rose to him and embraced him,
and said to him, How art thou with this infidel woman? He
therefore answered him, and he informed him of that which
he had seen, of the river, and the birds upon the tree. And
when the sheykh heard his words, he said to him, Beware of
her, and know that the birds that were upon the tree were all

young men, strangers, whom she loved, and she transformed them by enchantment into birds; and that black bird that thou sawest was of the number of her guards. She used to love him greatly; but he cast his eye upon one of the female servants; so she transformed him by enchantment into a black bird; and whenever she desireth to visit him, she transformeth herself by enchantment into a bird; for she still loveth him greatly. And when she knew that thou wast acquainted with her case, she meditated evil against thee; and she doth not offer thee a sincere affection. But thou shalt suffer no harm from her so long as I have a care for thee; therefore fear not; for my name is 'Abd-Allah, and there is not in my age anyone more skilled in enchantment than I: yet I make not use of enchantment save when I am constrained to do so. Often do I annul the enchantment of this accursed woman, and deliver people from her; and I care not for her, since she hath no way of injuring me: on the contrary, she feareth me violently, as also doth every one in the city who is an enchanter like her, after this manner: they all fear me, and all of them are of her religion, worshipping fire instead of the Almighty King. But to-morrow come to me again, and acquaint me with that which she shall do to thee; for this night she will exert herself to destroy thee, and I will tell thee what thou shalt do with her that thou mayest save thyself from her artifice.

Then the King Bedr Basim bade farewell to the sheykh, and returned to her, and found her sitting expecting him. And when she saw him, she rose to him and seated him, welcoming him; and she brought him food and drink. So they ate until they were satisfied, and washed their hands; after which, she gave orders to bring the wine. It was therefore brought, and they drank until midnight, when she served him with the cups, and she continued to ply him until he was intoxicated, and lost his sense and his reason. And when she saw him in this state, she said to him, By Allah, I conjure thee, and by the Object of thy worship, if I ask thee concerning a thing, tell me, wilt thou inform me thereof truly, and reply to my question? So he answered her, being in a state of intoxication, Yes, O my mistress. And she said to him, O my master, and light of mine eye, when thou awokest from thy sleep, and foundest me not, thou searchedst for me, and earnest to me in the garden, and sawest the black bird. Now I will acquaint thee with the truth of the case of this bird. He was one of my guards, and I loved him greatly; but he cast his eye one day upon one of my servants; so jealousy came upon me, and I transformed him by enchantment into a black bird. And as to the girl, I killed her. But now I cannot bear to be absent from him one hour; and whenever I desire to visit him, I transform myself by enchantment into a bird, and go to him. Art thou not on this account incensed against me, although I, by the fire and the light and the shade and the heat, have increased in love for thee, and made thee my worldly portion?—So he said, being intoxicated, Verily what thou hast understood, as to my anger being on that account, is true; and there is no cause for my anger except that. And she kissed him, after which he slept. And when it was midnight, she rose; and the King Bedr Basim was awake; but he pretended he was asleep, and kept stealing looks, and observing what she did; and he found that she had taken forth, from a red bag, something red, which she planted in the midst of the palace; and, lo, it became a stream running

like a large river. She then took a handful of barley, scattered
it upon the dust, and watered it with this water; whereupon
it became eared corn: and she took it and ground it into fine
flour, after which she put it in a place, and returned and
slept until the morning.

So when the morning came, the King Bedr Basim arose,
and, having washed his face, asked permission of the Queen
to go to the sheykh; and she gave him permission. He therefore repaired to the sheykh, and acquainted him with that
which she had done, and what he had beheld; and when the
sheykh heard his words, he laughed, and said, By Allah, this
infidel enchantress hath formed a mischievous scheme against
thee; but never care thou for her. He then produced to him
as much as a pound of sawik,[13] and said to him, Take this
with thee, and know that when she seeth it she will say to
thee, What is this, and what wilt thou do with it? Answer
her, A superfluity of good things is good:—and do thou eat
of it. And when she produceth her sawik, and saith to thee,
Eat of this sawik—pretend to her that thou eatest of it, but
eat of this, and beware of eating aught of her sawik, even one
grain; for if thou eat of it even one grain, her enchantment
will have power over thee, and she will enchant thee, saying
to thee, Quit this human form. So thou wilt quit thy form,
and assume whatsoever form she desireth. But if thou eat not
of it, her enchantment will be frustrated, and no harm will
result to thee from it; wherefore she will become in a state of
the utmost abashment, and will say to thee, I am only jesting
with thee. And she will make profession of love and affection

---

13 Barley-meal, made into a thin gruel.

to thee; but all that will be hypocrisy and artifice in her. Do thou, however, make a show of love to her, and say to her, O my mistress, and light of mine eye, eat of this sawik, and see how delicious it is. And when she hath eaten of it, if only one grain, take some water in thy hand, and throw it in her face, and say to her, Quit this human form—and tell her to assume whatsoever form thou desirest. Thereupon, leave her, and come to me, that I may contrive for thee a mode of proceeding.

Bedr Basim then bade him farewell, and pursued his way until he went up into the palace and entered into her presence; and when she saw him, she said to him, A friendly and free and an ample welcome! She rose to him and kissed him, and said to him, Thou hast wearied me by thy delay, O my master. He replied, I was with my uncle. And he saw with her some sawik, and said to her, And my uncle hath given me to eat of this sawik, and we have sawik better than it. Then she put his sawik into a dish, and hers into another, and said to him, Eat of this, for it is nicer than thy sawik. So he pretended to her that he ate of it; and when she believed that he had eaten of it, she took in her hand some water, and sprinkled him with it, and said to him, Quit this form, O young wretch, O villain, and assume the form of a one-eyed mule of hideous appearance! But he changed not. So when she saw him in his proper state, unchanged, she rose to him, and kissed him between the eyes, and said to him, O my beloved, I was only jesting with thee; therefore be not changed in mind toward me on that account. And he replied, By Allah, my mistress, I am not at all changed toward thee; but am convinced that thou lovest me; eat then of this my sawik. She therefore took a morsel of it, and ate it; and when it had settled in her stomach, she was agitated; and the King Bedr Basim, having taken some water in his hand, sprinkled her with it upon her face, saying to her, Quit this human form, and assume the form of a dapple mule. And she saw not herself save in that form; whereupon her tears began to run down upon her cheeks, and she rubbed her cheeks upon his feet. He then betook himself to bridle her; but she allowed not the bridle to be put. He therefore left her, and repaired to the sheykh, and acquainted him with what had happened; upon which the sheykh rose and produced to him a bridle, and said to him, Take this bridle, and bridle her with it. So he took it and went to her; and when she saw him, she advanced to him, and he put the bit in her mouth, and, having mounted her, went forth from the palace, and repaired to the sheykh 'Abd-Allah, who, on seeing her, rose to her, and said to her, May God (whose name be exalted!) abase thee by affliction, O accursed woman! Then the sheykh said to Bedr Basim, O my son, thou hast no longer an abode in this city; so proceed to whatsoever place thou wilt, and beware of giving up the bridle to anyone. The King Bedr Basim therefore thanked him, and bade him farewell, and departed.

He ceased not in his journey for three days; after which he came in sight of a city, and there met him a sheykh, of comely hoariness, who said to him, O my son, whence art thou come? He answered, From the city of this enchantress. The sheykh then said to him, Thou art my guest this night. And he consented, and proceeded with him along the way. And, lo, there was an old woman, who, when she saw the mule, wept, and said, There is no deity but God! Verily this mule resembleth the mule of my son, which hath died, and my heart is troubled for her. I conjure thee by Allah, then, O my master, that thou sell her to me.—He replied, By Allah, O my mother, I cannot sell her. But she rejoined, I conjure thee by Allah that thou reject not my petition; for my son, if I buy not for him this mule, will inevitably die. Then she urged her request in many words; whereupon he said, I will not sell her but for a thousand pieces of gold. And Bedr Basim said within himself, How can this old woman procure a thousand pieces of gold? But upon this she took forth from her girdle a thousand pieces of gold. So when the King Bedr Basim saw this, he said to her, O my mother, I am only jesting with thee, and I cannot sell her. The sheykh, however, looked at him and said to him, O my son, no one may utter a falsehood in this city; for everyone who uttereth a falsehood in this city they slay. The King Bedr Basim therefore alighted from the mule, and delivered her to the old woman; and she drew forth the bit from her mouth, and, having taken some water in her hand, sprinkled her with it, and said, O my daughter, quit this form, and return to the form in which thou wast! And she was transformed immediately, and returned to her first shape; and each of the two women approached the other, and they embraced each other.

So the King Bedr Basim knew that this old woman was the mother of the Queen, and that the stratagem had been accomplished against him, and he desired to flee. But, lo, the old woman uttered a loud whistle; whereupon there presented himself before her an 'Efrit like a great mountain; and the King Bedr Basim feared, and stood still. The old woman mounted upon his back, took her daughter behind her, and the King Bedr Basim before her, and the 'Efrit flew away with them, and there elapsed but a short time before they arrived at the palace of the Queen Lab; after which, when she had seated herself upon the throne of her kingdom, she looked at the King Bedr Basim, and said to him, O young wretch, I have arrived at this place, and attained what I desired, and I will shew thee what I will do with thee and with this sheykh, the grocer. How many benefits have I conferred upon him, and he doth evil unto me! And thou hadst not attained thy desire but by his means.—Then she took some water, and sprinkled him with it, saying to him, Quit this form in which thou now art, and assume the form of a bird of hideous appearance, the most hideous of birds! And he was transformed immediately, and became a bird of hideous appearance; upon which she put him into a cage, and withheld from him food and drink.

But a servant girl looked at him, and had compassion on him, and she fed him, and gave him to drink, without the knowledge of the Queen. Then the servant found her mistress gone out one day, and she went forth and repaired to the sheykh, the grocer, and acquainted him with the case, saying to him, The Queen Lab is resolved upon the destruction of the son of thy brother. So the sheykh thanked her, and said to her, I must surely take the city from her, and make thee Queen in her stead. He then uttered a loud whistle, and there came forth to him an 'Efrit who had four wings, and he said to him, Take this girl, and convey her to the city of Jullanar of the Sea, and to her mother Farasheh; for they two are the most skillful in enchantment of all existing upon the face of the earth.

And he said to the girl, When thou hast arrived there, inform them that the King Bedr Basim is a captive in the hands of the Queen Lab. The 'Efrit therefore took her up, and flew away with her, and but a short time had elapsed when he alighted with her upon the palace of the Queen Jullanar of the Sea. So the girl descended from the roof of the palace, and, going in to the Queen Jullanar, kissed the ground, and acquainted her with the events that had happened to her son from first to last; upon which, Jullanar rose to her, and treated her with honor, and thanked her. The drums were beaten in the city to announce the good tidings, and she informed her people, and the great men of her empire, that the King Bedr Basim had been found.

After this, Jullanar of the Sea, and her mother Farasheh, and her brother Salih, summoned all the tribes of the Jinn, and the troops of the sea; for the Kings of the Jinn had obeyed them after the captivity of the King Es-Semendel. Then they flew through the air, and alighted upon the city of the enchantress, and they plundered the palace, and slew all who were in it. They also plundered the city, and slew all the infidels who were in it in the twinkling of an eye. And Jullanar said to the girl, Where is my son? The girl therefore took the cage, and brought it before her, and pointing to the bird that was within it, said, This is thy son. So the Queen Jullanar took him forth from the cage, and she took in her hand some water, with which she sprinkled him, saying to him, Quit this form, and assume the form in which thou wast! And her words were not ended when he shook, and became a man as he was before; and when his mother beheld him in his original form, she rose to him and embraced him, and he wept violently, as did also his maternal uncle Salih, and his grandmother Farasheh, and the daughters of his uncle; and they began to kiss his hands and his feet. Then Jullanar sent for the sheykh 'Abd-Allah, and thanked him for his kind conduct to her son; and she married him (the sheykh) to the girl whom he had sent to her with the news of her son. So he took her as his wife; and Jullanar made him King of that city. And she summoned those people who remained of the inhabitants of the city, and made them vow allegiance to the shekyh 'Abd-Allah, covenanting with them, and making them swear, that they would obey and serve him; and they said, We hear and obey.

Then they bade farewell to the sheykh 'Abd-Allah, and departed to their city; and when they entered their palace, the people of their city met them with the drums to celebrate the good news, and with rejoicing. They decorated the city for three days, on account of their exceeding joy at the arrival of their King Bedr Basim, rejoicing greatly at his return. And after that, the King Bedr Basim said to his mother, O my mother, it remaineth only that I marry, and that we all be united. So she replied, O my son, excellent is the idea that thou hast formed; but wait until we inquire for a person suitable to thee among the daughters of the Kings. And his grandmother Farasheh, and the daughters of his uncle, and his maternal uncle, said, We, O Bedr Basim, will all immediately assist thee to attain what thou desirest. Then each of those females arose, and went to search through the countries, and Jullanar of the Sea also sent her female servants upon the necks of the 'Efrits, saying to them, Leave not a city, nor one of the palaces of the Kings, without attentively viewing all who are in it of the beautiful damsels. But when the King Bedr Basim saw the pains that they were taking in this affair, he said to his mother Jullanar, O my mother, leave this affair; for none will content me save Jawharah the daughter of the King Es-Semendel, since she is a jewel as her name importeth. So his mother replied, I know thy desire. She then sent immediately persons to bring to her the King Es-Semendel, and forthwith they brought him before her; whereupon she sent to Bedr Basim; and when he came, she acquainted him with the arrival of the King Es-Semendel. He therefore went in to him; and as soon as the King Es-Semendel saw him approaching, he rose to him and saluted him and welcomed him. Then the King Bedr Basim demanded of him in marriage his daughter Jawharah; and he replied, She is at thy service. And the King Es-Semendel sent some of his companions to his country, commanding them to bring his daughter Jawharah, and to inform her that her father was with the King Bedr Basim, the son of Jullanar of the Sea. So they flew through the air, and were absent awhile; after which they came back accompanied by the Queen Jawharah; who, when she beheld her father, advanced to him and embraced him. And he looked at her and said, O my daughter, Know that I have married thee to this magnanimous King, and bold lion, the King Bedr Basim, the son of the Queen Jullanar, and that he is the handsomest of the people of his age, and the most lovely of them, and the most exalted of them in dignity, and the most noble of them in rank: he is not suitable to any but thee, nor art thou suitable to any but him. And she replied, O my father, I cannot oppose thy wish: therefore do what thou wilt.

So thereupon they summoned the Kadis and the witnesses, and they performed the ceremony of the contract of the marriage of the King Bedr Basim, the son of the Queen Jullanar of the Sea, to the Queen Jawharah. The people of the city decorated it, sent forth the announcers of the glad tidings, and released all who were in the prisons; and the King clothed the widows and the orphans, and conferred robes of honor upon the lords of the empire, and the emirs and other great men. Then they celebrated a grand festivity, made banquets, and continued the festivities evening and morning for a period of ten days. After this, the King Bedr Basim conferred a dress of honor upon the King Es-Semendel, and restored him to his country and his family and his relations; and they ceased not to pass the most delightful life, and the most agreeable days, eating and drinking, and enjoying themselves, until they were visited by the terminator of delights and the separator of companions.

This is the end of their story.—The mercy of God be on them all!

The Story of 'Ala-ed-Din; or,
The Wonderful Lamp

In a large and rich city of China, there once lived a tailor, named Mustapha. He was very poor. He could hardly, by his daily labor, maintain himself and his family, which consisted only of his wife and a son.

His son, who was called 'Ala-ed-Din, was a very careless and lazy fellow. He was disobedient to his father and mother, and would go out early in the morning and stay out all day, playing in the streets and public places with idle children of his own age.

When he was old enough to learn a trade, his father took him into his shop and taught him how to use a needle; but all Mustapha's endeavors to keep his son to work were vain, for no sooner was his back turned than the boy was gone for the day. Mustapha chastised him, but 'Ala-ed-Din clung to the habits he had formed and his father was forced to abandon him to his idleness; and this was such a grief to Mustapha that he fell sick and died in a few months.

'Ala-ed-Din, who was now no longer restrained by the fear of a father, gave himself entirely over to his idle habits, and was never out of the streets. This course he followed till he was fifteen years old, without giving his mind to any useful pursuit or the least reflection on what would become of him. As he was one day playing, according to custom, in the street, with his bad companions, a stranger passing by stopped to observe him.

This stranger was a sorcerer, known as the African magician. He had but two days before arrived from Africa, his native country.

The African magician, seeing in 'Ala-ed-Din's countenance some thing which assured him that he was a fit boy for his purpose, inquired his name and history of his companions, and when he had learnt all he desired to know, went up to him, and, taking him aside from the other lads, said, Child, was not your father called Mustapha the tailor?

Yes, sir, answered the boy; but he has been dead for many years.

At these words the African magician threw his arms about 'Ala-ed-Din's neck and kissed him several times, with tears in his eyes, and said: I am your uncle. Your worthy father was my own brother. I knew you at first sight, you are so like him.

Then he gave 'Ala-ed-Din a handful of small money, saying, Go, my son, to your mother, give my love to her, and tell her I will visit her to-morrow, that I may see where my good brother lived so long, and ended his days.

'Ala-ed-Din ran to his mother, overjoyed at the money his uncle had given him. Mother, said he, have I an uncle?

No, child, replied his mother, you have no uncle by your father's side or mine.

I am just now come, said 'Ala-ed-Din, from a man who says he is my uncle and my father's brother. He cried and kissed me when I told him my father was dead, and gave me money, sending his love to you, and promising to come to pay you a visit, that he may see the house my father lived and died in.

Indeed, child, replied the mother, your father had no brother, nor have you an uncle.

The next day the magician found 'Ala-ed-Din playing in another part of town, and, embracing him as before, put two pieces of gold into his hand and said to him: Carry this, child, to your mother. Tell her that I will come to see her to-night, and bid her get us something for supper; but first show me the house where you live.

'Ala-ed-Din showed the African magician the house and carried the two pieces of gold to his mother, who went out and bought provisions; and considering she wanted various utensils, borrowed them of her neighbors. She spent the whole day in preparing the supper; and at night, when it was ready, said to her son: Perhaps the stranger knows not how to find our house. Go and bring him, if you meet him.

'Ala-ed-Din was just ready to go when the magician knocked at the door and came in loaded with all sorts of fruits, which he brought for a dessert. After he had given what he brought into 'Ala-ed-Din's hands, he saluted the boy's mother and began to talk with her. My good sister, said he, do not be surprised at your never having seen me all the time you have been married to my brother Mustapha of happy memory. I have been forty years absent from this country, and during that time have traveled into the Indies, Persia, Arabia, and Syria, and afterward crossed over into Africa, where I took up my abode. At last, as is natural, I was desirous to see my native country again, and to embrace my dear brother; and finding I had strength enough to undertake so long a journey, I made the necessary preparations, and set out. Nothing ever afflicted me so much as hearing of my brother's death. But

God be praised for all things! It is a comfort for me to find, as it were, my brother in a son, who has almost the same features.

The African magician, perceiving that the widow wept at the remembrance of her husband, changed the conversation, and turning toward her son, asked him: What business do you follow? Are you in any trade?

At this question the youth hung his head, and was not a little abashed when his mother answered: 'Ala-ed-Din is a lazy fellow. His father, when alive, strove all he could to teach him his trade, but could not succeed; and since his death, notwithstanding all I can say to him, he does nothing but idle away his time in the streets, as you saw him, without considering he is no longer a child; and if you do not make him ashamed of it, I despair of his ever coming to any good. For my part I am resolved, one of these days, to turn him out of doors and let him provide for himself.

After these words, 'Ala-ed-Din's mother burst into tears, and the magician said: This is not well, nephew. You must think of helping yourself and getting your livelihood. There are many sorts of trades. Perhaps you do not like your father's, and would prefer another. I will endeavor to help you. If you have no mind to learn any handicraft, I will take a shop for you, and furnish it with all sorts of fine stuffs and linens. Tell me freely what you think of my proposal. You shall always find me ready to keep my word.

This plan just suited 'Ala-ed-Din, who hated work. He told the magician he had a greater inclination to the business suggested than to any other, and that he should be much obliged to him for his kindness.

Well, then, said the African magician, I will take you with me to-morrow, clothe you as handsomely as the best merchants in the city, and afterward we will open a shop as I mentioned.

The widow, after his promises of kindness to her son, no longer doubted that the magician was her husband's brother. She thanked him for his good intentions; and after having exhorted 'Ala-ed-Din to render himself worthy of his uncle's favor, served up supper, at which they talked of several indifferent matters; and then the magician went away.

He came again the next day and took 'Ala-ed-Din with him to a merchant, who sold all sorts of clothes for different ages and ranks ready made, and a variety of fine stuffs, and bade 'Ala-ed-Din chose those he preferred, which he paid for.

When 'Ala-ed-Din found himself so handsomely equipped, he returned his uncle thanks, who thus addressed him, As you are soon to be a merchant, it is proper you should frequent these shops and be acquainted with them.

He then showed him the largest and finest mosques, went with him to the khans where the merchants and travelers lodged, and afterward to the Sultan's palace, and at last brought him to his own khan, where, meeting with some merchants he had become friendly with since his arrival, he gave them a treat, to make them and his pretended nephew acquainted.

This entertainment lasted till night, when 'Ala-ed-Din would have taken leave of his uncle to go home. The magician would not let him go by himself, but conducted him to his mother, who, as soon as she saw him so well dressed, was transported with joy, and bestowed a thousand blessings on the magician.

Early the next morning the magician called again for 'Ala-ed-Din and said he would take him to spend that day in the country, and on the next he would purchase the shop. He then led him out at one of the gates of the city, past some magnificent palaces, to each of which belonged beautiful gardens, into which anybody might enter. At every building he came to he asked 'Ala-ed-Din if he did not think it fine.

By this artifice the cunning magician led 'Ala-ed-Din some way into the country; and as he meant to carry him farther, to execute his design, he pretended to be tired, and took an opportunity to sit down in one of the gardens, on the brink of a fountain of clear water, which discharged itself by the mouth of a bronze lion into a basin. Come, nephew, said he, you must be weary as well as I. Let us rest ourselves, and we shall be better able to pursue our walk.

The magician pulled from his girdle a handkerchief in which were cakes and fruit, and while they ate he exhorted his nephew to leave off bad company, and to seek that of wise and prudent men to improve by their conversation; for, said he, you will soon be at man's estate, and you cannot too early begin to imitate their example.

When they had eaten as much as they wanted, they got up and pursued their walk beyond the gardens and across the country.

At last they arrived between two mountains of moderate height and equal size, divided by a narrow valley. This was the place where the magician intended to execute the design that had brought him from Africa to China. We will go no farther now, said he to 'Ala-ed-Din; I will show you here some extraordinary things, which, when you have seen, you will thank me for; but while I prepare to strike a light, gather up all the loose dry sticks you can see to kindle a fire with.

'Ala-ed-Din found so many dry sticks that he soon collected a great heap. The magician presently set them on fire; and when they were in a blaze, threw in some incense, pronouncing several magical words which 'Ala-ed-Din did not understand.

He had scarcely done so when the earth opened just before the magician, and exposed a stone with a brass ring fixed in it. 'Ala-ed-Din was so frightened that he would have run away, but the magician caught hold of him and gave him such a blow on the ear that he knocked him down. 'Ala-ed-Din got up trembling, and with tears in his eyes said to the magician, What have I done, uncle, to be treated in this severe manner?

I supply the place of your father, answered the magician; and you ought to make no reply. But, child, added he, softening, do not be afraid, for I shall not ask anything of you except that you obey me punctually. Only thus can you reap the advantages I intend for you. Know, then, that under this stone there is hidden a treasure, destined to be yours, and which will make you richer than the greatest monarch in the world. No person but yourself is permitted to lift this stone or enter the cave, and you must do exactly what I may command, for it is a matter of great consequence both to you and to me.

'Ala-ed-Din, amazed at all he saw and heard, forgot what was past, and rising, said: Well, uncle, what is to be done? Command me, I am ready to obey.

I am overjoyed, child, said the African magician, embracing him. Take hold of the ring and lift up that stone.

Indeed, uncle, replied 'Ala-ed-Din, I am not strong enough. You must help me.

You have no occasion for my assistance, answered the magician; if I help you, we shall be able to do nothing. Take hold of the ring and lift up the stone. You will find it will come easily.

'Ala-ed-Din did as the magician bade him, raised the stone with ease, and laid it at one side.

When the stone was pulled up, there appeared a staircase about three or four feet in length, leading to a door. Descend those steps, my son, said the African magician, and open that door. It will let you into a palace divided into three great halls. In each of the halls you will see four large brass cisterns full of gold and silver; but take care you do not meddle with them. Before you enter the first hall, be sure to tuck up your robe, wrap it about you, and then pass through the second into the third without stopping. Above all things, have a care that you do not touch the walls even with your clothes; for if you do, you will die instantly. At the end of the third hall, you will find a door which opens into a garden planted with fine trees loaded with fruit. Walk directly across the garden to a terrace, where you will see a niche before you, and in that niche a lighted lamp. Take the lamp down and blow out the light. When you have thrown away the wick and poured out the liquid the lamp contains, put it in your waistband and bring it to me. Do not be afraid that the liquid will soil your clothes, for it is not oil, and as soon as it is poured out the lamp will be dry.

After these words the magician drew a ring off his finger and put it on one of 'Ala-ed-Din's, saying, It is a talisman against all evil so long as you obey me. Go, therefore, boldly, and we shall both be rich all our lives.

'Ala-ed-Din descended the steps, and, opening the door, found the three halls just as the African magician had described. He went through them with all the precaution the fear of death could inspire, crossed the garden without stopping, took down the lamp from the niche, threw out the wick and the liquid, and put it in his waistband. But as he came down from the terrace, he stopped in the garden to observe the trees, which were loaded with extraordinary fruit of different colors. Some trees bore fruit entirely white, and some clear and transparent as crystal; some red, some green, blue, and purple, and others yellow; in short, there was fruit of all colors. The white fruit were pearls; the clear and transparent, diamonds; the red, rubies; the green, emeralds; the blue, turquoises; the purple, amethysts; and the yellow, sapphires. 'Ala-ed-Din, ignorant of their value, would have preferred figs, or grapes, or pomegranates; but he resolved to gather some of every sort. Having filled two new purses, he wrapped some up in his robe and crammed his bosom as full as it could hold.

'Ala-ed-Din, having thus loaded himself with riches of which he knew not the value, returned through the three halls and soon arrived at the mouth of the cave, where the African magician awaited him with the utmost impatience. As soon as 'Ala-ed-Din saw him, he cried out, Pray, uncle, lend me your hand, to help me out.

Give me the lamp first, replied the magician; it will be troublesome to you.

Indeed, uncle, answered 'Ala-ed-Din, I cannot now, but I will as soon as I am up.

The African magician was determined that he would have the lamp before he would help him up; and 'Ala-ed-Din, who had encumbered himself so much with his fruit that he could not well get at it, refused to give it to him till he was out of the cave. The African magician, provoked at this obstinate refusal, flew into a passion, threw a little of his incense into the fire, and pronounced two magical words, when the stone which had closed the mouth of the staircase moved into its place, with the earth over it in the same manner as it lay at the arrival of the magician and 'Ala-ed-Din.

This action of the magician plainly revealed to 'Ala-ed-Din that he was no uncle of his, but one who designed him evil. The truth was that he had learnt from his magic books the secret and the value of this wonderful lamp, the owner of which would be made richer than any earthly ruler, and hence his journey to China. His art had also told him that he was not permitted to take it himself, but must receive it as a voluntary gift from the hands of another person. Hence he employed young 'Ala-ed-Din, and hoped by a mixture of kindness and authority to make him obedient to his word and will. When he found that his attempt had failed, he set out to return to Africa, but avoided the town, lest any person who had seen him leave in company with 'Ala-ed-Din should make inquiries after the youth. 'Ala-ed-Din, being suddenly enveloped in darkness, cried, and called out to his uncle to tell him he was ready to give him the lamp; but in vain, since his cries could not be heard. He descended to the bottom of the steps, with a design to get into the palace, but the door, which was opened before by enchantment, was now shut by the same means. He then redoubled his cries and tears, sat down on the steps without any hopes of ever seeing light again, and in expectation of a speedy death. In this great emergency he said, There is no strength or power but in the great and high God; and in joining his hands to pray he rubbed the ring which the magician had put on his finger.

Immediately a Jinni of frightful aspect appeared, and said, What wouldst thou have? I am ready to obey thee. I serve him who possesses the ring on thy finger, I and the other servants of that ring.

At another time 'Ala-ed-Din would have been frightened at the sight of so extraordinary a figure, but the danger he was in made him answer without hesitation, Whoever thou art, deliver me from this place.

He had no sooner spoken these words than he found himself on the very spot where the magician had last left him, and no sign of cave or opening, nor disturbance of the earth. Returning God thanks to find himself once more in the world, he made the best of his way home. When he got within his mother's door, the joy to see her and his weakness for want of food made him so faint that he fell down and remained for a long time as dead. As soon as he recovered, he related to his mother all that had happened to him, and they were both very vehement in denouncing the cruel magician. 'Ala-ed-Din slept soundly till late the next morning, when the first thing he said to his mother was, that he wanted something to eat, and wished she would give him his breakfast.

Alas! child, said she, I have not a bit of bread to give you. You ate up all the provisions I had in the house yesterday; but I have a little cotton which I have spun. I will go and sell it, and buy something for our dinner.

Mother, replied 'Ala-ed-Din, keep your cotton for another time, and give me the lamp I brought home with me yesterday. I will sell it, and the money I shall get will serve both for breakfast and dinner, and perhaps supper too.

'Ala-ed-Din's mother took the lamp, and said to her son: Here it is, but it is very dirty. If it was a little cleaner, I believe it would bring something more.

She took some fine sand and water to clean it; but had no sooner begun to rub it than in an instant a hideous Jinni of gigantic size appeared before her, and said to her in a voice of thunder: What wouldst thou have? I am ready to obey thee as thy servant, and the servant of all those who have that lamp in their hands; I and the other servants of the lamp.

'Ala-ed-Din's mother, terrified at the sight of the Jinni, fainted. 'Ala-ed-Din, who had seen such a phantom in the cavern, snatched the lamp out of his mother's hand and said to the Jinni boldly, I am hungry, bring me something to eat.

The Jinni disappeared immediately, but promptly returned with a large silver tray, on which were twelve covered dishes of the same metal, containing the most delicious viands. He set down the tray and disappeared. This was done before 'Ala-ed-Din's mother recovered from her swoon.

'Ala-ed-Din fetched some water and sprinkled it in her face to revive her. Whether that or the smell of the meat effected her cure, it was not long before she came to herself. Mother, said 'Ala-ed-Din, be not afraid. Get up and eat. Here is what will put you in heart, and at the same time satisfy my extreme hunger.

His mother was much surprised to see the great tray and twelve dishes, and to smell the savory odor which exhaled from the food. Child, said she, to whom are we obliged for this great plenty and liberality? Has the Sultan been made acquainted with our poverty and had compassion on us?

It is no matter, mother, said 'Ala-ed-Din, let us sit down and eat, for you have almost as much need of a good breakfast as myself. When we have done I will answer your questions.

Accordingly, both mother and son sat down, and ate with the better relish as the table was so well furnished. But all the time 'Ala-ed-Din's mother could not forbear looking at and admiring the tray and dishes, though she could not judge whether they were silver or some other metal.

The mother and son sat at breakfast till it was noon, and then they thought it would be best to eat dinner; yet, after this they found they should have enough left for supper, and two meals for the next day.

When 'Ala-ed-Din's mother had taken away what was left, she went and sat down by her son on the sofa, saying, I expect now that you will satisfy my impatience, and tell me exactly what passed between the Jinni and you while I was in a swoon.

She was as greatly amazed at what her son told her as at the appearance of the Jinni, and said to him, But, son, what have we to do with the Jinn? I never heard that any of my acquaintances had ever seen one. How came that vile Jinni to address himself to me, and not to you, to whom he had appeared before in the cave?

Mother, answered 'Ala-ed-Din, the Jinni you saw is not the one who appeared to me. If you remember, he that I first saw called himself the servant of the ring on my finger; and this you saw called himself the servant of the lamp you had in your hand; but I believe you did not hear him, for I think you fainted as soon as he began to speak.

What! cried the mother, was your lamp then the occasion of that cursed Jinni addressing himself rather to me than to you? Ah! my son, take it out of my sight, and put it where you please. I had rather you would sell it than run the hazard of being frightened to death again by touching it; and if you would take my advice, you would part also with the ring, and not have anything to do with the Jinn, who, as our prophet has told us, are only devils.

With your leave, mother, replied 'Ala-ed-Din, I shall now take care how I sell a lamp which may be so serviceable both to you and me. That false and wicked magician would not have undertaken so long a journey to secure this wonderful lamp if he had not known its value exceeded that of gold and silver. And since we have honestly come by it, let us make a profitable use of it, though without any great show to excite the envy and jealousy of our neighbors. However, since the Jinni frightens you so much, I will take it out of your sight, and put it where I may find it when I want it. The ring I cannot resolve to part with, for without that you had never seen me again; and though I am alive now, perhaps, if it was gone, I might not be so some moments hence. Therefore, I hope you will give me leave to keep it, and to wear it always on my finger.

'Ala-ed-Din's mother replied that he might do what he pleased; but for her part, she would have nothing to do with the Jinn, and ordered him never to say anything more about them.

By the next night they had eaten all the provisions the

Jinni had brought; and the following day 'Ala-ed-Din put one of the silver dishes under his vest, and went out early to sell it. He addressed himself to a peddler whom he met in the streets, took him aside, and pulling out the plate, asked him if he would buy it. The cunning man took the dish, examined it, and as soon as he found that it was good silver, asked 'Ala-ed-Din at how much he valued it. 'Ala-ed-Din, who had never been used to such traffic, told him he would trust to his judgment and honor. The peddler was somewhat confounded at this plain dealing; and doubting whether 'Ala-ed-Din understood the material or the full value of what he offered to sell, took a piece of gold out of his purse and gave it to him, though it was but the sixtieth part of the worth of the plate. 'Ala-ed-Din received the money very eagerly and retired with so much haste that the peddler, not content with his great profit, was vexed he had not penetrated into 'Ala-ed-Din's ignorance. He was going to run after him, to endeavor to get some change out of the piece of gold; but 'Ala-ed-Din ran so fast, and had got so far, that it was impossible for the man to overtake him.

Before 'Ala-ed-Din went home, he called at a baker's, bought some cakes of bread, changed his money, and on his return gave the rest to his mother, who went and purchased provisions enough to last them some time. After this manner they lived, till 'Ala-ed-Din had sold the twelve dishes one by one, as necessity pressed, to the same peddler, who paid each time the same money as for the first, because he durst not offer less, in fear of losing so good a bargain. When he had sold the last dish, he still had the tray, which weighed ten times as much as the dishes, and he would have carried it to his old purchaser, but it was too large and cumbersome. Therefore he was obliged to bring him home to his mother's, where, after the man had estimated the weight of the tray, he laid down ten pieces of gold, with which 'Ala-ed-Din was very well satisfied.

When all the money was spent, 'Ala-ed-Din had recourse again to the lamp. He took it in his hand and looked for the part where his mother had rubbed it with the sand and water. There he rubbed it also, when the Jinni immediately appeared and said: What wouldst thou have? I am ready to obey thee as thy servant, and the servant of all those who have that lamp in their hands; I, and the other servants of the lamp.

I am hungry, said 'Ala-ed-Din, bring me something to eat.

The Jinni disappeared, and presently returned with a tray, containing the same number of covered dishes as before, set them down, and vanished.

As soon as 'Ala-ed-Din found that their provisions were again gone, he took one of the dishes, and went to look for his peddler; but passing by a goldsmith's shop, the goldsmith perceiving him, called to him and said: My lad, I imagine that you have something to sell to the peddler, whom I often see you visit; but perhaps you do not know that he is a great rogue. I will give you the full worth of what you have to sell, or I will direct you to other merchants who will not cheat you.

This offer induced 'Ala-ed-Din to pull his plate from under his vest and show it to the goldsmith, who at first sight saw that it was made of the finest silver, and asked him if he had sold such as that to the peddler. 'Ala-ed-Din told him that he had sold the man twelve such, for a piece of gold each.

What a villain! cried the goldsmith. But, added he, my son, what is past cannot be recalled. By showing you the value of this plate, which is of the finest silver we use in our shops, I will let you see how much that man has cheated you.

The goldsmith took a pair of scales, weighed the dish, and assured 'Ala-ed-Din that his plate would fetch by weight sixty pieces of gold, which he offered to pay immediately.

'Ala-ed-Din thanked him for his fair dealing, and never after went to any other person.

Though 'Ala-ed-Din and his mother had a boundless treasure in their lamp, and might have had whatever they wished for, yet they lived with the same frugality as before, and it may easily be supposed that the money for which 'Ala-ed-Din had sold the dishes and tray was sufficient to maintain them some time.

During this interval, 'Ala-ed-Din frequented the shops of the principal merchants, where they sold cloth of gold and silver, linens, silk stuffs, and jewelery, and oftentimes joining in their conversation, acquired a knowledge of the world and a desire to improve himself. By his acquaintance among the jewelers he came to know that the fruits which he had gathered when he took the lamp were, instead of colored glass, stones of immense value; but he had the prudence not to mention this to anyone, not even to his mother.

One day as 'Ala-ed-Din was walking about the town, he heard an order proclaimed, commanding the people to shut up their shops and houses, and keep within doors, while the Princess Bedr-el-Budur, the Sultan's daughter, went to the bath and returned.

This proclamation inspired 'Ala-ed-Din with eager desire to see the princess's face, and he determined to gratify this desire by placing himself behind the door of the bath, so that he could not fail to see her face as she went in.

'Ala-ed-Din had not long concealed himself before the princess came. She was attended by a great crowd of ladies and servants, who walked on each side and behind her. When she came within three or four paces of the door of the bath, she took off her veil, and gave 'Ala-ed-Din a chance for a full view of her features.

The princess was a noted beauty. Her eyes were large, lively, and sparkling; her smile bewitching; her nose faultless; her mouth small; her lips vermilion. It is not therefore surprising that 'Ala-ed-Din, who had never before seen such a blaze of charms, was dazzled and enchanted.

After the princess had passed by, and entered the bath, 'Ala-ed-Din quitted his hiding-place and went home. His mother perceived him to be more thoughtful and melancholy than usual, and asked what had happened to make him so, or if he was ill. He then told his mother all his adventure, and concluded by declaring, I love the princess more than I can express, and am resolved that I will ask her in marriage of the Sultan.

'Ala-ed-Din's mother listened with surprise to what her son told her; but when he talked of asking the princess in marriage, she laughed aloud. Alas! child, said she, what are you thinking of? You must be mad to talk thus.

I assure you, mother, replied 'Ala-ed-Din, that I am not mad, but in my right senses. I foresaw that you would reproach me with folly and extravagance; but I must tell you once more, that I am resolved to demand the princess of the Sultan in marriage; nor do I despair of success. I have the servants of the lamp and of the ring to help me, and you know how powerful their aid is. And I have another secret to tell you:

those pieces of glass, which I got from the trees in the garden of the underground palace, are jewels of inestimable value, and fit for the greatest monarchs. All the precious stones the jewelers have in Baghdad are not to be compared to mine for size or beauty; and I am sure that the offer of them will secure the favor of the Sultan. You have a large porcelain dish fit to hold them. Fetch it, and let us see how they will look, when we have arranged them according to their different colors.

'Ala-ed-Din's mother brought the china dish, and he took the jewels and placed them in order, according to his fancy. But the brightness and luster they emitted, and the variety of the colors, so dazzled the eyes both of mother and son that they were astonished beyond measure. 'Ala-ed-Din's mother, emboldened by the sight of these rich jewels, promised to carry them the next morning to the Sultan. 'Ala-ed-Din rose before daybreak and awakened his mother, urging her to get admittance to the Sultan's palace, if possible, before the Grand Wezir and the great officers of state went in to take their seats in the assembly, where the Sultan always attended in person.

'Ala-ed-Din's mother took the china dish in which they had put the jewels the day before, wrapped it in two fine napkins, and set forward for the Sultan's palace. When she came to the gates, the Grand Wezir and most distinguished lords of the court were just gone in; but not withstanding the crowd of people was great, she got into a spacious hall, the entrance to which was very magnificent. She placed herself just before the Sultan, who sat in council with the Grand Wezir, and the great lords, on his right and left hand. Several cases were called, according to their order, pleaded and adjudged, until the time the assembly generally broke up, when the Sultan, rising, returned to his apartment, attended by the Grand Wezir. The other Wezirs and ministers of state then retired, as also did all those whose business had called them thither.

'Ala-ed-Din's mother, seeing all the people depart, concluded that the Sultan would not appear again that day, and resolved to go home; and on her arrival said, with much simplicity: Son, I have seen the Sultan, and am very well persuaded he has seen me too, for I placed myself just before him; but he was so much taken up with those who attended on all sides of him that I pitied him, and wondered at his patience. At last I believe he was heartily tired, for he rose suddenly, and would not hear a great many who were ready prepared to speak to him, but went away, at which I was well pleased, for indeed I began to lose all patience, and was extremely fatigued with staying so long. But there is no harm done. I will go again to-morrow. Perhaps the Sultan may not be so busy.

The next morning she repaired to the Sultan's palace with the present, as early as the day before; and she went six times afterward on the days appointed, placing herself always directly before the Sultan, but with as little success as the first morning.

On the sixth day, however, when the Sultan returned to his own apartment, he said to his Grand Wezir: I have for some time observed a certain woman, who attends constantly every day that I give audience, with something wrapped up in a napkin. She always stands from the beginning to the breaking up of the audience, and places herself just before me. If this woman comes to our next assembly, do not fail to call her, that I may hear what she has to say.

On the next audience day, when 'Ala-ed-Din's mother

went to the assembly, and placed herself in front of the Sultan as usual, the Grand Wezir immediately called an officer, and pointing to her, bade him bring her before the Sultan. The old woman at once followed the officer, and when she reached the Sultan, bowed her head down to the carpet which covered the platform of the throne, and remained in that posture till he bade her rise, which she had no sooner done than he said to her: Good woman, I have observed you standing many days, from the beginning to the end of the assembly. What business brings you here?

After these words, 'Ala-ed-Din's mother prostrated herself a second time; and when she arose, said, Monarch of monarchs, I beg you to pardon the boldness of my petition, and to assure me of your pardon and forgiveness.

Well, replied the Sultan: I will forgive you, be it what it may, and no hurt shall come to you. Speak boldly.

When 'Ala-ed-Din's mother had taken all these precautions, for fear of the Sultan's anger, she told him faithfully the errand on which her son had sent her.

The Sultan hearkened to this discourse without showing the least anger; but before he gave her any answer, asked her what she had brought tied up in the napkin. She took the china dish which she had set down at the foot of the throne, untied it, and presented it to the Sultan.

The Sultan's amazement and surprise were inexpressible when he saw so many large, beautiful, and valuable jewels collected in the dish. He remained for some time lost in admiration. At last, when he had recovered himself, he received the present from the hand of 'Ala-ed-Din's mother, saying, How rich, how beautiful!

After he had admired and handled all the jewels one after another, he turned to his Grand Wezir, and showing him the dish, said, Behold, admire, wonder! and confess that your eyes never saw jewels so rich and beautiful before.

The Wezir was charmed. Well, continued the Sultan, what sayest thou to such a present? Is it not worthy of the princess my daughter? And ought I not to bestow her on one who values her at so great a price?

I cannot but own, replied the Grand Wezir, that the present is worthy of the princess; but I beg of your majesty to grant me three months before you come to a final resolution. I hope before that time, my son, whom you have regarded with your favor, will be able to make a nobler present than this 'Ala-ed-Din, who is an entire stranger to your majesty.

The Sultan granted his request, and he said to the old woman, Good woman, go home, and tell your son that I agree to the proposal you have made me; but I cannot let him marry the princess my daughter for three months. At the expiration of that time come again.

'Ala-ed-Din's mother returned home much more gratified than she had expected, and told her son the answer she had received from the Sultan's own mouth; and that she was to come to the assembly again in three months.

'Ala-ed-Din thought himself the most happy of all men at hearing this news, and thanked his mother for the pains she had taken in the affair, the success of which was of so great importance to his peace, that he counted every day, week, and even hour as it passed. When two of the three months were gone, his mother one evening having no oil in the house, went out to buy some, and found there was a general rejoicing. The houses were decorated with flowers, silks, and carpeting, and the people were all striving to show their joy. The streets were crowded with officers in costumes of ceremony, mounted on horses richly caparisoned, each attended by a great many footmen. 'Ala-ed-Din's mother asked the oil merchant what was the meaning of all this public festivity. Whence came you, good woman, said he, that you don't know the Grand Wezir's son is to marry the Princess Bedr-el-Budur, the Sultan's daughter, to-night? She will presently return from the bath; and these officers are to assist at the cavalcade to the palace, where the ceremony is to be solemnized.

'Ala-ed-Din's mother, on hearing this news, ran home very quickly. My son, cried she, you are undone! the Sultan's fine promises will come to naught. This night the Grand Wezir's son is to marry the Princess Bedr-el-Budur.

At this account, 'Ala-ed-Din was thunderstruck, and he bethought himself of the lamp, and of the Jinni who had promised to obey him; and without indulging in idle words against the Sultan, the Wezir, or his son, he determined, if possible, to prevent the marriage.

When 'Ala-ed-Din had got into his chamber, he took the lamp, and rubbed it. Immediately the Jinni appeared, and said to him: What wouldst thou have? I am ready to obey thee as thy servant, I and the other servants of the lamp.

Hear me, said 'Ala-ed-Din; thou hast hitherto done everything I ordered, but now I am about to impose on thee a harder task. The Sultan's daughter, who was promised me as my bride, is this night to marry the son of the Grand Wezir. Bring them both hither to me as soon after the ceremony as they are alone.

Master, replied the Jinni, I obey you.

'Ala-ed-Din supped with his mother as was their habit, and then went to his own apartment, to await the return of the Jinni.

In the meantime the festivities in honor of the princess's marriage were conducted in the Sultan's palace with great magnificence. The ceremonies were at last brought to a conclusion, and the princess and the son of the Wezir retired to the apartment prepared for them. No sooner had they entered it, and dismissed their attendants, than the Jinni, the faithful servant of the lamp, to the great amazement and alarm of the bride and bridegroom, took them up and by an agency invisible to them transported them in an instant into 'Ala-ed-Din's room, where he set them down. Remove the bridegroom, said 'Ala-ed-Din to the Jinni, and keep him a prisoner till to-morrow at dawn, and then return with him here.

On 'Ala-ed-Din being left alone with the princess he endeavored to calm her fears, and explained to her the treachery practiced on him by the Sultan her father. He then went outside the door and laid himself down and there stayed till morning. At break of day, the Jinni appeared bringing back the bridegroom, and by 'Ala-ed-Din's command transported the bride and bridegroom into the palace of the Sultan.

At the instant that the Jinni had set them down in their own apartment, the Sultan came to offer his good wishes to his daughter.

Having been admitted, he kissed the princess on the forehead, but was extremely surprised to see her look so melancholy. She only cast at him a sorrowful look, expressive of great affliction. He suspected there was something extraordinary in this silence, and thereupon went immediately to his wife's apartment, told her in what a state he found the princess, and how she had received him.

I will go see her, said the princess's mother.

The princess greeted her with sighs and tears, and signs of deep dejection. Her mother urged her to tell her thoughts, and at last she gave a precise description of all that happened to her during the night; on which her mother enjoined the necessity of silence and discretion, as no one would give credence to so strange a tale. The Grand Wezir's son, elated with the honor of being the Sultan's son-in-law, kept silence on his part, and the events of the night were not allowed to cast the least gloom on the festivities of the following day, in continued celebration of the royal marriage.

When night came, the bride and bridegroom were again attended to their apartment with the same ceremonies as on the preceding evening. 'Ala-ed-Din, knowing that this would be so, had already given his commands to the Jinni of the lamp; and no sooner were they alone than they were removed in the same mysterious manner as on the preceding evening; and having passed the night in the same unpleasant way, they were in the morning conveyed to the palace of the Sultan. Scarcely had they been replaced in their apartment when the Sultan came to make his compliments to his daughter. The princess could no longer conceal from him the unhappy treatment she had suffered, and told him all that had happened, as she had already related it to her mother. The Sultan, on hearing these strange tidings, consulted with the Grand Wezir; and finding from him that his son had been subjected to even worse treatment by an invisible agency, he determined to declare the marriage canceled, and to order all the festivities, which were yet to last for several days, ended.

This sudden change in the mind of the Sultan gave rise to various reports. Nobody but 'Ala-ed-Din knew the secret, and he kept it with the most perfect silence; and neither the Sultan nor the Grand Wezir, who had forgotten 'Ala-ed-Din and his request, had the least thought that he had any hand in the strange adventures that befell the bride and bridegroom.

On the very day that the three months contained in the Sultan's promise expired, the mother of 'Ala-ed-Din again went to the palace and stood in the same place in the assembly. The Sultan knew her and directed his Wezir to have her brought before him.

After having prostrated herself, she made answer, in reply to the Sultan, Sire, I come at the end of three months to ask of you the fulfillment of the promise you made to my son.

The Sultan little thought the request of 'Ala-ed-Din's mother was made to him in earnest, or that he would hear any more of the matter. He therefore took counsel with his Wezir, who suggested that the Sultan should attach such conditions to the marriage that no one could possibly fulfill them. In accordance with this suggestion of the Wezir, the Sultan replied to the mother of 'Ala-ed-Din: Good woman, it is true sultans ought to abide by their word, and I am ready to keep mine by making your son happy in marriage with the princess my daughter. But as I cannot let her marry without some further proof of your son's ability to support her in royal state, tell him I will fulfill my promise as soon as he shall send me forty trays of massy gold, full of the same sort of jewels you have already made me a present of, and carried by the same number of servants, all dressed magnificently. On these conditions I am ready to bestow the princess my daughter upon him. Therefore, good woman, go and tell him so, and I will wait till you bring me his answer.

'Ala-ed-Din's mother prostrated herself a second time before the Sultan's throne and retired. On her way home she laughed within herself at her son's foolish imagination. Where, said she, can he get so many large gold trays and such precious stones to fill them? It is altogether out of his power, and I believe he will not be much pleased with my visit this time.

When she came home, full of these thoughts, she told 'Ala-ed-Din all the circumstances of her interview with the Sultan, and the conditions on which he consented to the marriage. The Sultan expects your answer immediately, said she; and then added, laughing, I believe he may wait long enough!

Not so long, mother, as you think, replied 'Ala-ed-Din. This demand is a mere trifle, and will prove no bar to my marriage with the princess. I will prepare at once to satisfy his request.

Ala-ed-Din retired to his own apartment and summoned the Jinni of the lamp, and required him to immediately prepare and present the gift, before the Sultan closed his morning audience, according to the terms in which it had been prescribed. The Jinni professed his obedience to the owner of the lamp and disappeared. Within a very short time a train of servants appeared opposite the house in which 'Ala-ed-Din lived. Each carried on his head a basin of massy gold, full of pearls, diamonds, rubies, and emeralds. 'Ala-ed-Din then addressed his mother: Mother, pray lose no time. Before the Sultan and the assembly rise, I would have you return to the palace with this present as the dowry demanded for the princess, that he may judge by my diligence and exactness of the ardent and sincere desire I have to procure myself the honor of this alliance.

As soon as this magnificent procession, with 'Ala-ed-Din's mother at its head, had begun to march from 'Ala-ed-Din's house, the whole city was filled with the crowds of people desirous to see so grand a sight. The graceful bearing and elegant form of each servant, their grave walk at an equal distance from each other, the luster of their jeweled girdles, and the brilliancy of the precious stones in their turbans excited the greatest admiration. As they had to pass through several streets to the palace, the whole length of the way was lined with files of spectators. Nothing, indeed, was ever seen so beautiful and brilliant in the Sultan's palace, and the richest robes of the officers of his court were not to be compared to the costly dresses of these servants.

As the Sultan, who had been informed of their approach, had given orders for them to be admitted, they met with no obstacle, but went into the assembly in regular order, one part turning to the right and the other to the left. After they were all entered, and had formed a semicircle before the Sultan's throne, the servants laid the golden trays on the carpet, prostrated themselves, touching the carpet with their foreheads. When they rose, they uncovered the trays, and then all stood with their arms crossed over their chests.

In the meantime 'Ala-ed-Din's mother advanced to the

foot of the throne, and having prostrated herself, said to the Sultan, Sire, my son knows this present is much below the notice of Princess Bedr-el-Budur; but hopes, nevertheless, that your majesty will accept it, and make it agreeable to the princess, and with the greater confidence since he has endeavored to conform to the conditions you were pleased to impose.

The Sultan, overpowered at the sight of such more than royal splendor, replied without hesitation to the words of 'Ala-ed-Din's mother, Go and tell your son that I wait with open arms to embrace him; and the more haste he makes to come and receive the princess my daughter from my hands, the greater pleasure he will do me.

As soon as 'Ala-ed-Din's mother had retired, the Sultan put an end to the audience; and rising from his throne, ordered that the princess's attendants should come and carry the trays into their mistress's apartment, whither he went himself to examine them with her at his leisure. The servants were conducted into the palace; and the Sultan, telling the princess of their magnificent apparel, ordered them to be brought before her apartment, that she might see through the lattices he had not exaggerated in his account of them.

In the meantime 'Ala-ed-Din's mother reached home and showed by her demeanor and countenance the good news she brought her son. My son, said she, you may rejoice you are arrived at the height of your desires. The Sultan has declared that you shall marry the Princess Bedr-el-Budur. He waits for you with impatience.

'Ala-ed-Din, enraptured with this news, made his mother

very little reply, but retired to his chamber. There he rubbed his lamp, and the obedient Jinni appeared. Jinni, said 'Ala-ed-Din, convey me at once to a bath, and supply me with the richest and most magnificent robe ever worn by a monarch.

No sooner were the words out of his mouth than the Jinni rendered 'Ala-ed-Din, as well as himself, invisible, and transported him into a bath of the finest marble, where he was washed with various scented waters, and when he returned into the hall he found, instead of his own poor raiment, a robe, the magnificence of which astonished him. The Jinni helped him to dress, and when he had done, transported him back to his own chamber, where he asked him if he had any other commands.

Yes, answered 'Ala-ed-Din, bring me a charger that surpasses in beauty and goodness the best in the Sultan's stables, with a saddle, bridle, and other caparisons to correspond with his value. Furnish also twenty servants, as richly clothed as those who carried the present to the Sultan, to walk by my side and follow me, and twenty more to go before me in two ranks. Besides these, bring my mother six female attendants to attend her, as richly dressed at least as any of the Princess Bedr-el-Budur's, each carrying a complete dress fit for any princess. I want also ten thousand pieces of gold in each of ten purses. Go and make haste.

As soon as 'Ala-ed-Din had given these orders, the Jinni disappeared, but presently returned with the horse, the forty servants, ten of whom carried each a purse containing ten thousand pieces of gold, and six women servants, each bearing on her head a different dress for 'Ala-ed-Din's mother, wrapped up in a piece of silver tissue, and gave them all to 'Ala-ed-Din.

He presented the six female servants to his mother, telling her they were hers, and that the dresses they had brought were for her use. Of the ten purses 'Ala-ed-Din took four, which he gave to his mother, telling her those were to supply her with necessaries; the other six he left in the hands of the servants who brought them, with an order to throw the gold by handfuls among the people as they went to the Sultan's palace. The six servants who carried the purses he ordered to march before him, three on the right hand and three on the left.

When 'Ala-ed-Din had thus prepared himself for his first interview with the Sultan, he dismissed the Jinni, and immediately mounting his charger began his march, and though he never was on horseback before, appeared with a grace the most experienced horseman might envy. The innumerable concourse of people through whom he passed made the air echo with their acclamations, especially every time the six servants who carried the purses threw handfuls of gold among the populace.

On 'Ala-ed-Din's arrival at the palace, the Sultan was surprised to find him more richly and magnificently robed than he had ever been himself, and was impressed with his good looks and dignity of manner, which were so different from what he expected in the son of one so humble as 'Ala-ed-Din's mother. He embraced him with demonstrations of joy, and when 'Ala-ed-Din would have fallen at his feet, held him by the hand and made him sit near his throne. He shortly after led him, amidst the sounds of trumpets and all kinds of music, to a magnificent entertainment, at which the Sultan and 'Ala-ed-Din ate by themselves, and the great lords of the court, according to their rank and dignity, sat at different tables. After the feast the Sultan sent for the chief Kadi, and commanded him to draw up a contract of marriage between the Princess Bedr-el-Budur and 'Ala-ed-Din. When the contract had been drawn, the Sultan asked 'Ala-ed-Din if he would stay in the palace and complete the ceremonies of the marriage that day.

Sire, said 'Ala-ed-Din, though great is my impatience to enter on the honor granted me by your majesty, yet I beg you to permit me first to build a palace worthy to receive the princess your daughter. I pray you to grant me sufficient ground near your palace, and I will have it completed with the utmost expedition.

The Sultan granted this request, and again embraced him, after which 'Ala-ed-Din took his leave with as much politeness as if he had always lived at court.

'Ala-ed-Din returned home in the manner he had come, amidst the rejoicings of the people, who wished him all happiness and prosperity. As soon as he dismounted, he retired to his own chamber, took the lamp, and summoned the Jinni as usual. Jinni, said 'Ala-ed-Din, build me a palace fit to receive the Princess Bedr-el-Budur. Let its materials be made of nothing less than porphyry, jasper, agate, and the finest marble. Let its walls be massive gold and silver bricks laid alternately. Let each front contain six windows, and let the lattices of these (except one, which I want left unfinished) be enriched with diamonds, rubies, and emeralds, so that they shall exceed anything of the kind ever seen in the world. Let there be an inner and outer court in front of the palace and a spacious garden; but above all things, provide a safe treasure-house, and fill it with gold and silver. Let there be also kitchens and storehouses, stables full of the finest horses and hunting equipage, officers, attendants, and servants to form a retinue for the princess and myself. Go and execute my wishes.

When 'Ala-ed-Din gave these commands to the Jinni, the sun was set. The next morning at daybreak the Jinni presented himself, and having obtained 'Ala-ed-Din's consent, transported him in a moment to the palace he had made. The Jinni led him through all the apartments, where he found officers and servants, habited according to their rank and the services to which they were appointed. The Jinni then showed him the treasury, which was opened by a treasurer, where 'Ala-ed-Din saw large vases of different sizes, piled up to the top with money, ranged all round the chamber. The Jinni thence led him to the stables, where were some of the finest horses in the world, and grooms busy in caring for them. Thence they went to the storehouses, which were filled with all things necessary both for food and ornament.

When 'Ala-ed-Din had examined every portion of the palace, and particularly the hall with the four-and-twenty windows, and found it to far exceed his fondest expectations, he said, Jinni, there is one thing wanting, a fine carpet for the princess to walk on from the Sultan's palace to mine. Lay one down immediately.

The Jinni disappeared, and 'Ala-ed-Din saw what he desired executed in an instant. The Jinni then returned and carried him to his own home.

When the Sultan's porters came to open the gates, they were amazed to find what had been an unoccupied garden filled up with a magnificent palace, and a splendid carpet extending to it all the way from the Sultan's palace. They told the strange tidings to the Grand Wezir, and he informed the Sultan, who exclaimed: It must be 'Ala-ed-Din's palace, which I gave him leave to build for my daughter. He has wished to surprise us, and let us see what wonders can be done in only one night.

'Ala-ed-Din, on being conveyed by the Jinni to his own home, requested his mother to go to the Princess Bedr-el-Budur and tell her that the palace would be ready for her reception in the evening. She went, attended by her servants, in the same order as on the preceding day. Shortly after her arrival at the princess's apartment, the Sultan himself came in and was surprised to find her, whom he knew as a suppliant at his assembly in such humble guise, to be now more richly and sumptuously attired than his own daughter. This gave him a higher opinion of 'Ala-ed-Din, who took such care of his mother and made her share his wealth and honors. A little while after her departure, 'Ala-ed-Din, mounting his horse and accompanied by his retinue of attendants, left his old home forever, and went to the palace in the same pomp as on the day before. Nor did he forget to take with him the wonderful lamp, to which he owed all his good fortune, nor to wear the ring which was given him as a talisman.

The Sultan entertained 'Ala-ed-Din with the utmost magnificence. At night, on the conclusion of the marriage ceremonies, the princess took leave of the Sultan her father. Bands of music led the procession. Four hundred of the Sultan's young pages carried torches on each side, which together with the illuminations of the Sultan's and 'Ala-ed-Din's palaces, made all the vicinity as light as day. The princess, conveyed in a superb litter and attended by her female servants, proceeded on the carpet which was spread from the Sultan's palace to that of 'Ala-ed-Din's. On her arrival 'Ala-ed-Din was ready to receive her at the entrance and led her into a large hall, illuminated with an infinite number of wax candles, where a noble feast was served. The dishes were of massy gold and contained the most delicate viands. The vases, basins, and goblets were gold, also, and of exquisite workmanship, and all the other ornaments of the hall were equal to this display. The princess, dazzled to see so much riches collected in one place, said to 'Ala-ed-Din, I thought, prince, that nothing in the world was so beautiful as the Sultan my father's palace, but the sight of this hall alone is sufficient to show I was deceived.

When the supper was ended, there entered a company of female dancers, who performed according to the custom of the country, singing at the same time verses in praise of the bride and bridegroom. About midnight 'Ala-ed-Din and his bride retired.

The next morning the attendants of 'Ala-ed-Din presented themselves to dress him, and brought him another costume, as rich and magnificent as that worn the day before. He then ordered one of the horses to be got ready, mounted him, and went in the midst of a large troop of servants to the Sultan's palace to entreat him to take a repast in the princess's palace. The Sultan consented with pleasure and, preceded by the principal officers of his palace and followed by all the great lords of his court, accompanied 'Ala-ed-Din.

The nearer the Sultan approached 'Ala-ed-Din's palace the more he was struck with its beauty; but when he entered it, came into the hall, and saw the windows enriched with diamonds, rubies, and emeralds, he was completely surprised and said to his son-in-law: This palace is one of the wonders of the world; for where in all the world besides shall we find walls built of gold and silver, and diamonds, rubies, and emeralds composing the windows? Yet what most surprises me is, that a hall of this magnificence should be left with one of its windows incomplete.

Sire, answered 'Ala-ed-Din, the omission was by design, since I wished that you should have the glory of finishing this hall.

I take your intention kindly, said the Sultan, and will give orders about it immediately.

At the close of the magnificent entertainment provided by 'Ala-ed-Din, the Sultan was informed that the jewelers and goldsmiths attended, upon which he returned to the hall and showed them the window which was unfinished. I sent for you, said he, to fit up this window in as great perfection as the rest. Examine them well, and make all the dispatch you can.

The jewelers and goldsmiths examined the three-and-twenty windows with great attention, and after they had consulted together to know what each could furnish, they returned and presented themselves before the Sultan. The principal jeweler, undertaking to speak for the rest, said, Sire, we are willing to exert our utmost care and industry to obey you; but among us all we cannot furnish jewels enough for so great a work.

I have more than are necessary, said the Sultan; come to

my palace, and you shall choose what may answer your purpose.

When the Sultan returned to his palace, he ordered his jewels to be brought out, and the jewelers took a great quantity, particularly those 'Ala-ed-Din had presented to him, which they soon used, without making any great advance in their work. They came again several times for more, and in a month's time had not finished half their work. In short, they used all the jewels the Sultan had, and borrowed of the Wezir, but yet the window was not half done.

'Ala-ed-Din, who knew that all the Sultan's endeavors to make this window like the rest were in vain, sent for the jewelers and goldsmiths, and not only commanded them to desist from their work, but ordered them to undo what they had begun, and to carry all the jewels back to the Sultan and to the Wezir. They undid in a few hours what they had been six weeks about and retired, leaving 'Ala-ed-Din alone in the hall. He took the lamp, rubbed it, and presently the Jinni appeared. Jinni, said 'Ala-ed-Din, I ordered thee to leave one of the four-and-twenty windows of this hall imperfect, and thou hast executed my commands. Now I would have thee make it like the rest.

The Jinni immediately disappeared. 'Ala-ed-Din went out of the hall, and returning soon after found the window, as he wished it to be, like the others.

In the meantime the jewelers and goldsmiths repaired to the palace, and were introduced into the Sultan's presence, where the chief jeweler presented the precious stones, which he had brought back. The Sultan asked them if 'Ala-ed-Din had given them any reason for so doing, and they answering that he had not, he ordered a horse to be brought, which he mounted, and rode to his son-in-law's palace, with some few attendants on foot, to inquire why he had ordered the completion of the window to be stopped. 'Ala-ed-Din met him at the gate, and without giving any reply to his inquiries conducted him to the grand reception hall, where the Sultan, to his great surprise, found that the window which was left imperfect was now exactly like the others. He fancied at first that he was mistaken, and examined the two windows on each side, and afterward all the four-and-twenty; but when he was convinced that the window which several workmen had been so long about was finished in so short a time, he embraced 'Ala-ed-Din and kissed him. My son, said he, what a man you are to do such surprising things always in the twinkling of an eye! There is not your fellow in the world. The more I know you, the more I admire you.

'Ala-ed-Din did not confine himself in his palace, but went with much state, sometimes to one mosque, and sometimes to another, to prayers, or to visit the Grand Wezir, or the principal lords of the court. Every time he went out, he caused two servants, who walked by the side of his horse, to throw handfuls of money among the people as he passed through the streets and squares. This generosity gained him the love and blessings of the people. Thus 'Ala-ed-Din, while he paid all respect to the Sultan, won by his affable behavior and liberality the affections of the people.

'Ala-ed-Din had conducted himself in this manner several years, when the African magician, who had never doubted but that he had destroyed him, determined to inform himself with certainty whether he perished, as he supposed, in the underground cave or not. After he had resorted to a long course of magic ceremonies to ascertain 'Ala-ed-Din's fate, what was his surprise to find that 'Ala-ed-Din, instead of dying in the cave, had made his escape, and was living in royal splendor by the aid of the wonderful lamp!

On the very next day the magician set out and traveled with the utmost haste to the capital of China, where, on his arrival, he took up his lodging in a khan.

He then quickly learnt about the wealth, charities, happiness, and splendid palace of Prince 'Ala-ed-Din. As soon as he saw the gold and silver walls and bejeweled windows of the palace, he knew that none but the Jinnis, the servants of the lamp, could have performed such wonders; and envious at 'Ala-ed-Din's high estate, he returned to the khan, with the purpose to find out where the lamp was—whether 'Ala-ed-Din carried it about with him, or where he left it. His magic art soon informed him, to his great joy, that the lamp was in the palace. Well, said he, rubbing his hands in glee, I shall have the lamp, and I shall make 'Ala-ed-Din return to his original poverty.

The next day the magician was told by the chief superintendent of the khan where he lodged that 'Ala-ed-Din had gone on a hunting trip that was to last for eight days, of which only three had expired. The magician wanted to know no more. He resolved at once on his plans. He went to a coppersmith and asked for a dozen copper lamps. The master of the shop told him he had not so many then, but if he would have patience till the next day, he would have them ready. The magician agreed to wait, and desired him to take care that they should be handsome and well polished.

The next day the magician called for the twelve lamps, paid the man his full price, put them into a basket hanging on his arm, and went directly to 'Ala-ed-Din's palace. As he approached, he began crying, Who will change old lamps for new ones?

As he went along a crowd of children collected, who hooted at him and thought he was a madman or a fool, as did all who chanced to be passing by, to offer to change new lamps for old ones.

The African magician regarded not their scoffs, hootings, or all they could say to him, but still continued crying, Who will change old lamps for new ones?

He repeated this so often, walking backward and forward in front of the palace, that the princess, who was then in the hall of the four-and-twenty windows, hearing a man shout something, and seeing a great mob crowding about him, sent one of her female servants to learn what he had to sell.

The woman returned laughing so heartily that the princess rebuked her. Princess, answered the woman, who can forbear laughing to see an old man with a basket on his arm, full of fine new lamps, asking to change them for old ones? The children and mob crowd about him so that he can hardly stir, and they make all the noise they can in derision of him.

Another servant, hearing this, said: Now you speak of lamps, I know not whether the princess may have observed it, but there is an old one on a shelf of the Prince 'Ala-ed-Din's robing-room, and whoever owns it will not be sorry to find a new one in its stead. If the princess chooses, she may have the pleasure of trying if this old man is so silly as to give a new lamp for an old one, without taking anything for the exchange.

The princess, who knew not the value of this lamp and the interest that 'Ala-ed-Din had to keep it safe, entered into the pleasantry and commanded a servant to take it and make the exchange. The servant obeyed, went out of the hall, and no sooner got to the palace gates than he saw the African magician, called to him, and showing him the old lamp, said, Give me a new lamp for this.

The magician never doubted but this was the lamp he wanted. There could be no other such in the place, where every utensil was gold or silver. He snatched it eagerly out of the woman's hand, and thrusting it as far as he could into his breast, held out his basket, and bade the servant choose which lamp he liked best. The servant picked out one, and carried it to the princess; and the change was no sooner made than the place rung with the shouts of the children, deriding the magician's folly.

The African magician stayed no longer near the palace, nor cried any more, New lamps for old ones, but made the best of his way to his khan. He had succeeded in his purpose, and by his silence he got rid of the children and the mob.

As soon as he was out of sight of the two palaces, he hastened down the least-frequented streets; and having no more occasion for his lamps or basket, set all down in a spot where nobody saw him. Then going down another street or two, he walked till he came to one of the city gates, and pursuing his way through the suburbs, which were very extensive, at length reached a lonely spot, where he stopped till the darkness of the night, as the most suitable time for the design he had in contemplation. When it became quite dark, he pulled the lamp out of his breast, and rubbed it.

At that summons the Jinni appeared and said: What wouldst thou have? I am ready to obey thee as thy servant, and the servant of all those who have that lamp in their hands; both I and the other servants of the lamp.

I command thee, replied the magician, to transport me immediately, and the palace which thou and the other servants of the lamp have built in this city, with all the people in it, to Africa.

The Jinni made no reply, but with the assistance of the other Jinn, the servants of the lamp, immediately transported him and the entire palace to the spot whither he had been desired to convey them.

Early the next morning, when the Sultan, according to custom, went to contemplate and admire 'Ala-ed-Din's palace, his amazement was unbounded to find that it was nowhere in sight. He could not comprehend how so large a palace, which he had seen plainly every day for some years, should vanish so soon and not leave the least remains behind. In his perplexity he ordered the Grand Wezir to be sent for with haste.

The Grand Wezir, who, in secret, bore no good will to 'Ala-ed-Din, intimated his suspicion that the palace was built by magic, and that 'Ala-ed-Din had made his hunting excursion an excuse for the removal of his palace with the same suddenness with which it had been erected. He induced the Sultan to send a detachment of his guards to seize 'Ala-ed-Din as a prisoner of state. When his son-in-law was brought before him, he would not hear a word from him, but ordered him to be put to death. The decree caused so much discontent among the people, whose affection 'Ala-ed-Din had secured by his largesses and charities, that the Sultan, fearful of an insurrection, was obliged to grant him his life. As soon as 'Ala-ed-Din found himself at liberty, he addressed the Sultan, and said, Sire, I pray you to let me know the crime by which I have lost thy favor.

Your crime! answered the Sultan, wretched man! do you not know it? Follow me, and I will show you.

The Sultan then took 'Ala-ed-Din into the apartment whence it was his habit to look at and admire his palace, and said, You ought to know where your palace stood; look, consider, and tell me what has become of it.

'Ala-ed-Din looked, and being utterly amazed at the loss of his palace, was speechless. At last recovering himself, he said: It is true, I do not see the palace. It is vanished; but I had no concern in its removal. I beg you to give me forty days, and if in that time I cannot restore it, I will offer my head to be disposed of at your pleasure.

I give you the time you ask, responded the Sultan, but at the end of the forty days forget not to present yourself before me.

'Ala-ed-Din went out of the Sultan's palace in a condition of exceeding humiliation. The lords who had courted him in the days of his splendor, now declined to have any words with him. For three days he wandered about the city, exciting the wonder and compassion of the multitude by asking everybody he met if they had seen his palace, or could tell him anything of it. On the third day he wandered into the country, and as he was approaching a river, he fell down the bank and rubbed the ring which the magician had given him. Immediately the same Jinni appeared whom he had seen in the cave where the magician had left him. What wouldst thou have? said the

Jinni. I am ready to obey thee as thy servant, and the servant of all those who have that ring on their finger, both I and the other servants of the ring.

'Ala-ed-Din, agreeably surprised at an offer of help so little expected, replied, Jinni, show me where the palace I caused to be built now stands, and transport it back where it first stood.

Your command, answered the Jinni, is not wholly in my power; I am only the servant of the ring, and not of the lamp.

I command thee, then, replied 'Ala-ed-Din, by the power of the ring, to transport me to the spot where my palace stands, in whatsoever part of the world it may be.

These words were no sooner out of his mouth than the Jinni transported him into Africa, to the midst of a large plain, where his palace stood at no great distance from a city, and placing him under the window of the princess's apartment left him.

Now it so happened that shortly after 'Ala-ed-Din had been transported by the servant of the ring to the neighborhood of his palace, that one of the attendants of the Princess Bedr-el-Budur looking through the window perceived him and instantly told her mistress. The princess, who could not believe the joyful tidings, hastened to the window, and seeing 'Ala-ed-Din, immediately opened it. The noise of opening the window made 'Ala-ed-Din turn his head that way, and perceiving the princess, he saluted her with an air that expressed his joy. I have sent to have the private door unlocked for you, said she. Enter, and come up.

The private door which was just under the princess's apartment was soon opened, and 'Ala-ed-Din was conducted up into the chamber. It is impossible to express the joy of both at seeing each other after so cruel a separation. They embraced and shed tears of joy. Then they sat down, and 'Ala-ed-Din said, I beg of you princess, to tell me what is become of an old lamp which stood on a shelf in my robing-chamber.

Alas! answered the princess, I was afraid our misfortunes might be owing to that lamp; and what grieves me most is, that I have been the cause of them. I was foolish enough to change the old lamp for a new one, and the next morning I found myself in this unknown country, which I am told is Africa.

Princess, said 'Ala-ed-Din, interrupting her, you have explained all by telling me we are in Africa. I desire you only to inform me if you know where the old lamp now is.

The African magician carries it in his robes, said the princess; and this I can assure you, because he pulled it out before me and showed it to me in triumph.

Princess, said 'Ala-ed-Din, I think I have found the means to deliver you and to regain possession of the lamp on which all my prosperity depends. To execute this design, it is necessary for me to go to the town. I shall return by noon, and will then tell you what must be done by you to insure success. In the meantime, I shall disguise myself, and I beg that the private door may be opened at the first knock.

When 'Ala-ed-Din was out of the palace, he looked round him on all sides, and perceiving a peasant going into the country, hastened after him; and when he had overtaken him, made a proposal to him to change clothes, which the man agreed to. When they had made the exchange, the countryman went about his business, and 'Ala-ed-Din entered the city. After traversing several streets, he came to that part of the town where the merchants and artisans had their particular streets according to their trades. He went into that of the druggists; and entering one of the largest and best furnished shops, asked the druggist if he had a certain powder which he named.

The druggist, judging 'Ala-ed-Din by his habit to be very poor, told him he had it, but that it was expensive, on which 'Ala-ed-Din pulled out his purse, and showing him some gold asked for half a dram of the powder, which the druggist weighed and gave him, telling him the price was a piece of gold. 'Ala-ed-Din put the money into his hand and hastened to the palace, which he entered at once by the private door. When he came into the princess's apartment, he said to her: Princess, you must take your part in the scheme which I propose for our deliverance. You must overcome your dislike of the magician and assume a most friendly manner toward him, and ask him to oblige you by partaking of a feast in your apartments. Before he leaves, ask him to exchange cups with you, which he, gratified at the honor you do him, will gladly do, when you must give him the cup containing this powder. On drinking it he will instantly fall dead, and we will obtain the lamp, whose Jinni will do all our bidding and restore us and the palace to the capital of China.

The princess obeyed to the utmost her husband's instructions. She assumed a look of pleasure on the next visit of the magician and asked him to a feast. He most willingly accepted the invitation, and at the close of the evening, during which the princess had tried all she could to please him, she asked him to exchange cups with her. Then she had the drugged cup brought to her, and gave it to the magician. He drank its contents, out of compliment to the princess, to the very last drop, when he fell back lifeless on the sofa.

The princess, expecting the success of her scheme, had so placed her women from the great hall to the foot of the staircase that the word was no sooner given that the African magician was fallen backward than the door was opened, and 'Ala-ed-Din admitted to the hall. The princess rose from her seat and ran overjoyed to embrace him; but he stopped her and said, Princess, retire to your apartment, and let me be left alone while I endeavor to transport you back to China as speedily as you were brought thence.

When the princess and her attendants were gone out of the hall, 'Ala-ed-Din shut the door, and going directly to the dead body of the magician opened his vest, and took out the lamp which was carefully wrapped up. He rubbed it, and the Jinni immediately appeared. Jinni, said 'Ala-ed-Din, I command thee to transport this palace instantly to the place whence it was brought hither.

The Jinni bowed his head in token of obedience and disappeared. Immediately the palace was transported into China, and its removal was only felt by two little shocks, the one when it was lifted up, the other when it was set down, and both in a very short interval of time.

On the morning after the restoration of 'Ala-ed-Din's palace the Sultan was looking out of his window and mourning over the fate of his daughter, when he thought he saw that the vacancy created by the disappearance of the palace was filled up. On looking more attentively, he was convinced beyond the power of doubt that he saw his son-in-law's palace. Joy and gladness succeeded to sorrow and grief. He at once ordered a horse to be saddled, which he mounted that instant, thinking he could not make haste enough to the place.

'Ala-ed-Din rose that morning by daybreak, put on one of the most magnificent habits his wardrobe afforded, and went up into the hall of twenty-four windows. Thence he perceived the Sultan approaching, and received him at the foot of the great staircase and helped him to dismount.

He led the Sultan into the princess's apartment. The happy father embraced her with tears of joy; and the princess, on her side, afforded similar proofs of her extreme pleasure. After a short interval devoted to explanations of all that had happened, the Sultan restored 'Ala-ed-Din to his favor and expressed his regret for the apparent harshness with which he had treated him. My son, said he, be not displeased at my proceedings against you. They arose from my paternal love, and therefore you ought to forgive them.

Sire, replied 'Ala-ed-Din, I have not the least reason to complain of your conduct, since you did nothing but what your duty required. This wicked magician, the basest of men, was the sole cause of my misfortune.

The African magician, who was thus twice foiled in his endeavor to ruin 'Ala-ed-Din, had a younger brother, who was as skillful a magician as himself, and exceeded him in wickedness and hatred of mankind. By mutual agreement they communicated with each other once a year, however widely separate might be their place of residence from each other. The younger brother not having received as usual his annual message, prepared to ascertain what the trouble was. By his magic art he found that his brother was no longer living, but had been poisoned; and that his body was in the capital of the kingdom of China; also that the person who had poisoned him was of humble birth, though married to a princess, a Sultan's daughter.

As soon as the magician had informed himself of his brother's fate, he resolved immediately to revenge his death and at once departed for China, where, after crossing plains, rivers, mountains, and deserts, he arrived, having endured many fatigues. When he came to the capital of China, he took a lodging at a khan. His magic art promptly revealed to him that 'Ala-ed-Din was the person who had been the cause of the death of his brother. He had not been long in the city before he noticed that everyone was talking of a woman called Fatimeh, who was retired from the world, and who wrought many miracles. As he fancied that this woman might be useful to him in the project he had conceived, he made minute inquiries, and requested to be informed more particularly who that holy woman was, and as to the sort of miracles she performed.

What! said the person whom he addressed, have you never seen her? She is the admiration of the whole town for her fasting and her exemplary life. Except Mondays and Fridays she never stirs out of her little cell, but on those days she comes into the town and does an infinite deal of good; for there is not a person who is diseased whom she does not put her hand on and cure.

Having ascertained the place where the hermitage of this holy woman was, the magician went at night and killed the good woman. In the morning he dyed his face the same hue as hers, arrayed himself in her garb, and taking her veil, the large necklace she wore round her waist, and her staff, went straight to the palace of 'Ala-ed-Din.

No sooner did the people see the holy woman, as they imagined him to be, than they gathered about him in a great crowd. Some begged his blessing, others kissed his hand, and others, more reserved, only the hem of his garment; while others, suffering from disease, stooped for him to lay his hands on them, which he did, muttering some words in form of prayer, and, in short, he pretended so well that everybody took him for the holy woman. He came at last to the square before 'Ala-ed-Din's palace. The crowd was so great and so noisy that the princess, who was in the hall of four-and-twenty windows, heard it and asked what was the matter. One of her women told her a vast number of people had collected about the holy woman to be cured of diseases by the laying on of her hands.

The princess, who had long heard of Fatimeh, but had never seen her, was very desirous to have some conversation with her. The chief officer perceiving this, told the princess it was an easy matter to bring the holy woman into the palace, if she desired and commanded it; and the princess expressing her wishes, he immediately sent four servants for the pretended Fatimeh.

As soon as the crowd saw the attendants from the palace, it made way; and the magician, perceiving that they were coming for him, advanced to meet them, overjoyed to find his plot was succeeding so well. Holy woman, said one of the servants, the princess wants to see you and has sent for you.

The princess does me great honor, replied the false Fatimeh; I am ready to obey her command, and he followed the servants to the palace.

When the pretended Fatimeh had bowed, the princess

said: My good mother, I have one thing to request which you must not refuse. It is to stay with me, that you may edify me with your way of living, and that I may learn from your good example.

Princess, said the false Fatimeh, I beg of you not to ask what I cannot consent to without neglecting my prayers and devotions.

That shall be no hindrance to you, answered the princess. I have a great many apartments unoccupied; you shall choose which you like best, and have as much liberty to perform your devotions as if you were in your own cell.

The magician, who really desired nothing more than to introduce himself into the palace, where it would be a much easier matter for him to work his designs, did not long excuse himself from accepting the obliging offer which the princess made him. Princess, said he, whatever resolution a poor wretched woman as I am may have made to renounce the pomp and grandeur of this world, I dare not presume to oppose the will and commands of so pious and charitable a princess.

On this the princess, rising, said, Come with me; I will show you what vacant apartments I have, that you may make choice of the one you like best.

The magician followed the princess, and of all the apartments she showed him, made choice of that which was the worst, saying it was too good for him, and he only accepted it to please her.

Afterward the princess would have brought him back into the great hall to make him dine with her; but he, considering that he should then be obliged to show his face, which he had always taken care to conceal with Fatimeh's veil, and fearing that the princess would find out that he was not Fatimeh, begged of her earnestly to excuse him, telling her that he never ate anything but bread and dried fruits, and desired to eat that slight repast in his own apartment. The princess granted his request, saying: You may be as free here, good mother, as if you were in your own cell. I will order you a dinner, but remember I want to talk with you as soon as you have finished your repast.

After the princess had dined, and the false Fatimeh had been sent for by one of the attendants, he again waited on her. My good mother, said the princess, I am overjoyed to see so holy a woman as yourself, who will confer a blessing on this palace. But now I am speaking of the palace, pray how do you like it? And before I show it all to you, tell me first what you think of this hall.

The false Fatimeh surveyed the hall from one end to the other. When he had examined it well, he said to the princess: So far as such a solitary being as I, who am unacquainted with what the world calls beautiful, can judge, this hall is truly admirable. There wants but one thing.

What is that, good mother? demanded the princess. Tell me, I conjure you. For my part, I always believed and have heard say it wanted nothing; but if it does, it shall be supplied.

Princess, said the false Fatimeh, with great deceit, forgive me the liberty I have taken; but my opinion is, that if a rukh's egg were hung up in the middle of the dome, this hall would have no equal in the four quarters of the world, and your palace would be the wonder of the universe.

My good mother, said the princess, what is a rukh, and where may one get an egg?

Princess, replied the pretended Fatimeh, it is a bird of prodigious size, which inhabits the summit of Mount Caucasus. The architect who built your palace can get you one of its eggs.

After the princess had thanked the false Fatimeh for what she believed her good advice, she conversed with her on other matters; but could not forget the rukh's egg, which she resolved to request of 'Ala-ed-Din when next he should visit her apartments. He returned in the course of the evening, and shortly after he entered, the princess thus addressed him: 'I always believed that our palace was the most superb, magnificent, and complete in the world; but I will tell you now what it wants, and that is a rukh's egg hung up in the midst of the dome.

Princess, replied 'Ala-ed-Din, it is enough that you think it wants such an ornament; you shall see by the diligence I use in obtaining it that there is nothing which I would not do for your sake.

'Ala-ed-Din left the Princess Bedr-el-Budur that moment, and went up into the hall of four-and-twenty windows, where, pulling out of his bosom the lamp, which after the danger he had been exposed to he always carried about him, he rubbed it, and the Jinni immediately appeared. Jinni, said 'Ala-ed-Din, I command thee, in the name of this lamp, bring a rukh's egg to be hung up in the middle of the dome of the hall of the palace.

'Ala-ed-Din had no sooner pronounced these words than the hall shook as if ready to fall, and the Jinni said in a loud and terrible voice: Is it not enough that I and the other servants of the lamp have done everything for you; and yet you, by an unheard-of ingratitude, command me to bring my master and hang him up in the midst of this dome? This attempt deserves that you, the princess, and the palace should be immediately reduced to ashes; but you are spared because this request does not come from yourself. Its true author is the brother of the African magician. He is now in your palace, disguised in the habit of the holy woman Fatimeh, whom he has murdered. At his suggestion your wife makes this wicked demand. His design is to kill you. Therefore take care of yourself.

After these words the Jinni disappeared.

'Ala-ed-Din resolved at once what to do. He returned to the princess's apartment, and without mentioning a word of what had happened sat down and complained of a great pain which had suddenly seized his head. On hearing this, the princess told him how she had invited the holy Fatimeh to stay with her, and that she was now in the palace, and could no doubt cure him. At 'Ala-ed-Din's request the princess ordered Fatimeh to be summoned at once.

When the pretended Fatimeh entered, 'Ala-ed-Din said: Come hither, good mother. I am glad to see you here at so fortunate a time. I am tormented with a violent pain in my head, and request your assistance and hope you will not refuse me that cure which you impart to afflicted persons.

So saying, he rose, but held down his head. The counterfeit Fatimeh advanced toward him with his hand all the time on a dagger concealed in his girdle under his gown. 'Ala-ed-Din observed this, and snatched the weapon from the magician's hand and pierced him to the heart with his own dagger.

My dear prince, what have you done? cried the princess, in surprise. You have killed the holy woman!

No, my princess, answered 'Ala-ed-Din, with emotion, I have not killed Fatimeh, but a villain, who would have assassinated me if I had not prevented him. This wicked man, added he, uncovering his face, is the brother of the magician who attempted our ruin. He has strangled the true Fatimeh and disguised himself in her clothes with intent to murder me.

'Ala-ed-Din then informed her how the Jinni had told him these facts, and how narrowly she and the palace had escaped destruction through the treacherous suggestion which had led to her request.

Thus was 'Ala-ed-Din delivered from the persecution of the two brothers who were magicians. Within a few years afterward the Sultan died in a good old age, and as he left no sons, the Princess Bedr-el-Budur succeeded him, and she and 'Ala-ed-Din reigned together many years.

The Story of 'Ali Baba
and the Forty Thieves

There once lived in a town of Persia two brothers, one named Kasim and the other 'Ali Baba. Their father divided a small inheritance equally between them. Kasim married a very rich wife and became a wealthy merchant. 'Ali Baba married a woman as poor as himself and lived by cutting wood and bringing it on three donkeys into the town to sell.

One day when 'Ali Baba was in the forest, and had just cut wood enough to load his donkeys, he saw at a distance a great cloud of dust which seemed to approach him. He observed it with attention and soon distinguished a body of horsemen, whom he suspected might be robbers. To save himself, he determined to leave his donkeys, and after driving them into a thicket out of sight he climbed a large tree, growing on a high rock. Its branches were thick enough to conceal him and yet enabled him to see all that passed.

The horsemen numbered forty, and were all well mounted and armed. They came to the foot of the rock on which the tree stood and there dismounted. Every man unbridled his horse, tied it to a shrub, and gave it a feed of corn from a bag he had brought with him. Then each of them removed his saddle-bag, which seemed to 'Ali Baba to be full of gold and silver from its weight. One, whom he took to be the captain, came under the tree in which 'Ali Baba was hidden, and making his way through some bushes, pronounced these words, Open, Simsim!

As soon as the captain of the robbers had thus spoken, a door opened in the rock; and after he had made all his troop enter before him, he followed them, when the door shut of itself.

The robbers stayed some time within the rock, while 'Ali Baba, fearful of being caught, remained in the tree.

At last the door opened again, and the captain came out first and stood to see the troop all pass by him, when 'Ali Baba heard him make the door close by pronouncing these words, Shut, Simsim!

Every man at once bridled his horse and mounted. When the captain saw them all ready, he put himself at their head, and they returned the way they had come.

'Ali Baba followed them with his eyes as far as he could see them, and afterward stayed a considerable time before he descended. Remembering the words the captain of the robbers used to cause the door to open and shut, he had the curiosity to try if his pronouncing them would have the same effect. Accordingly he went among the bushes, and perceiving the door concealed behind them, stood before it and said, Open, Simsim!

The door instantly flew wide open. 'Ali Baba, who expected a dark, dismal cavern, was surprised to see a well-lighted and spacious chamber, which received the light from an opening at the top of the rock. In the chamber were all sorts of provisions, rich bales of silk, brocade, and valuable carpeting piled on one another, gold and silver ingots in great heaps, and money in bags. The sight of all these riches made him suppose that this cave must have been occupied for ages by robbers who had succeeded one another.

'Ali Baba went boldly into the cave and collected as much of the gold coin as he thought his three donkeys could carry. The gold was in bags, and when he had loaded the donkeys, he laid wood over the bags in such a manner that they could not be seen. When he had passed in and out as often as he wished, he stood before the door, and said, Shut, Simsim! the door closed of itself. He then made his way to town.

When 'Ali Baba got home, he drove his donkeys into his little yard, shut the gates very carefully, threw off the wood that covered the panniers, carried the bags into his house, and ranged them in order before his wife. He then emptied the bags, which raised such a great heap of gold as dazzled his wife's eyes, and he told her the whole adventure from beginning to end, and, above all, recommended her to keep it secret.

The wife rejoiced greatly at their good fortune and wanted to count all the gold, piece by piece. Wife, said 'Ali Baba, you do not know what you undertake when you speak of counting the money. You will never get done. I will dig a hole and bury it. There is no time to be lost.

You are in the right, husband, replied she; but let us know, as quickly as possible, how much we have. I will borrow a measure and measure it while you dig the hole.

Away the wife ran to the house of her brother-in-law, Kasim, who lived just by, and addressing herself to his wife, desired the loan of a measure for a little while. Her sister-in-law asked her whether she would have a great or a small one, and she asked for a small one.

The sister-in-law fetched it, but as she knew 'Ali Baba's poverty, she was curious to learn what his wife wanted to measure, and artfully putting some suet at the bottom of the measure, brought it to her, with an excuse that she was sorry she had made her stay so long, but that she could not find it sooner.

'Ali Baba's wife went home, set the measure on the heap of gold, filled it, and emptied it, till she had done. She was very well satisfied to find the number of measures amounted to so many as they did, as was also her husband, who had now finished digging the hole. While 'Ali Baba was burying the gold, his wife, to show her exactness and diligence to her sister-in-law, carried the measure back, but without taking notice that a piece of gold had stuck to the bottom. Sister, said she, giving it to her, you see that I have not kept your measure long. I am obliged to you for it and return it with thanks.

As soon as 'Ali Baba's wife was gone, Kasim's wife looked at the bottom of the measure and was surprised to find a piece of gold sticking to it. Envy immediately possessed her breast. What! said she, has 'Ali Baba gold so plentiful as to measure it? Whence has he all this wealth?

Kasim her husband was at his counting-house. When he came home, his wife said to him: Kasim, I know you think yourself rich, but 'Ali Baba is infinitely richer than you. He does not count his money, but measures it.

Kasim desired her to explain the riddle, which she did by telling him the stratagem she had used to make the discovery, and showed him the piece of money, which was so old that they could not tell when it was coined.

Kasim after he had married the rich widow had never treated 'Ali Baba as a brother, but neglected him; and now, instead of being pleased, he conceived a base envy at his brother's prosperity. He could not sleep all that night and went to him in the morning before sunrise. 'Ali Baba, said he, I am surprised at you; you pretend to be miserably poor, and yet you measure gold. My wife found this at the bottom of the measure you borrowed yesterday.

By this discourse, 'Ali Baba perceived that Kasim and his wife knew what he had so much reason to conceal; but what was done could not be undone. Therefore, without showing the least surprise or trouble, he confessed all, and offered his brother part of the treasure to keep the secret.

I must know exactly where this treasure is, replied Kasim haughtily; and how I may visit it myself when I want. Otherwise I will go and inform against you. Then you will not only get no more, but will lose all you have, and I shall receive a share for my information.

'Ali Baba told him all he desired to know, even to the very words he was to use to gain admission into the cave.

Kasim rose the next morning long before the sun and set out for the forest with ten mules bearing great chests, which he planned to fill with gold. He followed the road 'Ali Baba had pointed out to him, and it was not long before he reached the rock and found the place by the tree and other marks of which his brother had told him. When he reached the entrance of the cavern, he said the words, Open, Simsim!

The door immediately opened, and when he was in, closed on him. In examining the cave, he was greatly astonished to find much more riches than he had expected from 'Ali Baba's relation. He quickly laid at the door of the cavern as many bags of gold as his ten mules could carry; but his thought were now so full of the great riches he should possess, that he could not think of the necessary word to make the door open. Instead of Open, Simsim! he said Open, Barley! and was much amazed to find that the door remained fast shut. He named several sorts of grain, but still the door would not open.

Kasim had never expected such an incident, and was so alarmed at the danger he was in that the more he endeavored to remember the word Simsim the more his memory was confounded, and he had as much forgotten it as if he had never heard it mentioned. He threw down the bags he had loaded himself with and walked distractedly up and down the cave, without having the least regard to the riches that were around him.

About noon the robbers visited their cave. As they approached they saw Kasim's mules straggling near the rock, with great chests on their backs. Alarmed at this, they galloped full speed to the cave. They drove away the mules, who strayed through the forest so far that they were soon out of sight. Then the robbers, with their naked sabers in their hands, went directly to the door, which, when their captain pronounced the proper words, immediately opened.

Kasim, who heard the noise of the horses' feet, at once guessed the arrival of the robbers and resolved to make one effort for his life. He rushed to the door, and no sooner saw it open than he ran out and threw the robber captain down, but could not escape the other robbers, who, with their swords, cut off his head.

The first care of the robbers after this was to examine the cave. They found all the bags which Kasim had brought to the door, ready to load on his mules, and carried them to their places, but they did not miss what 'Ali Baba had taken away before. Then holding a council, and deliberating on the occurrence, they guessed that Kasim, when he was in, had not been able to get out, but could not imagine how he had learned the secret words by which alone he could enter. They could not deny the fact of his being there; and to terrify any person or accomplice who should attempt the same thing, they agreed to cut Kasim's body into four quarters and hang two on one side and two on the other, within the door of the cave. They had no sooner taken this resolution than they put it in execution; and when they had nothing more to detain them, left the place of their hoards well closed. They mounted their horses, and went to beat the roads again and attack the caravans they might meet.

In the meantime Kasim's wife was very uneasy when night came and her husband had not returned. She ran to 'Ali Baba in great alarm and said: I believe, brother-in-law, that you know Kasim has gone to the forest and on what account. It is now night, and he has not come back. I am afraid some misfortune had happened to him.

'Ali Baba told her that she need not frighten herself, for Kasim would certainly not think it proper to come into the town till the night was pretty far advanced.

Kasim's wife, considering how much it concerned her husband to keep the business secret, was easily persuaded to believe her brother-in-law. She went home and waited patiently till midnight. Then her fear redoubled, and her grief was the more marked because she was forced to keep it to herself. She repented her foolish curiosity and cursed her desire to pry into the affairs of other people. She spent all the night in weeping; and as soon as it was day, went to her brother- and sister-in-law, telling them by her tears the cause of her coming.

Ali Baba did not wait for his sister-in-law to ask him to go to see what was become of Kasim, but begging her to moderate her affliction, departed immediately with his three donkeys. He went to the forest, and when he came to the rock, having seen neither his brother nor the mules on the way, was seriously alarmed at finding some blood near the door. He took this for an ill omen; but when he had pronounced the proper words, and the door had opened, he was struck with horror at the dismal sight of his brother's body. He was not long in determining how he should pay the last dues to his brother, and having loaded one of his donkeys with the body, covered it over with wood. The other two donkeys he loaded with bags of gold, covering them with wood also as before. Then he bid the door shut and came away; but was so cautious as to stop some time at the end of the forest, that he might not go into the town before night. When he reached home he drove the two donkeys loaded with gold into his little yard and left the care of unloading them to his wife, while he led the other to his sister-in-law's house.

'Ali Baba knocked at the door, which was opened by Marjaneh, a clever, intelligent servant, who was fruitful in inventions to meet the most difficult circumstances. When he came into the court, he unloaded the donkey, and taking Marjaneh aside said to her: You must observe close secrecy. I have brought your master's body. We must bury him as if he had died a natural death. Go now and tell your mistress. I leave the matter to your wit and skillful devices.

'Ali Baba helped to place the body in Kasim's house and then returned with his donkey.

Marjaneh went out early the next morning to a druggist, and asked for a sort of lozenge which was considered efficacious in the most dangerous disorders. The apothecary inquired who was ill? She replied with a sigh, My good master Kasim himself, and he can neither eat nor speak.

In the evening Marjaneh went to the same druggist again, and with tears in her eyes asked for an essence which they used to give to sick people only when at the last extremity. Alas! said she, taking it from the apothecary, I am afraid that this remedy will have no better effect than the lozenges, and that I shall lose my good master.

Moreover, as 'Ali Baba and his wife were often seen going between Kasim and their own house all that day, and seemed melancholy, nobody was surprised in the evening to hear the lamentable shrieks and cries of Kasim's wife and of Marjaneh, who gave out everywhere that Kasim was dead. The next morning at daybreak, Marjaneh went to an old cobbler whom she knew to be always early at his stall, and bidding him good morrow, put a piece of gold into his hand, saying, Baba Mustapha, bring with you your sewing tackle and come with me; but I must tell you, I shall blindfold you when you come to a certain place.

Baba Mustapha hesitated a little at these words. Oh! oh! replied he, you would have me do something against my conscience or against my honor?

God forbid that I should ask anything contrary to your honor! said Marjaneh, putting another piece of gold into his hand. Only come along with me and fear nothing.

Baba Mustapha went with Marjaneh, who, after she had bound his eyes with a handkerchief at the place she had mentioned, guided him to her deceased master's house, and never unloosed his eyes till he had entered the room where she had the corpse. Baba Mustapha, said she, you must make haste and sew the parts of this body together; and when you have finished, I will give you another piece of gold.

When Baba Mustapha had finished his task, she blindfolded him again, gave him the third piece of gold as she had promised, and recommending secrecy to him, led him back to the place where she first bound his eyes. There she pulled off the bandage, and let him go home, but watched him till he was quite out of sight to make sure that he returned toward his stall. The next day four neighbors carried the corpse to the burying-ground, following the priest, who recited some prayers. 'Ali Baba came after with some neighbors. Marjaneh, who had been a servant to the deceased, came last in the procession, weeping, beating her breast, and tearing her hair. Kasim's wife stayed at home mourning, uttering woeful cries with the women of the neighborhood, who came, according to custom, during the funeral, and joining their wailings with hers, filled the quarter far and near with sounds of sorrow.

The manner of Kasim's melancholy death was concealed and hushed up between his widow, Marjaneh, and 'Ali Baba, with so much contrivance that nobody in the city had the least knowledge or suspicion of the cause of it. Three or four days after the funeral, 'Ali Baba removed his few goods openly to his sister-in-law's house, where it was agreed that he should in future live; but the money he had taken from the robbers he conveyed thither by night. Lastly, he entrusted his eldest son with the entire management of Kasim's warehouse.

While these things were being done, the forty robbers again visited their retreat in the forest. Great, then, was their surprise to find Kasim's body taken away, with some of their bags of gold. We are certainly discovered, said the captain. The removal of the body and the loss of more of our money plainly shows that the man whom we killed had an accomplice; and for our own lives' sake, we must try to find him. What say you, my lads?

All the robbers approved of the captain's proposal.

Well, said the captain, one of the boldest and most skillful among you must go into the town, disguised as a traveler and a stranger, to try if he can hear any talk of the man whom we have killed, and endeavor to find out who he was and where he lived. This is a matter of the first importance, and for fear of treachery, I propose that whoever undertakes this business without success, even though the failure arises only from an error of judgment, shall suffer death.

Without waiting for the sentiments of his companions, one of the robbers started up and said, I submit to this condition and think it an honor to expose my life to serve the troop.

After this robber had received great commendations from the captain and his comrades, he disguised himself; and taking his leave of the troop that night, went into the town just at daybreak, and walked up and down, till accidentally he came to Baba Mustapha's stall, which was always open before any of the shops.

Baba Mustapha was seated with an awl in his hand, just going to work. The robber saluted him, bidding him good morrow; and perceiving that he was old, said: Honest man, you begin to work very early. Is it possible that one of your age can see so well? I question, even if it were somewhat lighter, whether you could see to stitch.

You do not know me, replied Baba Mustapha; for old as I am I have extraordinary good eyes; and you will not doubt it when I tell you that I sewed the body of a dead man together in a place where I had not so much light as I have now.

Where was that? asked the robber.

You shall know no more, answered Baba Mustapha.

The robber felt sure that he had discovered what he sought. He pulled out a piece of gold, and putting it into Baba Mustapha's hand, said to him: I do not want to learn your secret, though I can assure you that you might safely trust me with it. The only thing I desire of you is to show me the house where you did this work.

If I were disposed to do you that favor, replied Baba Mustapha, I assure you I cannot. I was taken to a certain place, whence I was led blindfold to the house, and afterward brought back in the same manner. You see, therefore, the impossibility of my doing what you desire.

Well, replied the robber, you may, however, have some remembrance of the way that you were led blindfold. Come, let me blind your eyes at the same place. We will walk together; perhaps you may be able to go where you did before, and as everybody ought to be paid for their trouble, there is another piece of gold for you. Gratify me in what I ask you.

So saying, he put another piece of gold into the shoe-maker's hand.

The two pieces of gold were great temptations to Baba Mustapha. He looked at them a long time in his hand, without saying a word, but at last he pulled out his purse and put them in it. I am not sure that I can remember the way exactly, said he to the robber; but since you desire, I will try what I can do.

At these words Baba Mustapha rose, to the great joy of the robber, and led him to the place where Marjaneh had bound his eyes. It was here that I was blindfolded, said Baba Mustapha; and afterward I turned this way.

The robber tied his handkerchief over the shoemaker's eyes and walked by him till he stopped directly before Kasim's house, where 'Ali Baba then lived. The thief marked the door with a piece of chalk, which he had ready in his hand, and then he pulled off the bandage from Baba Mustapha's eyes and asked him if he knew whose house that was. Baba Mustapha replied he did not live in the neighborhood, and he could not tell.

The robber, finding he could discover no more from Baba Mustapha, thanked him for the trouble he had taken and left him to go back to his stall, while he returned to the forest, persuaded that he should be very well received.

A little after the robber and Baba Mustapha had parted, Marjaneh went out of 'Ali Baba's house on some errand, and on her return, seeing the mark the robber had made, stopped to observe it. What can be the meaning of this mark? said she to herself. Somebody intends my master no good. However, with whatever intention it was done, it is advisable to guard against the worst.

Accordingly, she fetched a piece of chalk and marked two or three doors on each side, in the same manner, without saying a word to her master or mistress.

By this time the robber had rejoined his troop in the

forest. He told the others of his success, rejoicing over his good fortune, in meeting so soon with the only person who could inform him of what he wanted to know. The robbers listened to him with the utmost satisfaction; and the captain, after commending his diligence, addressed himself to them all, and said: Comrades, we have no time to lose. Let us set off well armed; but that we may not excite any suspicion, let only one or two go into the town together and we will meet at the great square. In the meantime our comrade who brought us the good news and I will go and find the house he has marked, that we may consult what had best be done.

This speech and plan were approved by all. They were soon ready, and filed off in parties of two each, and got into the town without being in the least suspected. The captain and he who had visited the town in the morning as a spy came in last. The spy led the captain into the street where he had marked 'Ali Baba's residence; and when they came to the first of the houses which Marjaneh had marked, he pointed it out. But the captain observed that the next door was chalked in the same manner and in the same place; and showing it to his guide, asked him which house it was, that or the first. The guide was so confounded that he knew not what answer to make, and he was still more puzzled when he and the captain saw five or six houses similarly marked. He assured the captain, with an oath, that he had marked but one, and could not tell who had chalked the rest, so that he could not distinguish the house which the cobbler had stopped at.

The captain, finding that their design had proved abortive, went directly to the great square where the robbers were to meet and told his troop that they had lost their labor and must return to their cave. He himself set them the example, and they separated in parties of two and returned as they had come.

When the troop were all got together, the captain told them the reason of their returning; and presently the robber who had acted as spy was declared deserving of death and was killed.

But as the safety of the troop required the discovery of the second intruder into the cave, another of the gang offered to go and seek out the intruder's dwelling. He promised himself that he should succeed better than his unlucky predecessor, and his offer being accepted, he went and corrupted Baba Mustapha, as the other had done; and being shown the house, marked it in a place more remote from sight with red chalk.

Not long afterward, Marjaneh, whose eyes nothing could escape, went out, and seeing the red chalk mark, and arguing that some evil was planned against her master, marked the neighboring houses in the same place and manner.

The robber, at his return to his company, prided himself much on the care he had taken. He believed he had adopted a sure way of distinguishing 'Ali Baba's house from the others, and the captain and all of them thought now they must succeed. They conveyed themselves into the town with the same caution as before; but when the robber spy and his captain came to the street where 'Ali Baba lived they found several doors marked instead of one, at which the captain was enraged, and the spy was in as great confusion as the former guide.

Thus the captain and his troop were forced to retire a second time, even more dissatisfied; and the robber, who had been the author of the mistake, underwent the same punishment as the other spy.

The captain, having lost two brave fellows of his troop, was afraid of diminishing it too much by pursuing this plan to get information of the residence of their plunderer. It was evident that their heads were not so good as their hands on such occasions, and he therefore resolved to take on himself the important commission.

Accordingly, he went and addressed himself to Baba Mustapha, who did him the same service he had done the other robbers. The captain did not set any particular mark on the house, but examined and observed it so carefully, that it was impossible for him to mistake it. Well satisfied with his attempt, and informed of what he wanted to know, he returned to the forest; and when he came into the cave, where the troop waited for him, said, Now, comrades, nothing can prevent our full revenge, as I am certain of the house; and on my way hither I have thought how to put the revenge into execution; but if anyone can form a better plan, let him communicate it.

He then told his plan, and as they approved of it, ordered them to go into the villages about and buy nineteen mules, with thirty-eight large leather jars, one full of oil and the others empty.

In two or three days' time the robbers had purchased the mules and jars, and the captain after having put one of his men into each jar with the weapons which he thought fit, leaving open the seam which had been undone to allow them a chance to breathe, he rubbed the jars on the outside with oil from the full vessel.

Things being thus prepared, the nineteen mules were loaded with thirty-seven robbers in jars and the jar of oil. Then the captain, as their driver, set out with them, and reached the town by the dusk of the evening, as he had intended. He led them through the streets till he came to 'Ali Baba's, at whose door he designed to knock; but 'Ali Baba was sitting in the doorway after supper to take a little fresh air. The robber stopped his mules, addressed 'Ali Baba, and said: I have brought some oil a great way to sell at to-morrow's market, and it is now so late that I do not know where to lodge. If I should not be troublesome to you, do me the favor to let me pass the night with you, and I shall be very much obliged by your hospitality.

Though 'Ali Baba had seen the captain of the robbers in the forest and had heard him speak, it was impossible to know him in the disguise of an oil merchant. He told him he was welcome, and immediately opened his gates for the mules to go into the yard. At the same time he called to a servant and ordered him, when the mules were unloaded, to put them into the stable and feed them; and then went to Marjaneh to bid her get a good supper for his guest. After they had finished supper, 'Ali Baba charged Marjaneh afresh to take care of his guest.

In the meantime the captain of the robbers went into the yard, and took off the lid of each jar, and gave his comrades orders what to do. Beginning at the first jar and so on to the last, he said to each man, As soon as I throw some pebbles from the chamber window where I lie, do not fail to come out, and I will immediately join you.

After this he returned into the house, and Marjaneh

taking up a light conducted him to his chambers. There she left him; and he, to avoid any suspicion, put the light out soon after and lay down in his clothes, that he might be the more ready to rise.

Marjaneh began preparations for the morrow's breakfast; but while she was doing this, the oil burned out of the lamp she was using, and there was no more oil in the house, nor any candles. What to do she did not know. A fellow-servant, seeing her very uneasy, said, Do not fret yourself, but go into the yard, and take some oil out of one of the jars.

Marjaneh thanked him for his advice, took the oil-pot, and went into the yard; when as she came nigh the first jar, the robber within said softly, Is it time?

Though naturally much surprised at finding a man in the jar instead of the oil she wanted she immediately felt the importance of keeping silence, as 'Ali Baba, his family, and herself might be in great danger; and collecting herself, without showing the least emotion, she answered, Not yet, but presently.

She went quietly in this manner to all the jars, giving the same answer till she came to the jar of oil.

By this means Marjaneh found that her master, 'Ali Baba had admitted thirty-eight robbers into his house, and that this pretended oil merchant was their captain. She made what haste she could to fill her oil-pot and returned to her kitchen, where, as soon as she had lighted her lamp, she took a great kettle, went again to the oil-jar, filled the kettle, set it on a large wood fire, and as soon as it boiled, went and poured enough into every jar to stifle and destroy the robber within.

When this action was executed without any noise, as she

had intended, she returned to the kitchen with the empty kettle; and having put out the fire she had made to boil the oil, and the lamp also, she remained silent, resolving not to go to rest till she had observed through a window of the kitchen, which opened into the yard, what might follow.

She had not waited long before the captain of the robbers got up, opened the window, and finding no light and hearing no noise, or anyone stirring in the house, gave the appointed signal by throwing little stones, several of which hit the jars, as he doubted not by the sound they gave. He then listened, but not hearing or perceiving anything whereby he could judge that his companions stirred, he began to grow very uneasy, and threw stones a second and also a third time. He could not comprehend the reason that none of his men should answer his signal. Much alarmed he went softly down into the yard, and going to the first jar, asked the robber whom he thought alive, if he was in readiness. Then he smelt the hot boiled oil, and suspected that his plot to murder 'Ali Baba and plunder his house was discovered. Examining all the jars, one after another, he found that all his gang were dead; and, enraged to despair at having failed in his design, he forced the lock of a door that led from the yard to the garden, and climbing over the garden wall made his escape.

When Marjaneh saw him depart, she went to bed, satisfied and pleased to have succeeded so well in saving her master and family.

'Ali Baba rose before day, and, followed by a servant, went to the baths, entirely ignorant of the important events which had happened at home.

When he returned, he was very much surprised to see

the oil-jars, and wondered that the merchant was not gone with them and the mules. He asked Marjaneh, who opened the door, the reason. My good master, answered she, God preserve you and all your family. You will be better informed of what you wish to know when you have seen what I have to show you.

As soon as Marjaneh had shut the door, 'Ali Baba followed her, and she requested him to look into the first jar and see if there was any oil. 'Ali Baba did so, and seeing a man started back in alarm and cried out. Do not be afraid, said Marjaneh, the man you see there is dead.

Ah, Marjaneh, said 'Ali Baba, explain yourself.

I will, replied Marjaneh. Moderate your astonishment and do not excite the curiosity of your neighbors, for it is of great importance to keep this affair secret. Look into the other jars.

'Ali Baba examined all the other jars, one after another; and when he came to that which contained oil, found the oil nearly gone. He stood for some time motionless, looking at the jars, without saying a word, so great was his surprise. At last, when he had recovered himself, he asked, And what is become of the merchant?

Merchant! answered Marjaneh; he is as much one as I am. I will tell you who he is and what is become of him; but you had better hear the story in your own room, for it is time that you had your broth after your bathing.

They went indoors and Marjaneh told all she had done, from first observing the mark on the house to the destruction of the robbers and the flight of their captain.

On hearing of these brave deeds from the lips of Marjaneh, 'Ali Baba said to her: God, by your means, has delivered me from the snares these robbers laid for my destruction. I therefore owe my life to you; and, for a token of my acknowledgment, I give you your liberty from this moment. I will complete your recompense later.

'Ali Baba's garden was very long and shaded at the farther end by a great number of large trees. Near these he and the servant dug a trench, long and wide enough to hold the bodies of the robbers; and as the earth was light, they were not long in doing it. When the burial was finished, 'Ali Baba hid the jars and weapons; and as he had no occasion for the mules, he sent them at different times to be sold in the market by his servant.

While 'Ali Baba took these measures, the captain of the forty robbers returned to the forest with inconceivable mortification. He did not stay long. The loneliness of the gloomy cavern became frightful to him. He determined, however, to avenge the fate of his companions and to accomplish the death of 'Ali Baba. For this purpose he returned to the town and took a lodging in a khan, and disguised himself as a merchant selling silks. Under this assumed character he gradually conveyed a great many sorts of rich stuffs and fine linen from the cavern to his lodging, but with all the necessary precautions to conceal the place whence he brought them. In order to dispose of the merchandise, he rented a warehouse, and it happened to be opposite Kasim's, which 'Ali Baba's son had occupied since the death of his uncle.

The robber took the name of Khoja Hoseyn. 'Ali Baba's son was from his vicinity, one of the first to converse with Khoja Hoseyn, and the robber strove to cultivate his friendship. Two or three days after Khoja Hoseyn was settled,

'Ali Baba came to see his son and the captain of the robbers recognized him at once. After this he became more attentive than ever to 'Ali Baba's son, made him some small presents, and often asked him to dine and sup with him, when he treated him very handsomely.

'Ali Baba's son did not choose to continue under such obligation to Khoja Hoseyn; but was so much straitened for want of room in his house that he could not entertain him. He therefore acquainted his father, 'Ali Baba, with his wish to invite Khoja Hoseyn in return.

'Ali Baba with great pleasure took the treat on himself. Son, said he, to-morrow get Khoja Hoseyn to accompany you, and as you pass by my door, call in. I will go and order Marjaneh to provide a supper.

The next day 'Ali Baba's son and Khoja Hoseyn met by appointment, took their walk, and as they returned, 'Ali Baba's son led Khoja Hoseyn through the street where his father lived, and when they came to the house, stopped and knocked at the door. This, sir, said he, is the home of my father. From the account I have given him of your friendship, he has charged me to procure him the honor of your acquaintance; and I desire you to add this pleasure to those for which I am already indebted to you.

'Ali Baba received Khoja Hoseyn with a smiling countenance and in the most obliging manner one could wish. He thanked him for all the favors he had done his son; adding withal, the obligation was the greater as his son was a young man, not much acquainted with the world, and that he might contribute to his information.

Khoja Hoseyn returned the compliment by assuring 'Ali

Baba that though his son might not have acquired the experience of older men, he had good sense equal to the experience of many others. After a little more conversation on different subjects, he offered to take his leave, when 'Ali Baba, stopping him, said: Where are you going, sir, in so must haste? I beg you would do me the honor to sup with me. Though my entertainment may not be worthy your acceptance, such as it is, I heartily offer it.

Sir, replied Khoja Hoseyn, I am thoroughly persuaded of your good-will; but the truth is, I can eat no victuals that have any salt in them. Therefore judge how I should feel at your table.

If that is the only reason, said 'Ali Baba, it ought not to deprive me of the honor of your company; for, in the first place, there is no salt ever put into my bread, and as to the meat we shall have to-night, I promise you there shall be none in that. Therefore you must do me the favor to stay.

'Ali Baba went into the kitchen and ordered Marjaneh to put no salt to the meat which was to be served that night.

Marjaneh, who was always ready to obey her master, could not help being surprised at his strange order. Who is this man, said she, who eats no salt with his meat? Your supper will be spoiled.

Do not be angry, Marjaneh, replied 'Ali Baba. He is an honest man. Therefore do as I bid you.

Marjaneh obeyed, though with no little reluctance, and had a curiosity to see this man who ate no salt. To this end, when she had finished what she had to do in the kitchen, she helped the servant to carry up the dishes; and looking at Khoja Hoseyn, knew him at first sight, notwithstanding his disguise, to be the captain of the robbers, and examining him very carefully perceived that he had a dagger under his garment.

When the servant came for the dessert of fruit and had put it with the wine and glasses before 'Ali Baba, Marjaneh retired, dressed herself neatly, girded her waist with a silver-gilt girdle, to which there hung a poniard with a hilt of the same metal, and put a handsome mask on her face. When she had thus arrayed herself she said to the servant, Take your tambourine, and let us go and divert our master and his son's friend.

He took his tambourine and played all the way into the hall before Marjaneh, who, when she came to the door, made a low obeisance by way of asking leave to exhibit her skill. Come in, Marjaneh, said 'Ali Baba, and let Khoja Hoseyn see what you can do, that he may tell us what he thinks of your performance.

Khoja Hoseyn, who did not expect this diversion after supper, began to fear he should not be able to take advantage of the opportunity he thought he had found; but hoped, if he now missed his purpose, to secure it another time, by keeping up a friendly intercourse with the father and son. Therefore, though he could have wished 'Ali Baba would have declined the dance, he pretended to be obliged to him for it, and expressed his satisfaction at what he saw.

As soon as 'Ali Baba and Khoja Hoseyn had done talking, the servant commenced to play on the tambourine and at the same time sung an air, to which Marjaneh, who was an excellent performer, danced in such a manner as would have created admiration in any company.

After she had danced several dances with much grace, she drew the poniard, and holding it in her hand, began a dance, in which she outdid herself by the many different figures, light movements, and the surprising leaps and wonderful exertions with which she accompanied it. At last she snatched the tambourine from the servant with her left hand, and holding the dagger in her right, presented the other side of the tambourine, after the manner of those who get a livelihood by dancing and solicit the liberality of the spectators.

'Ali Baba put a piece of gold into the tambourine, as did also his son; and Khoja Hoseyn seeing that she was coming to him, had pulled his purse out of his bosom to make her a present. But while he was putting his hand in the purse, Marjaneh plunged the poniard into his heart.

'Ali Baba and his son, shocked at this action, cried out aloud. Unhappy woman! exclaimed 'Ali Baba, what have you done to ruin me and my family?

It was to preserve, not to ruin you, answered Marjaneh; for see here, continued she, opening the pretended Khoja Hoseyn's garment and showing the dagger, what an enemy you had entertained! Look well at him and you will find him to be both the false oil merchant and the captain of the gang of forty robbers. Before I saw him, I suspected him as soon as you told me you had such a guest. You now find that my suspicion was not groundless.

'Ali Baba, who immediately felt the new obligation he had to Marjaneh for saving his life a second time, embraced her. Marjaneh, said he, I gave you your liberty and then promised you that my gratitude should not stop there, but that I would soon give you higher proofs of its sincerity, which I now do by making you my daughter-in-law.

Then addressing himself to his son, he said: I believe you, son, to be so dutiful a child that you will not refuse Marjaneh for your wife. You see that Khoja Hoseyn sought your friendship with a design to take away my life; and if he had succeeded, there is no doubt but he would have sacrificed you also to his revenge. Consider that by marrying Marjaneh you marry the preserver of my family and your own.

The son, far from showing any dislike, readily consented to the marriage, not only because he would not disobey his father, but also because it was agreeable to his inclination. After this they buried the captain of the robbers with his comrades. A few days later, 'Ali Baba celebrated the wedding of his son and Marjaneh with a great feast and the usual dancing, and had the satisfaction to see that his friends and neighbors whom he invited had no knowledge of the true motives of the marriage.

'Ali Baba did not visit the robbers' cave for a whole year, as he supposed the other two members of the troop, whom he could get no account of, might be alive. At the year's end, when he found they had not made any attempt to disturb him, he had the curiosity to make another journey to the place where the treasure was concealed in the forest. He mounted his horse, and when he came to the cave he alighted and tied his horse to a tree. Then approaching the entrance he pronounced the words, Open, Simsim! and the door opened.

He entered the cavern, and by the condition he found things in judged that nobody had been there since the captain had fetched the goods for his shop. It was quite evident that all the robbers who knew of the cave were dead, and 'Ali Baba believed he was the only person in the world who had the secret of opening it, and that all the treasure was at his sole disposal. He put as much gold into his saddle-bags as his horse would carry, and returned to town. Some years later he carried his son to the cave and taught him the secret of opening and shutting the door. The son handed the secret down to his posterity, who, using their good fortune with moderation, lived in great honor and splendor.

Conclusion

Shahrazad, during this period, had borne the King three male children; and when she had ended these tales, she rose upon her feet, and kissed the ground before the King, and said to him, O King of the time, and incomparable one of the age and period, verily I am thy servant, and during a thousand and one nights I have related to thee the history of the preceding generations, and the admonitions of the people of former times: then have I any claim upon thy majesty, so that I may request of thee to grant me a wish? And the King answered her, Request: thou shalt receive, O Shahrazad. So thereupon she called out to the nurses, and said to them, Bring ye my children. Accordingly they brought them to her quickly; and they were three male children: one of them walked, and one crawled, and one was at the breast. And when they brought them, she took them and placed them before the King, and, having kissed the ground, said, O King of the age, these are thy children, and I request of thee that thou exempt me from slaughter, as a favor to these infants; for if thou slay me, these infants will become without a mother, and will not find among women one who will rear them well. And thereupon the King wept, and pressed his children to his bosom, and said, O Shahrazad, May God bless thee, and thy father and thy mother, and thy root and thy branch! I call God to witness against me that I have exempted thee from everything that might injure thee.—So she kissed his hands and his feet, and rejoiced with exceeding joy; and she said to him, May God prolong thy life, and increase thy dignity and majesty!

Joy spread through the palace of the King until it became diffused throughout the city, and it was a night not to be reckoned among lives: its color was whiter than the face of day. The King rose in the morning happy, and with prosperity inundated; and he sent to all the soldiers, who came; and he conferred upon his Wezir, the father of Shahrazad, a sumptuous and magnificent robe of honor, saying to him, May God protect thee, since thou hast married to me thy generous daughter, who hath been the cause of my repenting of slaying the daughters of the people. Moreover, God hath blessed me by her with three male children; and praise be to God for this abundant favor!—Then he conferred robes of honor upon all the wezirs and emirs and lords of the empire, and gave orders to decorate the city thirty days; and he caused not any one of the people of the city to expend aught of his wealth; for all the expense and disbursements were from the King's treasury. So they decorated the city in a magnificent manner, the like of which had not been seen before, and the drums were beaten and the pipes were sounded, and all the performers of sports exhibited their arts, and the King rewarded them munificently with gifts and presents. He bestowed alms also upon the poor and needy, and extended his generosity to all his subjects, and all the people of his dominions. And he and the people of his empire continued in prosperity and joy and delight and happiness until they were visited by the terminator of delights and the separator of companions.

Extolled be the perfection of Him whom the vicissitudes of times do not destroy, and to whom no change happeneth, whom no circumstance diverteth from another circumstance, and who is alone distinguished by the attributes of perfection! And blessing and peace be on the Imam of his Majesty, and the elect from among his creatures, our lord Mohammad, the lord among mankind, through whom we supplicate God for a happy end!